THE UNITED STA...
BE...
THE UNITED STAT...

If they can survive Baalphor of the Shikazu, where the warriors who can never be conquered stalk the conquerors who can never win...

If they can absorb Draco, the planet of pale reptilians which most humans can't stand— and which some can't leave...

If they can defeat Rhana, last of the rebel worlds, where the final battle is being fought to protect man from his worst enemy—himself!

MANIFEST DESTINY

A saga of mankind's highest adventure on the frontier of the far future

BARRY B. LONGYEAR

MANIFEST DESTINY

BERKLEY BOOKS, NEW YORK

"The Jaren" first appeared under the name Frederick Longbeard in the fall 1979 issue of *Isaac Asimov's Science Fiction Magazine*.

"Enemy Mine" first appeared in the September 1979 issue of *Isaac Asimov's Science Fiction Magazine*.

"Savage Planet" first appeared in the February 1980 issue of *Analog*.

MANIFEST DESTINY

A Berkley Book / published by arrangement with
the author

PRINTING HISTORY
Berkley edition / May 1980
Second printing / March 1981

ISBN: 0-425-04530-7

A BERKLEY BOOK® TM 757,375
PRINTED IN THE UNITED STATES OF AMERICA

Text Designed by Michael Serrian

To Adele Leone
and
Marguerete S. Digby

Contents

THE RESOLVE

WHEREAS the success and continued prosperity of the Human Race presupposes ever-increasing room for the expansion of its population, and

WHEREAS this same success and prosperity is dependent upon the continued acquirement of scarce resources to exploit, and

WHEREAS the recent discovery of lower alien lifeforms may indicate the existence of higher, advanced lifeforms that may pose a threat to this Human Destiny,

NOW, THEREFORE, BE IT RESOLVED:
That the Legislative Assembly of the Government of the United States of Earth, in all related matters that shall come before it, will decide all such matters in accordance with the Manifest Destiny of Man, that He shall reign supreme in this and in any and all other galaxies of the Universe.

Legislative Assembly Resolution 991
4 September 2032 A.D.
Adopted without Dissent

Adopted as official Executive Branch policy,
President General's order 621,
6 September 2032 A.D.

Reconsidered upon the discovery of intelligent alien lifeforms,
16 February 2044 A.D.

Affirmed by vote of the Legislative Assembly,
18 February 2044 A.D.
Against Repeal: 824; For Repeal: 127

Legislative Assembly

of the

UNITED STATES OF EARTH

LEGISLATIVE RECORD

November 5, 2052

SPEAKER. The chair recognizes the senior representative of the East European Union, Mister Kovsky.

MISTER KOVSKY. Madam Speaker, honorable members of the Assembly, I rise to speak on the matter of Legislative Document 1134, "A Declaration of a State of War between the Peoples of the United States and Planets of Earth and the Shikazu Empire of the Four Stars." I wish to move the committee's Out to Pass report.

(The motion was seconded by Mister Tiolini of the Fourth Italian Socio-Republic.)

SPEAKER. The chair recognizes the third representative of the Latin American States, Mister Diaz.

MISTER DIAZ. Madam Speaker, members of the Assembly, the states of this planet, and the over two hundred planets that form the union we call the United States of Earth, have left a trail of blood in humanity's attempts at becoming the dominant

5

race of this Galaxy. And here we gather once more to discuss waging war on our fellow beings. In response to our actions of the past twenty years, and in response to other races of our attitude, the rest of the Galaxy is banding together to form a union of quadrants through which races such as ours—races too vicious to let live—may be controlled or eradicated.

I see in this proposed enterprise only death, hardship, and expense. And I see them as unnecessary and a threat to the destiny of our race should we push the tempers of the Galaxy too far with our clumsy reaches into space. I urge the defeat of the committee's report.

SPEAKER. The chair recognizes the most junior member of the Arab-Israeli Compact, Mrs. Stitch.

MRS. STITCH. Madam Speaker, members. We have seen the Assembly tied hand and foot these past eleven days with debates on this issue, when other, more pressing business waits in the clerk's docket, expiring from the lack of the Assembly's attention. The Armed Force Committee and the State Committee in their exhaustive joint sessions have investigated and discussed every aspect of this Declaration of War, and the joint committee has made its recommendation. I would move to end debate on this question, and proceed to the vote on Mister Kovsky's motion.

(The motion was seconded by Mister Thurlough of the North American Union.)

SPEAKER. The motion to end debate being made and seconded, the Assembly shall now proceed to the vote.

(317 yea; 102 nay.)

Two thirds of the Assembly voting in favor of the motion, the motion is carried. The Assembly shall now proceed to vote on L.D. 1134, "A Declaration of a State of War between the Peoples of the United States and Planets of Earth and the Shikazu Empire of the Four Stars."

(296 yea; 123 nay.)

A majority of the voting representatives voting in favor of the motion, the motion is carried. Upon the signature of the

President-General, a state of war between the United States of Earth and the Shikazu Empire will be in effect. The next order of business ...

The Jaren

The hunting on Baalphor, as always, was good. My party had bagged its limit of the elusive Haak goats, and we sat around a fire that night—Dr. Velstock, Jamie Fender, the developer Wiggins, and I. The night was warm, yet we stoked the fire for its light—light that prompted memories and loosened tongues almost as well as the Purim that we were drinking in quantities that would have been distressing had we been in more civilized surroundings. But, the campfire after the hunt was as ingrained in the race of humans as was the grasp for land, or money, and much older.

We had taken on an old Shikki when we reached Baalphor, to cook, clean up, and haul some of our gear. They are unreliable, to say the least. I don't think anyone has seen one of the dark-skinned humanoids sober—I never have. But, they are cheap, and sufficiently obedient when clearheaded enough to understand orders. Our Shikki had gathered wood for the fire, and had retired to the edges of the clearing surrounding our camp, with a bottle of Purim. The old fellow seemed to sock the stuff away in quantities that we found not distressing, but astounding.

The developer Wiggins, his legs stretched out and his back

9

leaning against a log, looked around at the firelight reflecting from the trees, then nodded. "You are right, Hill," he said to me, "this planet has many possibilities." He waved a hand at the night. "Chief among them is no bugs."

I laughed. "I thought you would see it my way, once you visited."

Wiggins nodded. "And you own all this property we have been on?"

"Yes, and quite a bit more. Land here is cheap, but not for long. Other developers have been looking here, as well."

The developer smiled, then looked in my direction. "When I like a place, the competition tends to fade away."

"I know. That is why I made an effort to interest you in my proposition. And, you like the place?"

Wiggins stared into the fire. "Yes, I think so." He turned toward me and smiled. "I confess that I was worried, never having been on this planet before."

Dr. Velstock leaned forward. "You weren't worried on account of the Mithad, I hope. They have been as docile a bunch as you could ever hope to see, even though they can now vote."

Wiggins shook his head. "My concern was about the Shikkies, but," he held out his hands, "there seems to be nothing to worry about from that quarter."

Jamie Fender laughed. "The Shikkies? You have nothing to worry about from the Shikkies, Wiggins. All they want is a bottle and a dry spot to sleep."

We all chuckled. Wiggins nodded, then turned toward Fender. "I see all this now, but on another planet it is hard to see things as clearly. Stories about the Shikkies are still used to frighten children where I come from." He cocked his head in the direction of our Shikki beast of burden. "But I see more clearly now."

Dr. Velstock nodded. "Since the Shikkies were conquered, they have been no trouble—"

"No!"

We all looked up. The old Shikki stood at the edge of the clearing, weaving as he held his precious Purim bottle around the neck with a tight grasp. Dr. Velstock laughed. "No offense, old fellow." He turned to Wiggins. "I can't imagine what's got into him."

The Shikki staggered toward us until he stood before the fire. He was tall, and his muscles spoke of a strong youth. His skin was almost black, his hair a shock of white streaked with yellow. His black eyes seemed to study us, but from the level in his Purim bottle, I passed it off to drunken behavior.

I stood and pointed my finger at the old Shikki. "Go back to your drinking, Eeola."

The Shikki held the bottle in his left hand. With his right, he pointed at Dr. Velstock. "We are not conquered, human. The Shikazu cannot be conquered."

Velstock shook his head and laughed. "I beg to differ with you, old fellow, but I am as familiar with the war of the four stars as anyone. I was in it."

The Shikki took a pull from his bottle, then squatted down beside the fire. "I too was in the war, human, and I say we were not conquered."

Jamie Fender snickered, then jabbed Dr. Velstock in the arm. "Perhaps our historians have lied, Doctor. I would hear this old fellow's version."

Wiggins laughed and poured himself another cup of Purim. "Let us hear this version. I would like to know why we rule Baalphor and the other Shikki planets, yet the Shikkies are not a conquered race." He turned toward the old Shikki. "Tell us your story, and if your throat gets dry our supply of Purim is handy."

Wiggins laughed roundly, and was soon joined by Fender and Velstock. Normally, I would have joined them, but for once I took a good look at a Shikki. He wore the same kind of leather shirt and black sarong-like underwrapping worn by all the Shikkies, but those eyes—there was a haunted brilliance there that I had never seen before. That dull-eyed, out-of-focus appearance I had come to associate with the Shikkies was gone. Eeola stood, observed my companions, then turned away. In a moment, he was gone from the clearing.

Velstock laughed and turned toward Wiggins. "I'm afraid you offended the old fraud."

Wiggins shrugged and took another swallow of his Purim.

Lowering the cup, he chuckled. "Shikkies do have a low entertainment value, don't they?" He faced Fender and Velstock. "Enough of that. Are both of you interested in this development proposal?"

I stood. "I should follow the old Shikki."

The developer waved a hand back and forth. "Don't bother. He bores me, anyway."

"I should make sure that the drunken old fool doesn't fall off a ledge and kill himself."

Fender nodded. "It would never do if we had to carry all our own things."

I smiled, then left my companions and turned into the jungle after the Shikki. He was not far. Eeola sat on a rocky outcropping overlooking a steep cliff. The jungle floor spread into the distance, and on the horizon stood the peculiar landmark that marked the center of my property. In the bright light of Adn, Baalphor's only moon, the feature seemed larger than I remembered seeing it during the day. It was a portion of the jungle floor, risen on a huge cake-shaped formation of rock. I turned from it to see the old Shikki finishing his bottle of Purim.

"My friends didn't mean to hurt your feelings. Come back to the fire."

Eeola issued one sharp laugh, then tossed his empty bottle over the cliff. He laughed again, then listened as the bottle smashed on the rocks below. "They do not hurt my feelings." He shook his head. "I should have said nothing, but this place," he held his hands out toward the landmark, "it loosens a drunken tongue."

I lowered myself and sat on a rock facing the Shikki. "This place has special meaning to you?"

Eeola shook his head. "It is of no interest to you."

I held out my hands. "Then why am I sitting here, and why did I ask?"

The Shikki shrugged. "To understand the meaning of this place to me, you must understand me, and for that . . ." He held up an arm and pointed at the sky, "you must understand from where I came." He dropped the arm into his lap and shook his head. "Too much understanding, from a human."

I was not used to Shikkies talking to me in that manner, and my face grew hot. But for some reason I held my peace. Eeola sat quietly, and for such a long time I felt certain the old fellow had passed out. I was about to leave when a pale blue shimmering began in the jungle below. It faded, then began again in a new place. It faded once again and I strained my eyes for it. I turned to Eeola to ask him about it, and the blue light passed between me and the Shikki, then seemed to settle beside him. I could not move; it was as though my buttocks had become rooted to the rock. After a few moments, another such light joined the first, then another, and another, until four separate lights made a circle, with Eeola forming a fifth part of it. Slowly, Eeola turned his head until he faced me.

"Then, listen, human, while I take words and grant life to those who I am not yet able to grant death."

*   *   *

I would tell you of my Jaren; of Vastar, our warrior *Di,* who took the charge in battle much as he did when we were children; of Gemislor, whose broad back and jokes held us together through flame and privation; of mighty Dob, whose ruthlessness on the field of battle was matched only by his gentleness with a lost or hungry animal; of Timbenevva, whose pipes could make flagging spirits soar, and whose sly tongue could talk the very stars from the sky; and, of myself. I, Eeola, was the youngest member of the Jaren.

The human historians—those who deign to mention it—pass off the Jaren as a military organization; a form of half-squad in human terms; but the Jaren is much more. True, it is the building block of the Shikazu infantry, but it is, as well, family, schoolmates, friends, and yet more even than this. You are the Jaren, and without the Jaren, you are not.

Before entering the military, before adulthood, before instruction at the village *kiruch* as naked children playing at war with moss forts and water guns, the Jaren is formed. Over forty Earth years ago, in my village on the planet Tenuet, my story begins.

Ahrm was but a tiny village, no more than a wide place in the road on the way to the golden city of Meydal, but its single dusty street crowded with wattle huts was the center of my universe.

As a *tikiruch*, a carefree preschooler running naked with my mates, nothing seemed more important to me than joining in Jaren with Vastar. All the children of Ahrm admired Vastar, for even as a callow *tikiruch*, he stood a head or better above the rest of us, could outrun us all, and could wrestle any three of his mates to the ground. In our games, he would choose them, organize them, then win them. When we would take our water guns and deploy through the jungle to ambush phantom armies and shadow monsters, Vastar would always lead us. Even the elders at the evening meeting fire would nod at him, knowing someday Vastar would *Di* a Jaren, and because of that the Jaren would be great and do heroic deeds. Such would reflect well on Ahrm. I would daydream, but deep in my heart I knew that when Vastar formed his Jaren, I would not find myself one of its five. But toothless old Jevvey, my grandmother, had the faith that I lacked. She once sat before her hut tending her evening meal, stripped *sa* wrapped in yanna leaves baked in the ground over a bed of turawood coals. She sat as motionless as a smoke-blackened carving, her straggles of thin white hair hanging at the sides of her head.

"The evening finds you sad, little one."

I looked down and nodded. "Yes, Grandmother."

"Must I pull the reason from you as the fishers drag eels from their holes?"

I sighed, then shrugged. "Grandmother, will I *never* be joined in Jaren?"

The old woman snorted. "You are the son of the Ice Flower and the Silver Bird, two respected Jarens. You ask foolish questions."

"But, I am small. Even you call me 'little one.' What Jaren would have me?"

Jevvey shook her head. "The ghosts of my Jaren mates weep at your foolishness. Take care, else they shall steal into your hut and rob you of your breath."

I frowned. "I am not a child, Grandmother. You can't frighten me with tales of ghosts."

Jevvey looked at me, her eyes soft and black. "Eeola, I am the last of my Jaren, yet my mates still stand with me. They will always be with me until they call me to the endless sleep." She poked at the steaming ground with a stick. "One day you shall be part of a respected Jaren, and, perhaps years from now, you will see that the Jaren is forever. We are but bone and flesh, but the Light that fills you as an adult never dies." She sniffed and began scooping off the dirt from the cooked *sa*. "It is time for you to go home, little one."

I stood, wished her a good night, then walked the darkening path to my father's hut. Had I not been despondent about my chances of being joined in Jaren, the talk of ghosts would have hurried my steps. Instead, my feet dragged through the dust as I listened to *tikiruch* being called to mealtime by their mothers.

One day a few of us joined Vastar on one of his daring exploits. The *kiruchta*, the older schoolers, were at a clearing deep in the jungle, practicing with shield and wand under the stern instruction of Lodar, the village fencing master. Although the wands were at low energy output, a burst or slash on naked skin would blister it. A stray beam could blind a wide-eyed *tikiruch*, which is why we were forbidden to watch them practice, and which is why we skulked through the jungle to observe our seniors being put through their drills.

Crouching on all fours, peering out from beneath broad yanna leaves, our disrespectful band watched with eager eyes as the *kiruchta*, paired off in twos and traded beams and parries. Each student wore the *be*, the half-dress wrapped around the waist with the tail pulled between the legs and tucked in front. Their skins were already the deep brown of rich soil, with streaks of pink on cheeks, shoulders and thighs showing where wands in quick hands had found their marks. Each student held the clear wand, each tipped with its burning blue jewel, in the left hand, while right hands clasped the grips of black deflection shields. We giggled watching the students going wall-eyed, with one eye on opponent and the other on Lodar. No student dared let a stray beam fall on the fencing master, for Lodar would take this as a challenge. The student would then have to square off with the master and take his licks.

Lodar strode among the sweating students, pointing here and commenting there. He wore the *nabe*, the forest green full-dress of an adult. His shield was slung on his back, but his wand was

kept at the ready in his left hand. After a few moments of
watching, we noticed one of the students being bested by an
opponent obviously his superior at arms. With wand and shield,
the hapless *kiruchta* defended himself in a blur of arms, but the
coins of chance were against him. As he backed away, the tail of
his *be* untucked and fell behind his scrabbling feet, where he
stepped upon it, pulling the entire dress from his waist.

As we pained at our stifled giggles, none of us noticed Lodar
slip into the jungle and come up behind us. The grizzled old
master must have smiled as he saw our row of brown bums
sticking out at him from under the yanna plants, but in the flash
of an eye our giggles turned to yelps. Our band jumped to its feet,
each one clutching a burning cheek in each hand. Lodar's skilled
wand had played across our buttocks, and for the next few days
there would be much sleeping on stomachs and eating while
standing in the village of Ahrm. The master scolded us and sent
us running back toward the village to nurse our dignities.

Each one of us bore a pink stripe as evidence of our
infraction, and we were reluctant to bring them to our huts, for
when we did our parents would discover our sin. Until the pain
of Lodar's wand eased, none of us could bear having the hard
hands of our angry fathers popping off of our burned and
chubby cheeks. Most of the others fled to hideouts of their own,
while Vastar, Gemislor, Dob, Timbenevva and I sulked in the
brush behind the village. None of the others were crying, but it
was almost more than I could do to swallow my own tears. The
Shikazu take humiliation hard, and our striped buttocks would
be cause for jokes and laughter for years to come. Our faces
burned more fiercely than did our bums.

While we stood sullenly, rubbing our humiliated flesh, I
remember thinking, with the perspective of youth, that I could
not possibly survive that moment. It was then that Vastar
laughed. The cream blond of his mane shook, then he threw his
head back and howled. Leaping atop a stump, he held out his
arms. "Gather 'round me, mates; gather 'round."

The four of us stood before the stump, our humiliation
temporarily forgotten in our concern for our friend's sanity. He
laughed at the sky, then looked down at us. "Mates, this day we

have all been blooded with the same wand, and it is no shame to have Lodar's fire kiss your skin." He smiled, then nodded. "We are one in this, mates, and I would now form my Jaren. Gemislor, will you join me?"

Gemislor nodded, his eyes glowing. The elders had commented at many fires at how slow our generation of *tikiruch* was in forming Jarens. Many of them thought it was a sign that the Shikazu spirit was on the wane, but the cause was nothing so profound. We were all waiting for Vastar to form his Jaren in the hopes of being among its number. "And, you, Dob. Will you join me?"

Dob's hulking shoulders pulled back as his spine straitened. "Aye, Vastar. Aye."

"And, you, Timbenevva?"

"Aye. Your Jaren I will join."

Vastar turned toward me. I was smaller than the others and the worst runner in Ahrm. My most outrageous dreams did not see me thus. I swear my heart jumped as Vastar spoke. "And, you, Eeola. Will you join me?"

My heart stopped as I felt my mouth ask the question it had to ask. "Why me, Vastar? Why do you choose me?" I waved my hand at the others. "The blind can see why you choose Gem, Dob and Tim; they are tall, strong, brave."

My lower lip trembled as Vastar stepped down from his stump and placed his hands on my shoulders. "Eeola, a great Jaren must have more than brawn and speed; it must also have brains. This is what my father has taught me, and he speaks the truth. You are the smartest *tikiruch* in Ahrm, except for me. What do you say? Will you join me?"

I nodded as my face exploded into smiles. Vastar smiled back, then turned and mounted his stump. "Our Jaren is formed, and we shall swear so before the meeting fire tonight."

"Vastar," called Timbenevva. "We may wear our paint now that the Jaren is formed. What shall our symbol be?"

Dob admired the blue-painted flying creature he had seen on the left arms of a Jaren from another village. Gem insisted on the bright yellow lightening bolts he had seen on a warrior's hairy chest. Tim and I were both shouting for attention when Vastar held up his hands for silence. "Listen, mates. Our sign shall be a single red bar," he turned around and pointed at the pink stripe across his bum, "worn here."

Vastar raised his brow at us, we stood in silence for an instant, then all laughed. We would be spared our fathers' wrath, for the paint would hide the evidence. Laughing so hard he was barely able to stand, Dob ran to the village to secure paint and brushes. In the span of a few seconds I had become locked in life with the finest Jaren Ahrm would ever see, and had adopted a curious sign that we would all be sworn to defend with our lives. Of such things arc symbols made and destinies forged.

That night the five of us stood across the meeting fire from the hedman of Ahrm and declared our Jaren, our brightly painted backsides facing the people of the village. As I stood with my four tall companions, I could feel the eyes of envy dancing on my back. The pungent smell of turawood came from the fire while the pops and hisses joined the flickering light creating an aura that took us all back to the primitive ages of the first Jarens. The hedman, his deep green *nabe* decked with golden chains, looked up from the village book wherein was entered the signs of all the village Jarens. His voice, though strong, was rough with age. Nevertheless, he fixed us all with an unblinking black-eyed gaze. "There is no record of a Jaren of the Redbar in Ahrm." He closed the book and held out his arms. "This, then, is the Jaren of the Redbar?"

"Aye." We all responded with our heads bowed.

"Do you swear that your lives, your fortunes, and your futures are now as one, in the name of the Light?"

"We swear it."

"And who shall *Di* the Jaren of the Redbar?"

All but Vastar lifted their heads. "Vastar of Ahrm is our *Di*."

"And, this shall ever be so?"

"Aye."

The hedman nodded, then looked at Vastar. "*Di* of the Jaren of the Redbar."

Vastar looked up. "I am Vastar."

"Do you swear to *Di* this Jaren with fairness, strength, wisdom, and to do your best to bring it before the Light?"

"I so swear."

The hedman looked down, opened the book and held out a single brush dipped in red paint. "Make the mark of the Redbar, then, Vastar, and bring honor to your village." The people of the village cheered as our *Di* walked around the fire, took the brush and made the mark of the Redbar in the book. When he rejoined us, the five of us turned and faced the people, our chests bursting with pride. Our fathers and mothers stood up from the seated people and came to us.

On the dark path leading to my father's hut, my mother kissed me, then swiftly ran ahead to relate the news to my grandmother. My father placed a massive hand on my shoulder. "Eeola, I am pleased for you—and proud. I can tell you now that, because of your size, I feared no Jaren would take you. But, this—it is more than I could have hoped for. Vastar will be a great *Di,* and you all will bring glory to the symbol of the Redbar."

I suppressed a desire to laugh and only nodded. "It is good that I pleased you, father."

We walked in silence for a time, then my father stopped, pulling me to a halt beside him. He had a curious expression on his face. "Eeola, might I ask you a question?"

"Of course, Father."

"The symbol of the Redbar; you wear it higher up than the others. Why is that?"

I felt my face flush in the dark. "It . . . it's because they are so much taller than I am . . . Father."

My father's right eyebrow went up, while the other curled into a frown. A twinkle grew in his black eyes, then his face relaxed. He nodded and resumed walking down the path. "Come, Eeola. It is time we were getting to our sleeping mats."

I gulped and followed.

In time, the Redbar was presented to the five Jarens of our fathers where we were feasted and given advice. Afterwards, we were presented to the five Jarens of our mothers, again feasted, and inspected as material for future husbands. Until the very last of the Redbar was snared and wed, the Jarens of all of our mothers would scour the village, bragging, begging and negotiating, keeping sharp eyes out for females well placed in respected Jarens of their own.

In the years that followed, the Redbar had little time for such thoughts. Vastar took the duties of the *Di* seriously, and we ran, trained, wrestled and boxed, stopping only to eat and sleep. In time, although they remained taller than I, with the patient help of my brothers I could run as well and even best them wrestling on rare occasion. However, once we donned our half-dress and began the *kiruch,* it was my turn to help my brothers keep up with me. In between our lessons before the village classmaster, we met in the jungle clearing with Lodar to drill in arms. Lodar would always single out the Redbar for his severest criticisms, and by the look in his eye, I eventually became aware that our painted bums had fooled no one.

After classes and drills, Vastar would take us to the banks of the River Gnawi, where we would take out shield and wand and begin our drills. One on one, two on one, three on one, four on one. Jump, flash, parry, turn, flash—until the five of us ached and our *bes* hung limp between our legs, soaked with sweat. Then, placing our weapons aside, we would plunge into the cool waters of the river.

One day as we made our way to the riverbank, we heard laughter and splashing. Usurpers had moved into our swimming place. We came through the trees and entered the clearing and spied a Jaren of village females, also *kiruchta,* using *our* water to cleanse themselves after their drills. Glowers on our faces, Vastar ordered the females from the water. They laughed and made rude suggestions. Our blood boiling, Vastar challenged the female *Di* to a match with wands and shields to decide the question.

The five females came naked from the water, reached to the trees for their half-dress *bes* and covered their lower halfs. We hefted our own weapons as they retrieved theirs from the grass, then we squared off. Disaster ensued. Back at the village, nursing our newly roasted hides, Vastar stormed up and down in front of us.

"None of us? None of us won?"

Dob shrugged. "Vastar, I could not keep my mind on my drills. She bounced so . . ."

"Bah!" Vastar stamped his foot. "We have seen females before! And those females—we grew up with them! We have seen them naked since our first crawls in the dust!"

Timbenevva shrugged. "It is different, somehow."

Vastar snorted. "Different! If that had been war, we would be dead! How can I bring this Jaren before the Light?"

Gemislor rubbed his chin, his eyes cast down. "This is all so true, Vastar, but explain why you didn't lay your wand on their *Di*?"

Vastar flushed. "Why, my attention was diverted because of the four of you stumbling moonfaces bending all effort to disgrace our Jaren."

Gem's expression did not change as he absorbed the explanation, but his eyes laughed. Vastar blushed, then laughed with us. "Very well, Redbar, but we must keep our minds on our drills. In the years to come, we will be presented with stronger attractions than that. Let us drill."

True to his word, Vastar drilled and drilled us, there in the village street, until the horizon drank the sun. That night, as I lay my aching bones on my sleeping mat, I closed my eyes and dreamt of the lithe black-haired beauty that had smiled so sweetly just before burning the wand from my hand.

In our years of the *kiruch*, the classmaster beat many things into our heads. Then, it seemed to be a blur of facts and items of legend. Only now is it clear that every moment of our instruction was aimed at instilling in us the pride of the Shikazu; the pride of the unconquered warrior race of the planet Tenuet. True, we had merchants, builders, and administrators, but any one of them could push papers, tools and cash boxes aside, heft wands and shields, and acquit themselves respectfully on a field of battle. The Shikazu cannot be conquered; this was our one eternal truth. And, through it, we came to accept that as individuals we could not be beaten, save by another Shikazu. We held nine planets of four solar systems under the wand, races more advanced, more numerous, and physically more impressive; but, we held the wand, for we were the Shikazu.

At fencing drill, Lodar taught us nothing of quarter nor of surrender. His one subject: conquer. Press the opponent until he is vanquished, then move on to the next opponent. Those who lost contests at drills were driven by their Jarens to improve, until nothing could stand before their wands. Those who would not, or could not, improve their skills were dropped from drills, and dropped from their Jarens where they would be replaced by the more worthy. No one could bear the shame of a *kazu*—one discarded as being unfit—and a few of these drifted away from the village to live out their lives in the jungle or to seek a place amongst the dregs of the large cities. Most *kazu*, however, simply removed the energy guards on their wands and turned them upon themselves. No one wept for them.

This fate, and the constant pressure of my Jaren mates, polished my own skill with wand and shield until the five of us could put our backs together and stand off any ten opponents. Nevertheless, as our skills sharpened, so did Lodar's tongue in his verbal abuse of the Redbar. As time passed we became confident in our prowess with the wand, and ever more ingrained with fierce pride in the Shikazu, our Jaren, and in ourselves as individuals. The day had to come when Vastar was enough sure of himself and of his Jaren to no longer accept Lodar's abuse. A *Di* with less wit would have seen red and challenged Lodar months before, but Vastar was exceptional as only befits the *Di* of the Redbar Jaren.

At drills one day, the Redbar was squared off with the Jaren of the White Star. The White Star was senior to us, but we were leaving them in tatters, when Lodar called a halt to the drill. The two Jarens bowed toward each other, and then toward Lodar. The fencing master spat on the clearing's short grass and motioned for the White Star Jaren to retire to the edge of the clearing. Turning to face us, Lodar sneered. "The blood of the Shikazu curdles at the thought of this Jaren calling itself 'Shikazu.'" Lodar's black eyes flashed as he swaggered to stand in front of me. "I cannot understand why this Jaren hasn't dropped this pitiful tree lizard. And you three," he swept his hand at Gem, Dob and Tim, "you should be pulling plows, such hulking, clumsy lumps." He faced Vastar. "How can you bear the shame of keeping this disgraceful Jaren together? Have you no pride?"

Vastar lifted his head, his blond mane held in place by a red band, and smiled at the fencing master. Our *Di* lifted his wand, ejected its energy shield, and held the weapon under Lodar's nose. "Pick your mates, old man. The Redbar is past suffering the senile jabberings of an aging treetoad." Dob, Gem, Tim and I hefted our wands and ejected the energy shields. The wands would still be at low output, but without the shields, the burns would be deep and possibly deadly. Vastar had challenged Lodar to the *vienda*, the Jaren duel whose winners would be those left standing. There is no first burn and bows with the *vienda*. Instead, the combatant fights until he either wins or can fight no longer.

Lodar tossed back his head and laughed. "Mates? I need no mates to spread this Jaren all over the drill ground. I could throw my wand away, take a switch off a tree and whip the five of you."

Vastar folded his arms, snorted and said in an almost bored voice. "Pick your mates, Lodar, or retire from the field. We have had enough wind."

The rest of the Redbar laughed. As Lodar narrowed his eyes, nodded and walked to the edge of the clearing to fill out a combat team five, I felt the battle blood in my veins for the first time: a clawing, pulsing *need* to join in battle, to fight, to win. I felt no doubt about our victory; we were the Jaren of the Redbar; we were Shikazu. I looked at my mates and saw the same blood pounding through their veins, narrowed eyes, teeth showing through tightly drawn lips of brown.

With his wand, Lodar picked out four *kiruchta* and motioned them to the center of the clearing. All four were *Di* of their respective Jarens, and known to us all as excellent fighters. Lodar's group squared off with the Redbar, ejected their energy shields and bowed. The Redbar returned the bow and came up at the ready. Lodar spat out the command: "Begin!"

My opponent, the *Di* of the Black Sword Jaren, sidestepped and brought his wand down in a diagonal slash. Without thinking, I instinctively reacted with the trick Vastar had perfected and that we had practiced until the drill was more familiar to us than our names. Squeezing the shaft of my wand, I directed a pulse to the edge of my opponent's deflection shield at the same time I moved from the path of his slash. The force of the beam on his shield caused him to tip off-balance the least bit, and as he brought his wand arm up to counter, my wand seared the underside of his arm. In a flash, he brought his shield around, but the damage had been done and he was on the defensive. I laid my wand across his knees, and he began lashing out wildly with his own wand. His eyes were wild as I deflected his attack, then let my wand linger on his left foot. He went down on his left knee, covering himself almost completely with his shield, his ill-directed wand denuding the yanna plants behind me. A flash of brown, and I roasted the edge of his shoulder. His shield went up to cover, and my wand burned into his right foot. As his wand went up, I ran forward and kicked his shield with my foot, sending him sprawling on his back. In less time than it took his shield to sail to the ground, my knee was planted in his chest and my deenergized wand was at his throat. With my shield I came down upon his wand hand, then brought my knee up under his chin. I backed off at the ready, but the *Di* of the Black Sword lay motionless save the heaving of his chest. I turned to aid my mates, but they were waiting for me; Gem and Tim rested with their arms on Dob's shoulders, while Vastar stood above Lodar, our *Di's* eyes wild with triumph. Lodar pushed himself to a sitting position while the four of us gathered behind Vastar. Our *Di* looked down at the fencing master. "There will be no more abuse, Lodar, and the Redbar will come and go to drills as it chooses." Lodar nodded and we left the field, shouting and punching each other, looking for some way to work off the pressure we still had inside of us. I glanced back to look once more upon our field of victory and saw Lodar standing in its center, hands on his hips, smiles wrinkling his face and hot pride burning in his eyes. Since we were the victors, the look confused me. Years later it dawned on me that Lodar's occupation was taking babies and turning them into highly skilled fighters. The Jaren of the Redbar was not the only victor that day.

It was not long after that the Jarens of our parents offered us up for adulthood. My father's Jaren, that of the Ice Flower, and my mother's Jaren, that of the Silver Bird, stood with me before the Light.

When I was but a *tikiruch*, I had feared this test of the Light.

But, that was when I was a *tikiruch*. As we walked the path to the temple, in my heart I was Shikazu. I feared nothing, and felt confident the Light would serve me, not destroy me. The procession entered the rough stone structure, and inside it was but native rock for a floor. In the center of the structure, an outcropping protruded, and was capped by a carved rock shell. Great chains were attached to the shell and led to the roof, then down again. I stood with my mates around the shell, while the Jarens of our parents hefted the chains and began pulling.

My mates and I joined hands as the chain's slack was taken up. The shell began to rise, and a blinding blue light filled the temple. Higher rose the shell, until it dangled over our heads. I looked toward the light and saw its pulsing shimmer. Throughout the planet Tenuet ran this substance that bound together the Shikazu. Wherever it broke through the surface, the Shikazu covered it with a temple, then brought its best to stand the test of adulthood.

Still holding hands, we knelt before the Light, moved our clasped hands forward, and touched it. Had we been but four, we would have died. Had we been more than five, there would have been nothing. But, we were five, and the Light fused us into one. As its power flowed through us, our Jaren became as the fingers on a single hand, while, in turn, our Jaren became a part of the Shikazu. As we touched the Light, I could *feel* the thoughts of my mates, as they could feel mine. More than that, I could feel us all being filled with the warrior blood, and the mission to defend Tenuet, and the Light, for without the Light, we became nothing.

Apher of the Black Pike Jaren, Vastar's father, called forth from his place at the chains the first stanza of the *Rhanakah*— the service of the Light. "And now you are one in life, as you shall one day be one in death."

The five of us answered. "For we are Shikazu."

Gem's father called forth next, followed by each male parent in turn. "The Light you touch now shall remain with you each, until the last of your Jaren meets the long sleep."

"For we are Shikazu; the Light is ours."

"Witness the power of the Light, and know what you are."

"We are Shikazu; we cannot be conquered."

"You are bound now to the Shikazu, our honor is as your own."

"We are Shikazu and shall serve no other race."

"Stand, then, Shikazu; stand, Jaren of the Redbar."

We stood, let our hands fall to our sides, and watched as our parents' Jarens lowered the rock shell over the Light. The shell in place, there was a moment of quiet, then our parents' Jarens rushed to us, grinning, laughing, cheering, pummeling our backs, then presenting us each with the forest-green *nabe*—the robes of adulthood.

All of the Redbar donned the full-dress *nabe* that night, and the next morning we lounged next to our waterhole near the Gnawi discussing our futures. We had long since chased the female Jaren from the area, and in fact we ruled supreme in the village of Ahrm. "We are too big for Ahrm," as Dob observed.

Tim played on his pipes, then fingered the green of his *nabe*. "We have yet to exploit adulthood here in the village. There are females to be learned, councils to attend, and pleasures to experience. Let us at least wrinkle our robes before we seek the road."

Gem sat up, crossed his legs and held out his hands. "Brothers, why do we not place our Jaren at the disposal of the Shikazu Infantry? They would beg to have us in their ranks, and the promise of action is there. A race challenges our territories toward the galactic center side of the four stars." Gem turned the spit on the four-legged *sa* we'd caught.

Dob nodded. "Aye, the humans."

Tim replaced the pipes in his robe, then scratched his chin. "What are they like?" He sniffed at the cooking *sa*.

"Like us. They come from the same stock, but they are smaller and have many colors."

Tim looked thoughtful. "How do they fight?" Dob only shrugged. "Vastar?"

Our *Di* lay flat on his back, watching through the treetops at the clouds. He closed his eyes, shook his head, then went back to looking at the clouds. "I know nothing of the humans, except that they control many worlds and would have ours as well." We all laughed, since nothing had ever sounded as absurd as this alleged human goal. No race takes from the Shikazu and lives to recount the experience. Vastar rolled his head in my direction. "What about you, Eeola? Are you finding the borders of Ahrm confining?"

I shrugged. "I go with my Jaren."

"What about the female? What's her name?"

I flushed. After we had squared off again at the waterhole with the female Jaren, that of the Golden Dart, I had begun seeing Carrina, the female that had, first, beaten me, but then had fallen to my wand. Neither my Jaren nor she understood why the scars I had caused her gave me pain. But, all the same, she let me kiss and caress them. "Her name is Carrina." I added a stick to the small fire.

"Carrina," Vastar repeated. "The Golden Dart is already a respected Jaren. Do you think our mother's Jarens would approve?"

I looked down and picked at my toenails. "I know not. But, it is no matter. The Golden Dart is sworn to enter the army. She must follow her Jaren as I must follow mine." I smiled. "And, I doubt that my brothers of the Redbar are agreeable to settling down to wife, home and brat at this early time—and neither am I."

Dob reached over a thigh-sized hand and clopped me on the shoulder. It was only by the grace of that shoulder having filled out with muscle over the years since the Jaren was formed that I was saved. "Aye, Eeola, we must seek our fortunes— adventure!" He turned to Vastar. "I have heard the humans take mates at will, at any time, and without ceremony; that they act love without love, and without pledges of honor. Is this true?"

Vastar nodded as he sprang to his feet, then crouched before the fire. He ripped a still bloody limb from the *sa,* tore at it with his teeth and wiped the grease from his hands upon his dusty feet. He looked at us all as he spoke around the mouthful of bloody meat. "They are animals."

That day beside the waters of the Gnawi, we decided to strike out on the trail toward Meydal the next morning to see some of the sights. I had never been beyond the limits of Ahrm, and long before the sun chased the shadows from the sky, I was up waiting impatiently by the dying coals of the meeting fire. I had a small shoulder pack filled with food and things I would need for travel. My shield was slung, and at my waist my wand dangled where it would be handy. As I waited, the smells of the village—the fire, the dust, the life-smell of fat orchids in the jungle—began tugging at my heart. This was my only home. As I knelt on the hard-packed soil of the meeting place, I pulled the short-knife my father had given me the night before from my sash. I forced the blade into the dirt, and as I dug Dob walked up beside me, knelt and began digging. He smiled at me as we completed our holes. We each took our knives, cut off locks of hair and buried them in the holes. Even if we died, our spirits would come back to Ahrm to reclaim their own. It was a child's fable, and I would have felt foolish had not Dob joined me in my childish ritual.

We heard a snort behind us and we stood to see Vastar, Gem and Tim, packs on shoulders, shields on backs, standing together looking at us. Vastar held out a hand toward the burying place. "Are we *tikiruch* to be planting hair?" Dob and I were speechless, caught as we were by our brothers. Then Vastar laughed, and the three of them pulled knives, knelt and planted their own. Moments later, my brothers and I left the dim glow of the meeting fire, walked the dusty street of Ahrm and entered the blackness of the jungle trail. In the east, the shadows were beginning to give back the sun.

We walked in single-file with Vastar in the lead. Although we fairly exploded to laugh and rough around at the beginning of our adventure, we maintained silence and kept our eyes on the jungle, for we were not *tikiruch* to be surprised by bandit Jarens or bands of starving *kazu*. Many times we passed Jarens walking in the other direction, and each time we raised our wand hands when they did and placed them across our breasts. As they passed, Vastar would bow his head to the other *Di* who would, in turn, bow his or hers. As the last one in our procession, I would keep watch on the passing Jaren until it went out of sight, while the last one in the passing file kept a watch on the Redbar. There were lone travelers, too, and on these we kept a careful eye. They could be parts of Jarens, but more often than not they would be *kazu* turned to waylaying their betters for food and weapons. When these passed, we would draw our wand arms across our breasts, but Vastar would not bow.

We walked all that morning, keeping a strong pace, and had entered a district where the *nabe* worn by the Jarens were brown when a lone traveler wearing a leather shirt and black *be* half-dress approached from the other direction. The wand side, his left, was clear, but we kept our eyes on him as he came near. When he came up next to Vastar, a wand came up in the fellow's *right* hand. Our wand hands were across our breasts, and there was nothing Vastar could do. But, standing behind Dob's hulk, the leather-shirted creature could not see my right hand speed to my sash, take my new knife from it and hurl it past Dob's shoulder at the fellow's head. It was a new knife, and I was not yet familiar with its balance. Instead of the blade sinking into the thief's brain, the hilt struck him on the forehead, splitting the skin. As the thief's lamps went out, he sank to the path. As he hit, we heard scampering feet and rustling leaves in the jungle around us. The fellow's companions appeared to have no desire to tangle with the Redbar.

While I retrieved my blade, Vastar stooped over the bandit and plucked the wand from the fellow's hand. Looking up, he nodded at Tim and Gem. "Keep a watch on the jungle. All of this creature's band may not have taken to the bush." Vastar looked at me as I tucked my knife into my sash. "You spared this bandit, Eeola, and he still lives. What do you suggest we do with him?"

I shrugged. "My mercy was unintentional, Vastar. It is my new knife who spared the scum."

Vastar frowned. "If you intend to keep your hair, Eeola, you must bend your new blade to your will." I nodded. Vastar turned back to the bandit. "Still, what shall we do with him?"

Dob nudged the bandit with his toe. "Why not leave him here, Vastar?"

Our *Di* shook his head. "I would not leave even a *kazu* to the mercy of the jungle and its creatures. Besides, if the creatures don't kill him, he will recover and use our mercy to waylay other travelers."

Dob rubbed his chin, then shrugged. "Kill him, then. We have the right."

Vastar stood and backed away from the bandit. "Very well, Dob; have at it."

"Me?" Dob looked at Vastar with wide eyes.

"It was your suggestion."

Dob frowned, grasped his wand and pulled it from his sash. He held the wand for an instant, then lowered it. "It is not as though he could fight, Vastar." Dob replaced his wand and cocked his head toward Vastar. "Our *Di* deserves the honor of our Jaren's first kill."

Vastar snorted, stood and held out the thief's wand in my direction. I took it and watched while our *Di* secured his own wand and aimed it at the thief. He grimaced, looked at Dob, then back at the thief.

I held up my hand. "Vastar, wait."

Vastar heaved a sigh and lowered his wand. "What is it, Eeola? I must be about the work that needs doing."

I held the thief's wand out to him. "Look. It has no power, and the jewel is shattered. If he was out to kill us, it was not with that."

Vastar took the wand, aimed it at an empty spot in the trail and pressed the handle. Nothing. "It is true."

Dob nudged the thief, again with his toe. "Attacking a wanded Jaren with nothing but wit and a lifeless stick bespeaks of no little courage, Vastar."

Vastar shook his head. "The courage of a bandit." He threw up his hands. "Now, what do we do with him?"

The thief moaned, opened his eyes and looked at our faces. "I live?"

Vastar threw the dead wand on the bandit's chest. "We will probably live to regret it. What is your name, thief?"

The bandit sat up, holding his head as though it were a sack of shattered glass. "A moment, my benefactors, while I calm the whistles between my ears." After a moment, he lowered his hands to his lap and raised a shaggy gray eyebrow in my direction. "You, small one; is it your skill I should be thankful for or your ineptitude?"

I pulled the knife from my sash, flipped it and caught it by the blade. "Perhaps we can judge this properly if I make another throw."

The bandit grinned through his stubble of gray whiskers and held up a hand. "No offense, lad. I but asked a simple question."

Vastar snapped his fingers. "Old bandit. Your name?"

"I am called Krogar by my friends."

"What do the rest of us call you?"

Krogar shrugged. "You hold the wands; you may call me anything you wish." The bandit pushed himself to his feet, stood weaving for a moment, then looked at our faces, stopping on Vastar. "Well?"

"Well, what, thief?"

"Am I to be spared or not? If I am, I'm sure we both have better things to do than standing here. You must be on your way, and I must make my living." Krogar shrugged and looked down. "If I'm not to live, then be done with the task and end this cursed headache that threatens to open the top of my skull."

Despite ourselves, we could but laugh at the old fellow's crust. Vastar looked at us, then waved a hand at the old bandit. "Keep your miserable life and your aching head, Krogar. But beware of this Jaren should we pass this way again." Vastar motioned to us and we fell in line and continued down the trail. I turned once to look back at Krogar, but the trail was empty.

For days we walked the trail, putting up nights in strange villages. At their meeting fires we would relate the news we had come across and the villagers would tell us things they had picked up from other travelers. Often there would be one or more other travelers at the fire, and it was from one of these that we heard of the human conquest of the planet Baalphor. The traveler had come from a town on the edge of the city of Meydal where the terrible news still ran hot through the streets. "The Jarens of Meydal and surrounding towns were entering the army in droves." The fellow scratched beneath his maroon *nabe*, then pointed in the direction we had come from. "I travel to my village of Tdist to gather up my Jaren. We will return to Meydal and enter."

Vastar snapped a stick he had been toying with, then threw the two pieces into the fire. His eyes blazed in the red light of the fire as he turned to the traveler. "I cannot believe Baalphor has fallen—not to *humans*."

The traveler shrugged. "They are numerous, and they have great, powerful weapons, as well as skill in their use."

Vastar made fists with his hands and shook them. "But, they are not *Shikazu!* Do you tell me the Shikazu have been *conquered?*"

"No. The Shikazu will remain unconquered until the last of us lays down the wand. The garrison on Baalphor has been destroyed, but even now I suspect the army is preparing to drive the humans off the planet."

Dob snorted and raised his brows in a show of contempt. "Vastar, the army will probably drive the scum from Baalphor long before we can reach the streets of Meydal."

The traveler shook his head. "I fear not, my gross friend. Many new ghosts shall walk before Baalphor falls. The Shikazu controls few planets compared to the humans."

"How many do the humans hold?" I asked.

"Over two hundred. We cannot be beaten, for we are the Shikazu; but, there will be a price."

The Shikazu's empire of nine planets had been difficult to imagine; at least, for one who had never been outside of Ahrm. An empire of two hundred planets—it was beyond imagination. I think I felt, at that moment, a touch of fear.

The next morning, we pointed our toes at Meydal to be sworn to the military. Our blood, the blood of the Shikazu, was up and boiling. In time, the trail widened and we came upon motor carts, as well as more travelers. The closer we came to the city, the wider and more congested the road became. Soon, the road was hard-surfaced and traveled only by sleek, many-colored crafts that would whiz by blowing the heat and dust from the road over us. The villages we traveled through were constructed of stone, metal and glass, while the villagers strutted upon upraised paths of stone wearing *nabe* that fought the eye for belief: metal gold, deep crimson stitched with silver, loud pinks, and stripes of every description. Next to the raised walks, merchants shouted of their wares amidst the bustle, and soon the human hoards were forgotten as the five villagers of Ahrm drank in this new world of flash and glitter. In the town of Adelone, we walked one of the upraised paths around a flowered hill upon which stood a grand house of smooth white pillars and arches, then stopped as though stunned as the main street of the town spread before us. The *size* of the buildings. The *crowds!*

Suddenly Vastar's angry face cut off my view. "Look at you! Mouths hanging open, eyes bugged! Get the straw out of your ears! Do you want these villagers to think us unsophisticated?" I looked at the others and realized that our *Di* had not singled me out, but was lashing all of us. He turned and pointed down the street. "There is a station. We need not go on to Meydal."

I followed the direction of his finger and saw the crossed pikes that symbolized the army standing out from the wall of a tall silver-and-glass building. I tugged at Vastar's *nabe*. "If this is only a town, Vastar, what could Meydal be like?"

Vastar shook his head. "We are here to enter the army; not to see the sights. There is a station, and we can be in service all the sooner."

Dob gained control of his gaping mouth long enough to comment upon Vastar's reasoning. "We will still be sent to the main station in Meydal, will we not? We will be sworn no faster, then, if we travel to Meydal and seek a station."

Vastar raised an eyebrow. "Gem, what say you?"

Gem shrugged. "I would see a little of this city before we are sworn."

There was no need to ask Timbenevva; his drooling tongue almost hung to the walk. Vastar's head gave a curt nod. "Very well, we shall see Meydal, but can we at least inquire at the station here about directions? All of these roads, streets and side streets are beginning to confuse me."

We stepped off, gawking at the buildings and people, our attention so absorbed that had we been attacked by two crippled, half-witted *tikiruch*, I doubt that victory would have fallen to the Redbar.

Compared to the city of Meydal, the town of Adelone that had stunned us with its grandeur was but a mud wallow. The army officer at the Adelone station had given us transportation passes, and told us we could report to one of the stations in Meydal—this, of course, after signing us up. We had two days to ourselves before reporting. The officer walked us to the pneumo station in the town, and put us on one of the cars. Moments after we lowered ourselves into the plush seats, the car shot along a tube much like a bullet through a blowpipe. Before we had really settled in, a voice from the brightly lit overhead barked at us. We were in Meydal.

As we stepped from the car onto a platform, we simply gawked. Passengers trying to disembark behind us shoved us rudely out of the way, but we hardly noticed. Like a forest of giant sword ferns, Meydal's incredible buildings towered above us. When we walked to the railed edge of the platform to have a better view, we backed away as we realized the platform was suspended high above the ground. We inched back and saw that the buildings extended below the platform just as far as they rose above it. Dob shook his head and laughed so hard he could not stop.

"What amuses you, brother?" I asked.

Dob waved his hand up and down at the magnificient spires of Meydal. "Do you remember how they marveled in Ahrm when my father built a hut with a loft above it, and how afraid I was to be up so high?" He laughed again, and I joined him. It was an overwhelming sight, and I believe we would be gawking there yet had not Larenz come along.

"Seeing the sights before entering the army, jungle cousins?" We turned to see a tall, black-maned fellow decked in crimson *nabe* embroidered along the edges with geometric shapes in gold thread.

Vastar cocked his head at us and spoke to the stranger. "We have already entered. We must report the morning of the day after tomorrow. Who might you be?"

The fellow in red bowed. "Please excuse my thoughtlessness. I am Larenz, *Di* of the Jaren of the Red Claw. Meydal is my city."

Vastar nodded. "We are the Jaren of the Redbar from Ahrm." At Larenz's puzzled expression, Vastar shrugged. "It is a village far to the south." Our *Di* introduced himself and the rest of us to Larenz.

The stranger smiled at us with a display of beautiful straight teeth that contrasted sharply with the dark brown of his face.

"Excellent. I am to report at the same time with my Jaren. Do you know someone in Meydal?"

Vastar frowned. "Why?"

"If you don't, I would be happy to show you the city. If you don't know your way around, you'll miss most of it."

Vastar turned to consult with us, bounced a single gaze off of our eager faces, then turned back to Larenz. "Very well, Larenz. We accept your invitation."

"Excellent. Then, cousins, be kind enough to follow me." Larenz turned and led us off the platform, through a glass door that opened without touching, then into a small box that dropped out from underneath us, disgorging us below at street level. All during our fall to the street, I mulled over the reasons I could think of for this apparent kindness from a stranger, and decided to keep my wand arm limber.

Using our army transportation passes, Larenz of the Red Claw led our Jaren through a maze of tubes and connections, stopping here and there to witness sights he thought would interest us. Of all the sights, the squat sprawl of the government district, with broad, tree-lined streets and gleaming white, metal and glass above smooth, well-tended lawns, impressed me the most. But between that and the park, the choice was hard—and the business buildings! The walks choked with bustling adults and children, the streets jammed with sleek dark vehicles. Meydal was, in truth, a city of wonders.

Even so, as my neck began aching at looking up at the buildings and my feet tired at being slapped upon the hard walks, my interest began flagging. It was at that point I noticed a curious thing: the citizens of Meydal carried neither shields nor wands. Here and there would be an individual properly armed, but his or her *nabe* branded the person as being out of the jungle as was the Redbar. Those decked in the garish finery I had come to associate with Meydalians, were unarmed. At one point in our travels, I found Larenz walking beside me, and asked him about this curious fact.

He laughed. "There is no need for arms in Meydal. Do you see slavering beasts crouching on the building ledges, or lurking in doorways?" He laughed again. "The jungle is a long way off, cousin."

I pointed at a few of the people passing in the other direction. "I see the most dangerous beast of all here, and in great numbers."

Larenz halted, stood on his toes and looked over the heads of the crowd on the walk. "You can never find one when you need . . . there!" He pointed. "Do you see the fellow in black *nabe* with the red stitching?"

"The one with the club?"

"Aye. It is his job, Eeola, to keep the citizens of Meydal from each other's throats—and purses." We turned and walked quickly to catch up with the others. "He is a member of a Jaren sworn to the police."

I shrugged. "I would not be comfortable leaving my protection to others, Larenz."

"It is our way, Eeola, and it works well enough. There is no need to go armed in Meydal except, perhaps, in the Human Quarter."

My eyes went wide. "Humans? Here on Tenuet?"

"Why, of course. There are many, many races in Meydal, including humans. Quite a number, too."

"But, Larenz, we are at war . . ."

He waved his hand. "We are at war with a government, Eeola, not a race. Everyone in the Human Quarter is a citizen of Tenuet, as are you and I."

"But . . . they are not Shikazu!"

"No, they are not Shikazu. Would you and your mates like to see the Human Quarter?"

My face felt drained of blood. I nodded and turned to ask the others, but they had been listening. Vastar nodded. "Show the way, Larenz. We would see your housebroken humans."

As gnarled, filth-covered roots are part of a beautiful flower, the Human Quarter was a part of Meydal. In a haze my mind recalls low, red-black row dwellings; narrow, refuse-strewn streets, strange music and hostile glances. The humans, pink, gray, yellowish, copper, and a few who could almost pass as Shikazu, except for their strange fuzzy hair, moved from the walks as we approached, keeping their eyes down, hands shoved into openings in the leg coverings they wore. Females hung from windows in the evil-smelling structures, chattering and shouting among themselves. Many younger humans sat on steps leading to entrances, while others stood along the walk in small groups, laughing and talking. Old ones stared blankly from open windows, seeing nothing.

I turned to Larenz. "Why, Larenz? Why do they live in this manner?"

Larenz only shrugged. "It is their way."

I snickered. "This is the race that rules two hundred worlds?" The others laughed. A group of young male humans turned at the sounds of the laughter and glowered at us.

Larenz waved his hand at the street. "These are not the only humans on Tenuet, Eeola. There are many in rich homes here in Meydal. But, every city of the nine worlds has a human quarter that looks much as this one does. My only explanation is that they are not Shikazu."

The group of male humans spread out across the walk in front of us. My eyes quickly noted that Larenz and my mates were the only Shikazu within sight. Several of the humans pulled knives or wands from garish-looking shirts while, two and three at a time, other humans joined their ranks carrying wands, knives, lengths of pipe and chain. My fingers stole around the handle of my wand.

A tall human, yellow with slanting eyes, stood above the others and in front of them. He threw up his head. "Looks like Baalphor hasn't taught the Shikkies anything."

Larenz waved his hand. "Stand out of the walk and let us pass."

The human spat on the walk. "And, if we don't, Shikki?"

Larenz laughed. "Why, we'll burn a path through the middle of you. Now, stand aside."

One of them from the end called, "Aye, shikkishikkishikki!"

A wand came up, and in the flash of an eye Vastar burned it from the human's hand. The Redbar unslung its shields and stood at the ready. The yellow human held up its hands and shook his head. "Hey, Shikki, we were just having a little fun. Ease off."

Vastar, his eyes bright with blood, dropped his shield a bit and lowered his wand. At that moment, a whirling length of chain sailed through the air at him. Vastar knocked it to the ground with his shield and screamed, "Shikazu!" He brought his wand across the chests of the front rank of humans and they dropped to the walk. The rest of us waded in, cutting and burning, the smell of roasted flesh strong in the air. Larenz picked a fallen wand from the walk and joined us, burning the scum with a skill the Redbar had rarely seen outside of its own performances. After only a few moments, the street animals broke and ran. I counted fifteen of the humans left on the walk by the time the police came. The females had stopped their chattering and were looking down upon us, their faces twisted with hate, some with grief. But, the old ones still stared through their windows, seeing nothing.

The police were numerous, and upon Larenz's advice, we surrendered our wands and shields to them. Other than those groaning on the walk, few of the humans were gathered up and placed in the holding cell with us. Larenz and Vastar explained that we must report soon to the army, but the police said there was nothing to be done about it. It would take all of five days to process us, get our statements and stand the hearing that would determine if we would have to stand trial. The holding cell was an enormous room, windowless and dark, which reflected our gloomy spirits. We had given our oaths to the army, but there seemed no way to abide by our word. Several times Vastar spoke sharply to Larenz. "A fine guide you are! 'Would you like to see the Human Quarter?' he says!" Vastar swept his arm at the few Shikazu and numerous humans in the cell. "Well, Larenz, we are in the Human Quarter. What now?" He sat on the cell floor with a thump, next to Dob.

Larenz, seated on the floor, leaned back against the cell wall, and stared at the humans seated in the opposite corner of the room. "I had not planned this, Vastar."

Vastar snorted. "I suppose it is nothing to you, but we of Ahrm are honor-bound to keep our oaths."

Larenz's eyes flashed at our *Di*. "The oath is no less sacred to a Meydalian, jungle runner!" He started up, but Dob's huge hand found Larenz's shoulder and held him to the floor.

Dob smiled. "Larenz, I would like to know why you singled us out on the platform. Why did we become the object of your generosity?"

Larenz's eyes went from one to the other of us, then he shrugged with his unclamped shoulder. "My Jaren reports soon to the army, as you know."

"As we know."

"My father's Jaren officers the Army of the Fourth Star. I have studied at the *Den-kiruch*, the military school, and after training, my Jaren shall officer an infantry group. Meydalians are good fighters—some say, none better. But, my father always speaks well of our jungle cousins. He advised me to put as many jungle Jarens into my group as I could get to join."

Dob nodded. "And, you would have us join your group when it is formed?"

"Yes."

Dob nodded again. "Truly a great honor, Larenz. I have a question—a matter that needs clearing up."

"What is that?"

Dob held his hands up indicating the cell. "The first thing that happened to the Jaren of the Redbar under your skilled leadership is that it was thrown into prison. If we join you, do you then lead us to the penal colony, or perhaps the execution block?"

The rest of us snickered. Larenz grimaced, then shook his head. "I had no reason to expect the humans to attack us here on the streets of Meydal. It has never happened before."

A human on the other side of the cell stood and shouted. "You Shikkies clamit! Some of us want to sleep."

As the human returned to his place, Vastar began getting to his feet. Dob's other meaty hand clamped our *Di* to the hard floor. "There must be thirty of them, Vastar. If you order it, I will happily join your attack, but it seems to me that we are already in enough trouble."

"They forget their place!"

Dob nodded. "But you forget our place." He nodded again at the cell walls.

Vastar shook his head. "We have given our word to the army!"

A shadowy figure, seated in a corner away from both the

humans and our group, stood, scratched itself and shambled across the floor to stand in front of Vastar. It laughed. "Well, well. My ears spoke truly. It is my benefactor from the trail south of Laronan." He turned to me. "We meet again, skull-cracker."

I squinted in the poor light. "Krogar? It is you."

Vastar snorted. "What do you want, *kazu*? Another crack on the head?"

Krogar squatted and pointed a finger at Vastar's chest. "I am no *kazu*, young one. Although I am alone and work the trails for a living, I am of a Jaren, that of the Green Dragon of the Village of Sarat."

Vastar raised an eyebrow. "Then where are your mates?"

Krogar looked at the cell floor, then back at Vastar. "They are ashes mixed with those of the defenders of Dashik. We were part of the force that secured the ninth planet for the Shikazu."

"You were in the army?"

"I think I already answered that."

Vastar threw up a hand, then let it fall back into his lap. "If you are Shikazu, and once of the army, why are you a thief? Why do you prey on Shikazu?"

I could not see Krogar's face, but a strange quality came into his voice—an empty, lost sound. "My Jaren was almost twenty years old when my mates walked as ghosts. It works on you in a way I hope you never have an opportunity to understand." Krogar waved his hand, dismissing the subject. "From the conversation I overheard, I detect a desire to quit these walls. Why are you here?"

Vastar pointed at the humans on the other side of the cell. "They attacked us. We will be set free after the hearing, but that means we will miss our reporting time."

Krogar looked over our faces and stopped on Larenz. "You have picked up a new companion."

Larenz returned Krogar's look. "I am Larenz of the Red Claw Jaren, here in Meydal. I too will miss my reporting time."

Krogar rubbed his chin. "Larenz . . . does not your father's Jaren officer the Fourth Army?"

"Yes."

"I suppose your father might look with favor, in a pecuniary fashion, upon one who rescued his son from this disgrace."

Larenz laughed. "It would appear, Krogar, that your position is no more mobile than ours."

Krogar stood, turned toward the humans and shouted: "Jailer, get these foul-smelling creatures out of our cell! Shikazu cannot be forced to share cells with such animals!" The humans began grumbling, and several got to their feet and began approaching Krogar. The thief turned back to us and grinned. "In confusion there is profit." He turned back to the humans, adopted a fighting stance, then rushed headlong into them, knocking four of them to the floor in a tangle of legs and arms.

Larenz and Vastar both stood at the same time and yelled, "Shikazu!" We all came to our feet, as did the humans, then closed battle in the center of the floor. A human rushed at me, fists swinging, but I sidestepped his attack and brought up my knee into his stomach. While I grappled with a second, a third planted a fist in my eye. I'm not sure, I didn't take the time to examine him, but I think I broke his neck. In a moment, I was buried under a mountain of cursing bodies. A moment later, I felt the bodies being plucked from me, then saw Dob—a human clutching to his back and one hanging from each leg, picking up my attackers by neck and drawers and flinging them across the cell.

Whistles shrieked, the cell door flew open, and four armed police entered. They carried clubs which they soon brought to bear upon the heads of the humans. In a moment, the full fury of the humans was concentrated upon the police, while Krogar, Larenz and the Redbar separated and went for the open door. Standing in the doorway, another of the police spied Krogar and lifted his club. Krogar shrugged as if to say, "I cannot be blamed for trying," then he half-turned away, turned back in a flash and caught the fellow with a foot in the stomach.

The seven of us rushed through the door and over the downed police into the corridor. Krogar waved, turned right and ran. We followed until we saw two more officers rushing in the opposite direction. These two hefted wands, rather than clubs, but Krogar did not hesitate for an instant. I saw him take a burst in the chest just as he leaped into the air to fall against the two police, knocking them to the floor. Gem reached to pick up one of the fallen officer's wands, but Krogar knocked Gem's hand away. "No! If we kill a police, they will never rest until they find us. Leave it." Krogar opened his leather shirt, looked at the ugly burn on his chest, then waved us on. I turned back and saw the corridor choked with police. Most went into the cell we vacated, but eight of them, armed with wands, came our way.

We pounded down the corridor, wand beams flashing about our heads and off the walls. We turned a corner, ran over a guard positioned there, and piled into an elevator. Krogar grabbed the control and the floor dropped out from beneath me. He cocked his head toward the door. "Be prepared to charge when it opens; they will be waiting for us."

Krogar brought the car to a sudden stop, pulled open the door, and joined us in our battle cry as we charged into the lobby of the police building. "Shikazu!" We stumbled into each other as those in front saw first that no one was waiting for us. A receptionist, seated behind a counter next to the elevator, looked at us with a puzzled expression. Krogar laughed, then began walking toward the door.

The receptionist stood. "One moment..."

A clanging sound filled the lobby, and we could see massive shutters slowly closing over the doors to the street. Krogar broke, ran and dived under a shutter, while the rest of us dived under other door shutters. Rolling on the walk outside the police building, I looked around and saw that we had all made it. Still, it would not be safe to linger out on the street for too long. Soon, police cruisers would arrive. Larenz turned to Krogar. "Where now?"

"To your father's house that I might collect my reward."

Dikahn of the Blue Cloud Jaren, Lord General of the Army of the Fourth Star and father of Larenz, reclined on his couch as Larenz recounted the history of the past few hours. Krogar stood at his side while the rest of us stood in a row behind him. Aside from the occasion, I was stunned at the grandeur of Dikahn's home. The one room we were in could fit over six of the huts entire families occupied in Ahrm. Dikahn himself was dressed in silver *nabe* and wore a bright red sash encrusted with medals. His black mane was shot with silver, and his black eyes, set in an impassive face as though they were jewels mounted in stone, studied his son. As Larenz finished, Dikahn turned toward Krogar. "You say you were once in the army?"

Krogar bowed. "Yes, Lord General. My Jaren served you in the capture of Dashik more than fifteen years ago."

Dikahn nodded, then turned toward Larenz. "You are an adult, my son, which precludes my warming your backside for today's foolishness. I hope your Jaren will accept your apology." He turned back to Krogar. "Since my son made your acquaintance in a prison, am I hasty in presuming that you were there for some reason?"

Krogar smiled. "My Lord General, it was nothing—a small dispute over property."

"Somebody else's, no doubt." The Lord General shrugged. "Still, I owe you for enabling my son to keep his word to his Jaren and to the army. Do you have something in mind for a reward?"

Krogar bowed. "I would not presume to instruct the Lord General in such a matter."

Dikahn nodded, a wry smile tugging at the corners of his mouth. "Tell me, Krogar; under what circumstances did you leave the army?"

The thief pursed his lips, then held out his hands. "It was nothing. A simple dispute over orders that resulted in a minor scuffle."

Dikahn nodded. "And who was the officer you struck?"

Krogar raised his eyebrows in a show of innocence, then he sighed. "A company officer named Vulnar, Lord General. But," he added, "no one served the Shikazu better than I. I was dismissed against my will, and for an unjust reason."

Again, Dikahn nodded. "Krogar, faithful old soldier, I believe your treatment to have been harsh, and I would correct this injustice. Tomorrow you will join my son and his new friends here and report to the barracks in Meydal for army service."

"But, but Lord General..."

Dikahn held up his hand. "No need to thank me, Krogar. This you have earned." The general turned toward Larenz. "You will bring special instructions from me to the station officer. It would not be wise to have you train on Tenuet. Therefore, you and your new comrades will be shipped to the Fourth Army and trained on Dashik. To put you any further away from Tenuet would require going outside the jurisdiction of the Shikazu."

Krogar held out his hands. "Lord General, it has been a long time since I saw service and I am over forty now, and perhaps the decision to discharge me wasn't as unjust as I thought . . ."

Dikahn held up a hand. "None of this will stand before my orders, Krogar. Please, let me do this for you for what you did for my son."

Krogar stood straight and cocked his head. "If I don't?"

The Lord General leaned forward on his couch, his eyes deep and cold. "Consider the alternative, my purse-lifting friend."

Krogar studied the general for an instant, then bowed. "Of course, the Lord General's wishes will be observed."

"Of course." Dikahn nodded at Larenz. "Find a servant and arrange quarters for your friends."

"Yes, Father." Larenz turned and the rest of us bowed, then turned to follow. Dikahn caught my eye as I was about to go through the door, then motioned for me to remain.

"Close the door."

I did so, then walked back and stood before Dikahn's couch. "Yes, Lord General?"

"Larenz said that your village was far south?"

"Yes, Lord General. The Jaren of the Redbar hails from Ahrm."

The general nodded. "Then your fencing master would have been Lodar?"

"Why, yes. Do you know him?"

Dikahn nodded. "He has served with me. He and his Jaren officered a group under me during the last war. A Shikazu is Lodar." Dikahn rubbed his chin, then studied me. "You know that, after training, my son's Jaren will officer a company?"

"Yes. He told us."

Dikahn nodded. "Tell me—what is your name?"

"Eeola."

"Tell me, Eeola. Would the Redbar apply to serve in my son's company?"

"I cannot speak for the Jaren, Lord General, but for myself, I would serve with him." I saw no change on the old general's face, but I had the feeling that I had said just the right thing.

Dikahn waved his hand. "Go and join your mates, Eeola, and thank you."

"Thank you, Lord General." I bowed and left the room.

Dashik is the second planet in the Minuraam system, the Fourth Star of the Shikazu. There is a large Shikazu population on the planet dominating the Borgunz, the squat, powerful, fur-covered creatures that were the planet's original masters. Dashik is lonely, and very, very hot. After our month-long flight from Tenuet, our first look at our new station, and after absorbing the molten wrath of Aragdan, the training instructor assigned to us, we appreciated all the more Lord General Dikahn's peculiar sense of humor.

Training by a field unit is different than group training at a station, such as the centers on Tenuet. Perhaps the station cadres are further removed from the threat of invasion. In any event, the instructors in a field unit know that any moment their charges may be called upon to fight, and fight well. Aragdan, therefore, was a merciless master, and we would have been continually sweat-soaked had not the air been so dry.

So much of it was so different from the jungle. Learning the jump racks was the first thing. The jump rack is designed to amplify body movements both in strength and speed. Standing by itself, the machine looks like a skeleton without a head. One backs into it, stands on the foot plates; then, beginning with the toe belts, the metal frame is strapped to the body, up the legs, waist, chest, shoulders, arms and wrists. The hands fit into three-fingered metal gloves. At first, our training group spent as much time ramming each other as we did drilling in the racks, but in time we learned the machines, making them parts of us. With them we could run great distances at high speeds carrying heavy weights, or jump to incredible heights, or down from such heights with the rack absorbing the shocks. When the backs of our machines were mounted with the heavy black cubes, we saw why the racks were necessary. To heft one of the cubes took two strong Shikazu, who would, nevertheless, be cursing, staggering and straining every muscle before they had to put the cube down moments later. Each Shikazu had to carry one, for the cubes powered the wands and shields we carried.

The new wands were connected to the cube by a clear cable, and they could slice metal as a hot dagger slices cheese. The black cube supplied the power. The shields were not the heavy black deflection squares we were used to, but instead were almost transparent nets, also connected to the power supply. The nets could absorb almost any kind of energy, including sunlight, and convert it in a flash to power that could be used by the wand. For the new weapons we had to learn new tactics, which meant new drills. The drills seemed unending, but in time the Jaren of the Redbar functioned again as the parts of a well-designed machine. In addition, the Redbar could function in a like manner with any other Jaren in our training group, and the entire group together made a formidable force. Despite his cursing, ridicule and constant haranguing, as we reached the end of our training, we could see the pride—the Shikazu—burning in Aragdan's eyes.

Sprinkled among our hundred and fifty recruits were several who had sworn to the army before, such as Krogar. Most of them were the remaining members of their respective Jarens. They were a curious lot. Some were like Krogar—wanderers, thieves, drunkards—pulled back into the army from outside. Others were more recently divested of their Jarens by the humans during the battle for Baalphor, Dashik's sister planet. These were sullen soldiers indeed. Watching them drill with us, I could not but help think of my own feelings should my mates be lost in battle. When I tried to imagine it, I felt hot rage trying to hold together a life shredded by emptiness and vengeance.

We knew that the old soldiers, as we called them, would officer the groups that were formed from our training group. Five Jarens make up a section, and five sections make up a company. The company is officered by another Jaren, and the odds and ends of old soldiers officered the sections. As was predicted, Larenz and his Jaren of the Red Claw excelled at everything, and a company was formed from our training group officered by the Red Claw. Krogar officered the section in which the Redbar found itself. Despite his light-fingered past, we had witnessed the old thief at drills, and were willing to serve him.

We knew from the first that we were being trained as part of the invasion force that would retake Baalphor. The human destruction of the Baalphor garrison, and the subsequent occupation of the planet by the humans, forged an aura of vengeance and somber purpose about those on Dashik who prepared to right the humiliation to the Shikazu. Army battle-cruisers had blockaded the planet and had fought the human space forces to a standstill. The rest was up to us. We were entered into the Fourth Army roster as the Second Company, Fifth Assault Group, Fifth Battle Force attached to the Baalphor Invasion Armada.

On an evening soon after, I was sent by Larenz to find Krogar and inform him of a meeting of company officers. The black of Dashik's night had almost swallowed the day, and cool breezes picked at my skin as the desert gave up its warmth. I found Krogar seated on a rock at the bottom of a draw cut into the desert floor by some long-dead stream. As I came up on him, my feet walked fine sand and he did not hear me. Then, when I could view the direction the old thief faced, I saw them—four pale apparitions glowing with the Light's color. I gasped, and Krogar turned his head and faced me. "Eeola?"

"Yes," I could hardly hear my own voice.

Krogar held out his hand toward the patches of glowing blue. "Be not afraid, Eeola. Meet my mates of the Jaren of the Green Dragon; Pegda, Yos, Aldaon, and our *Di*, Radier."

I watched the glows. They were unmoving, yet they seemed to flow within themselves as something bearing life. I swallowed. "Krogar, are they . . . ghosts?"

The old soldier placed his elbows on his knees, clasped his hands, and rested his grizzled chin upon them as he studied the representations of his mates. "Ghosts? I wonder. The *Rhanakah* tells us that our brothers stand with us in death as they did in life. Perhaps they are." Krogar remained silent for a long moment, then shook his head. "Perhaps they are nothing more than projections of my mind made visible by what little of the Light remains in me. This is what some would have you believe."

"And you, Krogar; what do you believe?"

The old soldier shrugged. "I do not concern myself. They are here, and I accept them." He turned and faced me. "Why have you come for me?"

"Larenz . . . he has called a meeting of officers."

Krogar stood. "Then I should be off." He again faced the spots of light. "Be off, my brothers. I am not ready to join you yet. Perhaps soon." The lights rose from the desert floor, faded into the rock wall of the draw, then disappeared. I jumped as Krogar slapped me on the shoulder. "Let us be off."

Our weeks of training concluded, we packed into landing shuttles and were moved to an army attack transport, where we were assigned a compartment. Our jump racks and weapons stood in the shuttles, a silent, motionless, mindless company awaiting only the direction of living bodies to wreak destruction upon the defenders of Baalphor. And how we longed—lusted—for that destruction. As we talked among ourselves during the days it took to reach our staging area around Baalphor, we would often speak of the great heroes that peopled the history of the Shikazu—epics all of us had long since memorized from childhood, but which never grew dull from the telling.

Larenz would bring Krogar with him and go from Jaren to Jaren in our section explaining such of the battle plan as applied to the company. If need be, any member of the company would be able to fill Larenz's place should he fall. Larenz would also recount his favorite Shikazu epics, and did so in a strong, clear voice that seemed louder than it was. Often he would leave the compartment and I would look around at my Jaren, my section, and all of those who made up my company. We were more than twenty-five separate Jarens with a common purpose. We were something of a unity, a single structure of new metal—a Jaren with a hundred and twenty-five mates.

At the staging area, as we stood silently in the landing shuttle, strapped into our racks, I could see the battle blood pounding through my company and could feel it in my own veins. The shuttle lurched downward, gradually pulled forward as it applied power, and swung several times as it maneuvered to make formation with the ship's other shuttles. In the front of the compartment, Larenz listened to the steady chatter of the tactical information channel. We could all hear that the invasion was going according to plan, which meant that our role had not changed. As we came abreast of the human battle lines, the top of the shuttle would open and we would jump out of the compartment into the steaming jungle below. After the area had been cleared of humans, we would strike through the lines and secure a rise in the jungle floor the humans had equipped and manned as a heavy-weapons position.

Once we entered the atmosphere, we could feel the shuttle being rocked as the humans threw up their defensive screen of weapons. Inside me, I felt frustration at being unable to strike back during the landing. About us, landing shuttles were being blown from the sky, and perhaps chance would favor us, perhaps not. I looked at my mates and saw none of this in their eyes. In them I read what we had been taught. Some will get through; enough to do what must be done. We train that, if we should be chosen by chance to avenge the Shikazu, we will be ready. If chance chooses us to die, others will be spared by the same chance—others that will assume our burden of revenge.

Larenz held out his hands as the shuttle leveled in its fall. "Stand ready!" At that moment, the shuttle was slammed by a huge fist of energy. Since the racks compensated for the lurch, none of us were knocked down to the deck, but Larenz entered into a heated conversation with the pilot. He turned back to us. "We cannot steer, and we have missed our jump point. Also, the doors will not open. The pilot will attempt to circle around to make our jump point again. At my command, use your wands to cut through the walls of the shuttle. When you land, clear your area, then regroup on the Red Claw. Watch for where we land."

As the shuttle lurched and wallowed, all of us reached to the part of our racks behind our waists and energized our wands and shields. A hum that almost drowned out the pounding of the humans' weapons filled the compartment. Larenz turned to us. "We can't make it! We will be far behind enemy lines when we land. When you land, clear and regroup." He hefted his wand and aimed it at the bulkhead. "Shikazu!"

Those of us against the walls turned our wands against them, unmindful of the splatters of molten metal that clung to our legs. It was soon impossible to see in the spark-and-smoke-filled compartment. Then one plate fell away, then another. The plate I worked on tore away exposing blue skies crossed with red beams and black smoke trails. I jumped, followed by others behind me. The wind tumbled me as an angry swarm of red streaks cut the air around me. Using my arms and legs as counter-weights, I gained control of my fall and began playing my wand on the jungle below. A red streak would emerge from the jungle, then I would sizzle that point, catching the return fire with my shield. Before I hit ground, my shield had overloaded and was deflecting, rather than absorbing, energy.

I crashed through the leaf cover and saw that I had landed in the center of a human heavy-weapons position. The weapon itself could not be used on me, but the crew quickly pulled hand weapons and fired them in my direction. As though they were stalks of guava cane, my wand swept the humans and cut them down. As I swapped fire with a pocket of the animals entrenched in a protected position, Gem joined me, and together we saw the last of them, then turned our wands upon the weapon to render it useless.

The jungle seemed strangely quiet as Gem, his face flushed with victory, turned toward me. "Ah, it is true! We are the Shikazu! We are unconquerable!"

"Gem, in which direction did the Red Claw land? I could not see."

"That way." Gem pointed into the jungle, gained control of himself, breathed a few times, then nodded. "Yes, this way. The company is strung out all along the enemy line."

We ran from the position into the jungle and were soon joined by one of the members of a Jaren in our section. His gleaming eyes and bared teeth reflected our own. In a few moments we were joined by a few more Shikazu, among them Krogar and Vastar. Krogar led us through the jungle, picking up more of the company as we went, until we walked into a wall of red light. The humans had brought up a unit to block our attempt to join up with the Red Claw. Entrenched in good defensive positions, their own kinds of weapons and shields deployed, this would be no area-clearing exercise. The main body of our small force, covered by our shields, played our wands over the human positions, while Krogar and the remainder of the force jumped to the right and out of sight. After a few moments, the screams from the human positions evidenced the success of Krogar's flanking maneuver. Krogar stuck his head out of the jungle and motioned us to follow. As I stepped through a row of brush, I saw a human staring at me, the wound in his shoulder and chest still smoking, leaving a sick, sweet smell of cooking flesh. He reached out his right hand toward one of their hand weapons, and without thought my wand passed across the creature's throat, severing its head from its body. The grisly orb rolled across the jungle floor and came to rest against a tree, eyes still staring.

"Eeola!" I lifted my head and saw Krogar looking at me from beyond a low wall of brush. "Over here! We must move quickly!" He turned and disappeared into the jungle. I hesitated, thinking for some reason that there was something I should do for the remains of this fallen enemy. I could think of nothing. Hefting my wand and shield, I took a last look at those eyes, then followed Krogar's path.

Except for a straggling human or two, the rest of our journey to join up with Larenz was without event. One of the scouts Krogar sent out reported back late in the day to inform him that contact with Larenz had been made. In an hour, we were again a company. Vastar, Gem and I searched the others, and when we found Dob and Tim, we hugged, slapped backs, joked and roughed around until we were ordered to silence. Other Jarens celebrated as they found their lost mates, but others wept. A third of the company had been lost; either killed or still wandering the jungle.

Larenz conferred with the section officers, then Krogar came back to our section. He gathered us around, then began in a low voice. "The officers have decided to try for our original objective." He pulled a map from his *nabe* and spread it on the jungle floor. He pointed one of his armored fingers at a spot on the map. "We are here. It is a half-day's walk to the hill." He stabbed another part of the map. "We will be coming up behind the enemy lines, which could be good or bad. If they do not expect us, we shall surprise them. If they expect us..." Krogar looked up at the circle of faces. "If they expect us, there will be that many more of them with which to fertilize the soil." Folding the map, Krogar stood. "Follow me."

Long after the horizon swallowed the sun, we crept through the brush, stopping only to either check or clear the trail ahead. In the night, the humans took to holes, using only remote equipment against us. We easily infiltrated their positions, slid into their holes and blessed them with eternal sleep. The jungle was our home.

In time a halt was ordered, pickets put out, and orders for rest given. I unstrapped myself from my rack and slid to the ground and was asleep in an instant. *My dreams, if dreams they were, showed Ahrm at the harvest season; the one dusty street piled with jeba cane, gahn roots and the bright yellow peppers that seared the tongue with a delicious fire. The large blue beln melons stacked in a pyramid, dusty* tikiruch *creeping in and out of the stands and people, then running into the jungle with their art-acquired fruit. The Redbar with its booty of melons, busting them against the trees and devouring the ice green flesh amidst gay laughter and fine belches...*

"Up." Vastar tapped my shoulder. I shook the sleep from my eyes and sprang to my feet to begin strapping myself into my jump rack. The sky was yet red as the shadows gave back the sun, and the broad-leafed trees and overhead vines stood out black against the sky. My stomach grumbled to remind me that the company had not eaten since landing. Had we put down as planned, we would be in contact with our forces and food brought up. Never mind. There would be food once we drove the humans from the hill.

The sky yellowed, and soon those of us at the edge of the clearing that opened before us could see the hill. It was nothing—little more than a bump in the carpet of the jungle. The top, however, bristled with heavy weapons, and on the lower slopes, freshly blasted human defensive positions could be seen. Perhaps because we had not taken our objective as planned, it remained as a human strongpoint, probably holding up the advance of the Shikazu. In every mind watching that hill ran the same thought: It is our error; therefore, it is ours to correct.

From where I stood I could see Larenz nod toward his widely dispersed section leaders, then move out, his mates of the Red Claw close at his back. We halted at the edge of the clearing at the base of the hill, then, upon Larenz's signal, we jumped our racks toward the hill, slashing our wands toward anything that moved or might move. The humans' return fire delayed only a few seconds, but in that time we were across the clearing and at their throats. The first line fell before us almost without loss, but as we worked our way uphill the second line of human defenders were reinforced. In addition, several of the heavy weapons on the crest of the hill were turned in our direction. I saw others fall as red beams eluded shields, burning great pulpy holes in Shikazu chests, but I paid them no heed for the blood was upon me. My wand could not find enough of the humans as it slashed and butchered all those it could find, my shield sucking up their beams to return them through my stick of death.

Still, battle blood or no, we slowed in front of the wall of force placed before us. The defenders—all well armed—numbered almost a thousand, and as my arm, then my leg caught human fire, even I cooled in my tracks. Then we saw it: a crossfire of countless red beams swept over Larenz. He fell, his pieces rolling in different directions down the slope.

Time stood still as a primeval roar erupted from the Shikazu. We moved forward as shields of blinding white fury made us gods of wrath, impervious to the feeble weapons of the humans. Our grief shot through our wands and scourged the hill and the humans melted before us, for they were mere mortals.

Night fell upon the hill, and I thought with amusement at the pockets of humans we had slaughtered—the outraged looks on their faces as we cut them down, their hands stretched over their heads, one or two waving little white flags. The human, says Vastar, has a strange concept of war. The human thinks it to be a game, and when one side bests the other the losers may throw up their hands, smile and retire to the sidelines to await the next round. The Shikazu expects no quarter, and gives none. If there were such a thing as a human worthy of being spared, what possible reason would the creature have for being on Baalphor? Hungry as we were, we only picked at our ration blocks. The wine that had been brought up, however, saw more enthusiastic custom. We knew Larenz such a short time—and would that there had been more time—that our grief could have been that much deeper. The top of the hill was almost bare of trees—not by nature's choice, but by ours—and as we sat crosslegged on the ground, downing great draughts of wine and picking at our rations, the stars spread out over our heads. We had no fires, and we did not recognize the stranger as he walked into our midst. "Is this the Second Company of the Fifth Assault?" The voice sounded hollow, but familiar.

I struggled to my feet. "Lord General Dikahn?"

The figure nodded. "Yes."

"It is Eeola . . . of the Redbar—"

The figure nodded again. "Yes, one of my son's companions from the prison." A chuckle worked its way through the old general's grief. Hearing his words, others stood and faced the general. He held up his hands, palms outward. "Please, resume your rest. No one has earned it more." We remained standing until the general nodded and lowered himself to the ground. The remains of Larenz's company in our area gathered around him and sat down. The general looked around at us. "Are you being fed well?"

Several voices muttered an affirmative. We watched as Dikahn bowed his head for a moment, then lifted it. "Who commands this company now?"

Vastar spoke. "The Red Claw still commands this company, Lord General, and will until either it or the company no longer remains."

Dikahn reached out a hand and clamped it on Vastar's shoulder. "Well said, soldier. Well said." He removed his hand, let it fall into his lap then faced us. "I have no military purpose here, my soldiers, and should be off. There is much for me to do." Dikahn started up, but Tim stood over him.

"Would the Lord General care to hear the song I have made in honor of his son?" Tim held out his pipes.

Dikahn rubbed his eyes and nodded. "I would hear your song, soldier. Play."

Tim began, the haunting strains of the tiny pipes marking well the grief of the company and, as well, the grief of a Lord

General. The simple tune washed over the listeners—sad, yet supported by a will of metal, until all the company had gathered to hear. As Tim ended the first refrain, and began the second, Krogar talked the song of death:

> *"Hear me, Universe,*
> *This was one of us,*
> *Our comrade Larenz.*
> *His fellows wish him well*
> *On his journey of endless night,*
> *Wishing only to be at his side,*
> *Slain in battle*
> *As Shikazu.*
> *Give us this, oh Universe,*
> *That we may be*
> *As our comrade Larenz;*
> *Shikazu."*

The notes of the pipes died, and the shadowed scene before my eyes could have been carved from black and dark gray stone. Lord General Dikahn then stood, turned and was swallowed by the night. One by one we drifted back to our wine and ration blocks.

The next morning, the humans counter-attacked with a fury we hardly expected. Those humans that lived were sent back down the hill, licking their wounds. Afterwards, the Jaren of the Redbar laid Timbenevva to rest. It is hard to explain the feeling of losing a Jaren mate. As an individual, you still live, but losing an arm or leg would cause less grief. No human can understand the desolation, the endless pain of a lost mate. In time, a scab of sorts forms, you go on, but it is missing—that fierce joy that filled us when we whipped Lodar on the drill ground. The feeling of superiority when we defeated the Jaren of the Golden Dart for the rights to the swimming hole. The Shikazu feeling when we took the hill from the humans. Victory still sat well, but it was something less than it was, despite his Light still being with us.

To fill out our military unit, we accepted Zeth, the sole remaining member of the Green Waters Jaren of the village of

Kurinaam. He was a jungle brother, but aloof—apart from us. His only two goals left little room for conversation between us. He would kill humans, and he would join his mates of the Green Waters in their endless night. Who could argue with him? He, and his mates, were Shikazu.

But the Redbar was not a unit. When the Company was pulled off the hill, there was still that battle blood—that kill-the-humans feeling—that fired our actions of old. I look back at it now and it seems that, of all things, we wanted victory. Next, we still wanted to live. We had not yet achieved Zeth's single-minded desire to die and, in the process, to take a host of humans with us. It was enough for us to send the humans on the trip.

Our racks were equipped with extra packs, and we carried our rations and shelters with us. Our company was assigned a place in the spearhead that would split the human forces of the Baalphorian Main Continent. In reality, the planet Baalphor has but one continent worthy of the name, but the original inhabitants and subsequent convention had designated several of the larger islands as continents. Neither the humans nor ourselves considered the fight for Baalphor to hinge on anything other than control of the Main. As with all modern armies, the human forces were mobile and widely scattered; however, there were several reinforced positions that commanded wide areas of surrounding ground. Between their defensive screens and well-entrenched fortifications, it was left to our infantry forces to destroy these positions. The most formidable of these positions, and the land headquarters of the human forces, was the Citadel; a batholith thrust from the jungle floor with sides so sheer that not even jungle vines or airborne seeds had found a niche. A single fissure in the west wall allowed access to the top—for those who controlled the heights above and along the fissure. The top of the feature was generally flat, with only trees and other jungle growth to soften its stark appearance. As night defeated day, the pale yellow glows of permanent defensive screens could be seen covering the top, while random bursts of fire cascaded down the fissure. To attack such a thing was madness; to let it remain unharmed, keeping an iron hand on our movement across the surrounding bush, was madness of another kind. We would attack.

Where the shields over the human positions overlapped, neutral slits existed. The nature of these fields was such that beams and high-speed projéctiles could not penetrate with effect. Slower-moving landing shuttles, however, might make it through. The strongest evidence supporting this was the deployment of the human forces beneath the screens. Diagrams prepared by orbital survey showed the areas surrounding each of the slits to be heavily defended. There was no trick plan. We would assault where and in the manner expected by the humans. We would cast the spirit of the Shikazu against that of the humans. Two waves of shuttles, a total of forty-six, would make the attack. The first wave was to fight through the initial defense ring and secure a position for the second wave. While the first wave held the position, the second would fight through the lines and knock out the screens. As soon as they accomplished their task, the might of the Fourth Army would fall on the position in a massive airborne assault, bringing the Citadel to its knees. Our company was assigned to the second wave.

As we prepared to move into the shuttles, the Jaren of the Redbar pledged the blood of its brother Timbenevva on the heads of the human defenders of the Citadel. Zeth, his mind wrapped in his own thoughts, stood apart from us. I could see that Vastar was bothered by this. A Jaren must work as the fingers of a hand and, clearly, Zeth was not one of us. The racks had already been moved inside our company's shuttle, and while we awaited the command to mount, we squatted outside in the narrow strip of shade cast by the landing craft. As were the others of the company, we discussed the coming battle. After the traditional round of boasts, brags and declarations of bloodletting, our group quieted as each of us played pictures in our minds of skilled wands and screaming Shikazu cutting down the humans. My imaginings were interrupted by a strange quality in Vastar's voice. "Zeth?"

Our new member came back from his own mental wanderings and looked at our *Di*. "Yes, Vastar?"

Vastar studied each of us in turn, then turned back to Zeth. "The Redbar has pledged the blood of its fallen mate on the heads of the enemy."

Zeth nodded, his eyes studying the ground in front of him. "I was listening."

Vastar nodded. "If you would join us, Zeth, in our pledge, we would join you in pledging the blood of your brothers of the Green Waters."

Zeth brought up his head sharply, his eyes examining Vastar's. His eyes grew bright as he slowly nodded, reached out both hands, clamped one on my shoulder and the other on Dob's. "Their names...Perra, our *Di*. Then, Vane, Dommis, and Arapen. Your brother's name?"

"Our brother's name is Timbenevva." We each extended our hands and clasped them in the center of our circle. Vastar's eyes studied us as he spoke. "Then, let the Light of our fallen brothers—Timbenevva, Perra, Vane, Dommis, and Arapen— go with the Jaren of the Redbar and Green Waters into battle. Let their strength fill us and their wands join us as the Jaren of the Redbar and Green Waters goes forth to avenge the deaths of its brothers."

We all stood, then hugged and slapped Zeth as we welcomed him to the Jaren, and he welcomed us. We would, again, work as the fingers of a hand; We were a Jaren.

Josahr of the Red Claw, Larenz's Jaren mate, stood in the front of the shuttle's compartment observing the tactical information as we fell toward the Citadel. We knew Josahr to be an excellent leader, and had resworn to him. The shuttle lurched as unseen forces slapped against its hull. Josahr turned to us. "The shuttles going through the slot—those that made it that far—are being burned out of the sky before they can discharge their companies. Only parts of three companies in the first wave have made it to the ground. Our orders have changed. We will turn and go out over the center of one of the screens and discharge *above* it. Those of us that make it to the ground should be close to the screen's projector battery. Questions?" There were none. Josahr nodded at the pilot, and a moment later the shuttle banked and swung to the left. A moment later, and the overhead of the craft was open. Screaming "Shikazu!" we leaped out over the Citadel.

The familiar wind blast struck my face as I emerged, then controlled my fall. Below me appeared to be nothing but the jungle-covered Citadel, but in a moment I felt myself slowed as the feeling of a thousand insects crawling on my body began.

The landscape below grew wavy and distorted, and all sound ceased. My rack lost all power, freezing me into a spread-legged position, my wand dead and helpless in my hand.

I had little time to think of these things as blinding pains shot through my head, chest and muscles. Then they were gone and I was falling. As the ground rushed up at me, I braced myself for the impact that would see my end, but power slowly came back to my jump rack and wand. Numerous streaks of red cracked and sizzled the air around us, but the source for most of these was a slight rise in the terrain almost directly below me. I directed my wand below my feet and roasted the site I had picked for landing. Most of the human fire was directed toward the slot where the main body of the second wave was attempting entrance, but I could see from the fire we were drawing that many of us would die. From the stiff, tumbling falls some were taking, I realized that not everyone's racks had gotten back power after falling through the shield.

Even with my rack absorbing most of the shock, striking the ground stunned me and I rolled downhill, coming to rest against a tree. The slashes of my wand had downed several of the humans, but many more remained, and only my unexpected roll saved me. The humans unleashed a red crossfire at my tumbling form, causing themselves much damage as the fire from one side fell into the other's ground. I came up beneath my shield, pulsing my wand at all movements. The red fire slackened as the humans still on their feet sought the safety of trees, rocks, and holes. Soon my shield could absorb no more energy and the red fire splashed off it as I worked my way up the hill. Further to my right, I caught sight of Krogar littering the ground with humans. Beyond him, there were others—all moving up the hill toward the projector. Still more humans broke from above and were cut down by our wands. I would have felt pity for the foolish creatures that stood before us, had not my mind been blinded to all but one thing: destroy the projector.

There was no organized assault, no cover fire and flank. We reached the top of the hill and faced trenches manned by humans determined to make a stand. Behind them stood a tracked vehicle mounted with a dull green dome—the projector. Our wands roasted the trenches while our shields swatted away the enemy fire. Some dropped, but still we moved forward until we

stood in the trenches and swept them of human life. The
projector crew fell clutching at ripped chests and severed limbs
before they could surrender. There was no need to destroy the
projector. Krogar climbed the stairs into a side hatch, executed
an operator who huddled on the deck whimpering, then reached
out a hand and turned off all the controls. I turned from the door
and watched as the sky filled with Fourth Army shuttles
discharging their companies. The Citadel had been broken.

A quick headcount showed Vastar, Gem and Zeth to be
among the dead; however, Dob and I could spare them little
thought. With the fall of the Citadel, the human lines were
rolling up. The revenge for the Baalphor garrison was at hand,
and the battle forces of the Baalphor Armada took only a deep
breath before locking with the remains of the human forces. A
shuttle moved the remains of our company from the Citadel to
the jungle below, where we joined other units of the Fifth
Assault Group.

A few human units attempted surrender, but their fates
removed this course from the list of human options. The battle
blood was running hot, and it would not cease until we ran out of
humans to kill. We saw only our small part of the advance, but
we heard the news from other units. Across the entire Main
Continent, the humans were folding and striking north. The
Second and Fifth Battle Forces deployed across the humans'
lines of retreat, and the rest was a matter of time and blood.
Afterwards, Baalphor rocked with our cries: "Shikazu!
Shikazu! Shikazu!"

Krogar joined me as I laid my last Jaren mate, Dob, to rest.
The pain of losing my mates mixed with the elation of victory
confused me. Krogar had brought extra rations of wine, but that
only confused me further. As the distance in time from our
victory increased, the elation diminished and the pain grew.

Krogar drank deeply from his bottle, lowered it, then studied
me for a long time. "At this moment, Feola, you wonder how
you will last out the pain. Perhaps, you wonder, as I once did, if
it is worth lasting out the pain." He shrugged. "I can't answer
that for you. For myself, something inside of me snapped—you

saw me on the trail. It was a death of sorts, living from moment to moment, thinking of nothing, of no one. But this," he lifted his free hand, "this has made me whole again. Our victory reminds us that we are Shikazu. I forgot that once, but never will again. You are Shikazu, Eeola."

I nodded, took a deep breath, and felt a great weight lift from my heart. There would still be pain, but being Shikazu was my shield. In a manner of speaking, all Shikazu belonged to a single great Jaren—a band sworn to our brothers and traditions, founded upon our one truth: the Shikazu cannot be conquered.

As I drank from my flask, Krogar stood and walked into the night. The air was warm, and as the wine relaxed my muscles, I leaned back against a tree and let my mind wander back to Ahrm, where my mates and I planted our hair. Only I had not returned to the village, but I swore to. At the end of my service I would once again walk that dusty path and smell the turawood and jungle orchids. Perhaps, even Carrina of the Golden Dart—if she lived. I would settle into the routine of an elder, wed my woman and raise a hut full of screaming brats, that I would see join Jarens and travel the road to adulthood. Perhaps, when Lodar feels his years, I will become the new fencing master, I thought. As these thoughts wandered through my mind, I noticed that on the other side of my skull there was a difference in the night.

I put down my flask and stood, holding my breath to listen. The tension in the air was wrapped around my heart as though it were some powerful snake. I heard murmurs, a wail, saw the discharge of an energy wand. A weeping figure staggered toward me from beyond the near trees. I could not recognize him. "You!" I shouted. As though the figure had no volition, it stopped and faced me. "What is it? Do you know?" The figure nodded, then hung its head. "What?"

"Tenuet—the Light—has been destroyed!"

*   *   *

Eeola hung his head, then raised it and looked at me. "Now, human, perhaps you can understand." He held out his hands toward the four shimmering lights. "That Light which remains in us—in our Jaren—waits for me." He dropped one hand to his lap, but pointed the other in my direction. "But, understand, we are not conquered. Since the war, no Jarens have been formed, no marriages have been made, and no babies conceived. In a few years there will be none of us left. As it came to our brothers and sisters, the endless sleep shall come to us. Is this how a conquered race behaves? The Mithad grows its young to serve you, but the Shikazu will not add to your subjects. Now, we are as the *kazu* wandering lost in the jungle—awaiting the final victory of time. We can be killed, but we can never be conquered. We are Shikazu."

The old Shikki stood, wandered off into the jungle, and was followed by the blue lights. I never saw him again. I looked at that landmark and realized that it was the Citadel. There, and in the jungle surrounding the feature, Eeola of the Redbar Jaren had lost his mates, then the Light that sustained his race.

Was it the old fellow's story that touched me, or was it because of the few schoolmates of my own that lost their lives on Baalphor during the war of the four stars? I don't know. I never signed the agreement with Wiggins—at least, not for that particular piece of property. Baalphor is a big planet, and I don't worry about Wiggins.

Instead, I go to that rocky outcropping every now and then, and watch. It doesn't happen often, but every now and then you can see the lights gathering to welcome one of their own to the endless sleep.

Legislative Assembly

of the

UNITED STATES OF EARTH

LEGISLATIVE RECORD

June 6, 2071

Speaker. Members of the Assembly, it is my honor and privilege to recognize, his excellency, Azdov Kuznikov, President-General of the United States of Earth.

President-General Kuznikov. Mister Speaker, honorable members of the Assembly, ladies and gentlemen. The matter I bring before you this morning strikes at the heart of the question "What is man, and what is man to become?" Shall we rule this Galaxy, or be ruled? Shall we follow our own destinies as free and independent men and women, or shall we submit to the despotism of a host of reptilian and insect-like creatures who would dictate to the human race where it may and may not exist? I speak, of course, in reference to this sham of a democratic league of planets that calls itself the United Quadrants of the Milky Way Galaxy.

It has been argued in this Assembly that, in our difficulties with the creatures from the planet Draco, if we were signatories of the Ninth Quadrant Charter, it would be the charter forces doing battle with the Dracs instead of humans. Ladies and gentlemen of the Assembly, I submit that the so-called forces of the Ninth Quadrant are paper armies, and that no force in this galaxy equals our own in its ability to protect and defend the interests of the human race.

Neither this government nor the Dracon Chamber are signatories to the Charter. If this body should act so irresponsibly as to vote in the affirmative on the bill now before it, the Dracs would be free to fight for the Dracs by and through the means they see best, while the United States of Earth Forces would be saddled by the supervision of a crowd of overgrown aquarium creatures.

The issue is simple. Do humans or Dracs rule this corner of space? Do we put forward our best effort to destroy the aggressors from Draco, or do we default by turning the conduct of human affairs over to this laughable association called the Ninth Quadrant Federation of Habitable Planets?

I say we are humans. As such, we can and will fight our own battles. I thank you.

Speaker. The chair recognizes the senior representative of the planetary government of Occam, Mister Vyuna.

Mister Vyuna. Mister Speaker, President-General Kuznikov, members of the Assembly. Through informal agreement the party leaderships are decided on ending debate and acting upon this matter without delay. Hence, I move the acceptance of the committee's Ought Not to Pass report on L.D. 2978, "An Act Mandating the President-General of the USE States and Planets to Sign the Charter of the Ninth Quadrant Federation of Habitable Planets."

Speaker. Since this is an informal agreement, individual members of the Assembly are not bound by it. Does anyone wish to speak to the issue? The chair recognizes the senior representative of the East African Union, Mrs. Tsambe.

Mrs. Tsambe. Mister Speaker, honorable guest, members of the Assembly. I see that, again, I am alone. How much is worth a statement for the record? A statement that you will turn deaf ears against. A statement that will lie buried in the *Legislative Record*, to be perhaps examined as a curiosity by some alien archaelogist some decades hence as the creature sorts through the rubble of our civilization. Nevertheless, for the record, I submit that the days of humanity's freewheeling rampage through the Galaxy are numbered. Just as we cannot let pass the threat to us from Draco, the races of this Quadrant cannot let pass our threat to them.

It is true that the Ninth Quadrant organization is weak, but this is a symptom of youth. With each passing second, the organization gains strength, while humanity insists upon following the insanity of acting as though it were the only race in the Universe.

The committee has seen fit to recommend against joining the Quadrant; the sentiments expressed by the members of the Assembly these past few days are unmistakable, as well as the sentiments expressed by our illustrious guest this morning. I can only add that I pray that none of us lives to see the results of this day's work.

Speaker. The Assembly will now proceed to the vote. The chair recognizes the second representative of the North American Union, Mrs. Baines.

Mrs. Baines. Mister Speaker, I rise to a point of order. The motion has not been seconded.

(The motion was seconded by Mister Kruz of United Germany.)

Speaker. The motion being made and seconded, the Assembly shall now proceed to the vote.

(438 yea; 62 nay.)

A majority of the voting representatives voting in favor of the motion, the committee's Ought Not to Pass report is accepted, defeating the signing of the Quadrant Charter. As the Speaker of this Assembly, I would like to express this chamber's gratitude to the President-General for coming before this body and expressing his views in person. We shall now proceed with the next order of business . . .

Enemy Mine

The Dracon's three-fingered hands flexed. In the thing's yellow eyes I could read the desire to either have those fingers around a weapon or my throat. As I flexed my own fingers, I knew it read the same in my eyes.

"*Irkmaan!*" the thing spat.

"You piece of Drac slime." I brought my hands up in front of my chest and waved the thing on. "Come on, Drac; come and get it."

"*Irkmaan vaa, koruum su!*"

"Are you going to talk, or fight? Come on!" I could feel the spray from the sea behind me—a boiling madhouse of whitecapped breakers that threatened to swallow me as it had my fighter. I had ridden my ship in. The Drac had ejected when its own fighter had caught one in the upper atmosphere, but not before crippling my power plant. I was exhausted from swimming to the gray, rocky beach, and pulling myself to safety. Behind the Drac, among the rocks on the otherwise barren hill, I could see its ejection capsule. Far above us, its people and mine were still at it, slugging out the possession of an uninhabited corner of nowhere. The Drac just stood there and I went over the phrase taught us in training—a phrase calculated to drive any Drac into a frenzy. "*Kiz da yuomeen, Shizumaat!*" Meaning: Shizumaat, the most revered Drac philosopher, eats Kiz excrement. Something on the level of stuffing a Moslem full of pork.

The Drac opened its mouth in horror, then closed it as black anger literally changed its color from yellow to reddish-brown. "Irkmaan, yaa stupid Mickey Mouse is!"

I had taken an oath to fight and die over many things, but that venerable rodent didn't happen to be one of them. I laughed, and continued laughing until the guffaws in combination with my exhaustion forced me to my knees. I forced open my eyes to keep track of my enemy. The Drac was running toward the high ground, away from me and the sea. I half-turned toward the sea and caught a glimpse of a million tons of water just before they fell on me, knocking me unconscious.

"*Kiz da yuomeen, Irkmaan, ne?*"

My eyes were gritty with sand and stung with salt, but some part of my awareness pointed out "Hey, you're alive." I reached to wipe the sand from my eyes and found my hands bound. A straight metal rod had been run through my sleeves and my wrists tied to it. As my tears cleared the sand from my eyes, I could see the Drac sitting on a smooth black boulder looking at me. It must have pulled me out of the drink. "Thanks, toadface. What's with the bondage?"

"*Ess?*"

I tried waving my arms and wound up giving an impression of an atmospheric fighter dipping its wings. "Untie me, you Drac slime!" I was seated on the sand, my back against a rock.

The Drac smiled, exposing the upper and lower mandibles that looked human, except instead of separate teeth they were solid. "*Eh, ne, Irkmaan.*" It stood, walked over to me and checked my bonds.

"Untie me!"

The smile disappeared. "*Ne!*" It pointed at me with a yellow finger. "*Kos son va?*"

"I don't speak Drac, toadface. You speak Esper or English?"

The Drac delivered a very human-looking shrug, then pointed at its own chest. *"Kos va son Jeriba Shigan."* It pointed again at me. *"Kos son va?"*

"Davidge. My name is Willis E. Davidge."

"Ess?"

I tried my tongue on the unfamiliar syllables. *"Kos va son Willis Davidge."*

"Eh." Jeriba Shigan nodded, then motioned with its fingers. *"Dasu, Davidge."*

"Same to you, Jerry."

"Dasu, dasu!" Jeriba began sounding a little impatient. I shrugged as best I could. The Drac bent over and grabbed the front of my jump suit with both hands and pulled me to my feet. *"Dasu, dasu, kizlode!"*

"All right! So *dasu* is 'get up.' What's a *kizlode?*"

Jerry laughed. *"Gavey 'kiz'?"*

"Yeah, I *gavey.*"

Jerry pointed at its head. *"Lode."* It pointed at my head. *"Kizlode, gavey?"*

I got it, then swung my arms around, catching Jerry upside its head with the metal rod. The Drac stumbled back against a rock looking surprised. It raised a hand to its head and withdrew it covered with that pale pus that Dracs think is blood. It looked at me with murder in its eyes. *"Gefh! Nu Gefh, Davidge!"*

"Come and get it, Jerry, you *kizlode* sonofabitch!"

Jerry dived at me and I tried to catch it again with the rod, but the Drac caught my right wrist in both hands and, using the momentum of my swing, whirled me around, slamming my back against another rock. Just as I was getting back my breath, Jerry picked up a small boulder and came at me with every intention of turning my melon into pulp. With my back against the rock, I lifted a foot and kicked the Drac in the midsection, knocking it to the sand. I ran up, ready to stomp Jerry's melon, but he pointed behind me. I turned and saw another tidal wave gathering steam, and heading our way. *"Kiz!"* Jerry got to its feet and scampered for the high ground with me following close behind.

With the roar of the wave at our backs, we weaved in and out of the black water-and-sand-ground boulders, until we reached Jerry's ejection capsule. The Drac stopped, put its shoulder to the egg-shaped contraption, and began rolling it uphill. I could see Jerry's point. The capsule contained all of the survival equipment and food either of us knew about. "Jerry!" I shouted above the rumble of the fast-approaching wave. "Pull out this damn rod and I'll help!" The Drac frowned at me. "The rod, *kizlode*, pull it out!" I cocked my head toward my outstretched arm.

Jerry placed a rock beneath the capsule to keep it from rolling back, then quickly untied my wrists and pulled out the rod. Both of us put our shoulders to the capsule, and we quickly rolled it to higher ground. The wave hit and climbed rapidly up the slope until it came up to our chests. The capsule bobbed like a cork, and it was all we could do to keep control of the thing until the water receded, wedging the capsule between three big boulders. I stood there, puffing.

Jerry dropped to the sand, its back against one of the boulders, and watched the water rush back out to sea. *"Magasienna!"*

"You said it, brother." I sank down next to the Drac, we agreed by eye to a temporary truce, and promptly passed out.

My eyes opened on a sky boiling with blacks and grays. Letting my head loll over on my left shoulder, I checked out the Drac. It was still out. First, I thought that this would be the perfect time to get the drop on Jerry. Second, I thought about how silly our insignificant scrap seemed compared to the insanity of the sea that surrounded us. Why hadn't the rescue team come? Did the Dracon fleet wipe us out? Why hadn't the Dracs come to pick up Jerry? Did they wipe out each other? I didn't even know where I was. An island. I had seen that much coming in, but where and in relation to what? Fyrine IV; the planet didn't even rate a name, but was important enough to die over.

With an effort, I struggled to my feet. Jerry opened its eyes and quickly pushed itself to a defensive crouching position. I waved my hand and shook my head. "Ease off, Jerry. I'm just going to look around." I turned my back on it and trudged off between the boulders. I walked uphill for a few minutes until I reached level ground.

It was an island, all right, and not a very big one. By eyeball estimation, height from sea level was only eighty meters, while the island itself was about two kilometers long and less than half that wide. The wind whipping my jump suit against my body was at least drying it out, but as I looked around at the smooth ground boulders on top of the rise, I realized that Jerry and I could expect bigger waves than the few puny ones we had seen.

A rock clattered behind me and I turned to see Jerry climbing up the slope. When it reached the top, the Drac looked around. I squatted next to one of the boulders and passed my hand over it to indicate the smoothness, then I pointed toward the sea. Jerry nodded. *"Ae. Gavey."* It pointed downhill toward the capsule, then to where we stood. *"Echey masu, nasesay."*

I frowned, then pointed at the capsule. *"Nasesay?* The capsule?"

"Ae, capsule *nasesay. Echey masu."* Jerry pointed at its feet.

I shook my head. "Jerry, if you *gavey* how these rocks got smooth," I pointed at one, "then you *gavey* that *masuing* the *nasesay* up here isn't going to do a damned bit of good." I made a sweeping up-and-down movement with my hands. "Waves." I pointed at the sea below. "Waves, up here;" I pointed to where we stood. "Waves, *echey*."

"Ae, gavey." Jerry looked around the top of the rise, then rubbed the side of its face. The Drac squatted next to some small rocks and began piling one on top of another. *"Viga, Davidge."*

I squatted next to it and watched while its nimble fingers constructed a circle of stones that quickly grew into a doll-house-sized arena. Jerry stuck one of its fingers in the center of the circle. *"Echey, nasesay."*

The days on Fyrine IV seemed to be three times longer than any I had seen on any other habitable planet. I use the designation "habitable" with reservations. It took us most of the first day to painfully roll Jerry's *nasesay* up to the top of the rise. The night was too black to work, and was bone-cracking cold. We removed the couch from the capsule which made just enough room for both of us to fit inside. The body heat warmed things up a bit, and we killed time between sleeping, nibbling on Jerry's supply of ration bars (they taste a bit like fish mixed with cheddar cheese) and trying to come to some agreement about language.

"Eye."

"Thuyo."

"Finger."

"Zurath."

"Head."

The Drac laughed. *"Lode."*

"Ho, ho, very funny."

"Ho, ho."

At dawn on the second day, we rolled and pushed the capsule into the center of the rise and wedged it between two large rocks, one of which had an overhang that we hoped would hold down the capsule when one of those big soakers hit. Around the rocks and capsule, we laid a foundation of large stones and filled in the cracks with smaller stones. By the time the wall was knee high, we discovered that building with those smooth, round stones and no mortar wasn't going to work. After some experimentation, we figured out how to bust the stones to give us flat sides with which to work. It's done by picking up one stone and slamming it down on top of another. We took turns, one slamming and one building. The stone was almost a volcanic glass, and we also took turns extracting rock splinters from each other. It took nine of those endless days and nights to complete the walls, during which waves came close many times, and once washed up ankle deep. For six of those nine days, it rained. The capsule's survival equipment included a plastic blanket, and that became our roof. It sagged in at the center, and the hole we put in it there allowed the water to run out, keeping us almost dry and with a supply of fresh water. If a wave of any determination came along, we could kiss the roof good-bye, but we both had confidence in the walls, which were almost two meters thick at the bottom and at least a meter thick at the top.

After we finished, we sat inside and admired our work for about an hour, until it dawned on us that we had just worked ourselves out of jobs. "What now, Jerry?"

"Ess?"

"What do we do now?"

"Now wait, we." The Drac shrugged. "Else what, *ne?"*

I nodded. *"Gavey."* I got to my feet and walked to the passageway we had built. With no wood for a door, where the walls would have met, we bent one out and extended it about three meters around the other wall with the opening away from the prevailing winds. The never-ending winds were still at it, but the rain had stopped. The shack wasn't much to look at, but looking at it stuck there in the center of that life-deserted island made me feel good. As Shizumaat observed: "Intelligent life making its stand against the universe." Or, at least, that's the sense I could make out of Jerry's hamburger of English. I shrugged and picked up a sharp splinter of stone and made another mark in the large standing rock that served as my log. Ten scratches in all, and under the seventh, a small "x" to indicate the big wave that just covered the top of the island.

I threw down the splinter. "Damn, I hate this place!"

"Ess?" Jerry's head poked around the edge of the opening. "Who talking at, Davidge?"

I glared at the Drac, then waved my hand at it. "Nobody."

"Ess va, 'nobody'?"

"Nobody. Nothing."

"Ne gavey, Davidge."

I poked at my chest with my finger. "Me! I'm talking to myself! You *gavey* that stuff, toadface!"

Jerry shook its head. "Davidge, now I sleep. Talk not so much nobody, *ne?"* It disappeared back into the opening.

"And so's your mother!" I turned and walked down the slope. *Except, strictly speaking, toadface, you don't have a mother—or father. "If you had your choice, who would you like to be trapped on a desert island with?"* I wondered if anyone ever picked a wet, freezing corner of Hell shacked up with a hermaphrodite.

Half of the way down the slope, I followed the path I had marked with rocks until I came to my tidal pool, that I had named "Rancho Sluggo." Around the pool were many of the water-worn rocks, and underneath those rocks below the pool's waterline lived the fattest orange slugs either of us had ever seen.

I made the discovery during a break from house-building and showed them to Jerry.

Jerry shrugged. "And so?"

"And so what? Look, Jerry, those ration bars aren't going to last forever. What are we going to eat when they're all gone?"

"Eat?" Jerry looked at the wriggling pocket of insect life and grimaced. "*Ne*, Davidge. Before then pickup. Search us find, then pickup."

"What if they don't find us? What then?"

Jerry grimaced again and turned back to the half-completed house. "Water we drink, then until pickup." He had muttered something about kiz excrement and my tastebuds, then walked out of sight.

Since then I had built up the pool's walls, hoping the increased protection from the harsh environment would increase the herd. I looked under several rocks, but no increase was apparent. And, again, I couldn't bring myself to swallow one of the things. I replaced the rock I was looking under, stood and looked out to the sea. Although the eternal cloud cover still denied the surface the drying rays of Fyrine, there was no rain and the usual haze had lifted.

In the direction past where I had pulled myself up on the beach, the sea continued to the horizon. In the spaces between the whitecaps, the water was as gray as a loan officer's heart. Parallel lines of rollers formed approximately five kilometers from the island. The center, from where I was standing, would smash on the island, while the remainder steamed on. To my right, in line with the breakers, I could just make out another small island, perhaps ten kilometers away. Following the path of the rollers, I looked far to my right, and where the gray-white of the sea should have met the lighter gray of the sky, there was a black line on the horizon.

The harder I tried to remember the briefing charts on Fyrine IV's land masses, the less clear it became. Jerry couldn't remember anything either—at least nothing it would tell me. Why should we? The battle was supposed to be in space, each one trying to deny the other an orbital staging area in the Fyrine system. Neither side wanted to set foot on Fyrine, much less fight a battle there. Still, whatever it was called, it was land and considerably larger than the sand and rock bar we were occupying.

How to get there was the problem. Without wood, fire, leaves or animal skins, Jerry and I were destitute compared to the average poverty-stricken caveman. The only thing we had that would float was the *nasesay*. The capsule. Why not? The only real problem to overcome was getting Jerry to go along with it.

That evening, while the grayness made its slow transition to black, Jerry and I sat outside the shack nibbling our quarter-portions of ration bars. The Drac's yellow eyes studied the dark line on the horizon, then it shook its head. "*Ne, Davidge. Dangerous is.*"

I popped the rest of my ration bar into my mouth and talked around it. "Any more dangerous than staying here?"

"Soon pickup, *ne*?"

I studied those yellow eyes. "Jerry, you don't believe that any more than I do." I leaned forward on the rock and held out my hands. "Look, our chances will be a lot better on a larger land mass. Protection from the big waves, maybe food..."

"Not maybe, *ne*?" Jerry pointed at the water. "How *nasesay* steer, Davidge? In that, how steer? *Ess eh* soakers, waves, beyond land take, *gavey? Bresha*," Jerry's hands slapped together. "*Ess eh bresha* rocks on, *ne*? Then we death."

I scratched my head. "The waves are going in that direction from here, and so is the wind. If the land mass is large enough, we won't have to steer, *gavey*?"

Jerry snorted. "*Ne* large enough; then?"

"I didn't say it was a sure thing."

"*Ess?*"

"A sure thing; certain, *gavey*?" Jerry nodded. "And for smashing up on the rocks, it probably has a beach like this one."

"Sure thing, *ne*?"

I shrugged. "No, it's not a sure thing, but what about staying here? We don't know how big those waves can get. What if one just comes along and washes us off the island? What then?"

Jerry looked at me, its eyes narrowed. "What there, Davidge? *Irkmaan* base, *ne*?"

I laughed. "I told you, we don't have any bases on Fyrine IV."

"Why want go, then?"

"Just what I said, Jerry. I think our chances would be better."

"Ummm." The Drac folded its arms. "*Viga*, Davidge, *nasesay* stay. I know."

"Know what?"

Jerry smirked, then stood and went into the shack. After a moment it returned and threw a two-meter-long metal rod at my feet. It was the one the Drac had used to bind my arms. "Davidge, I know."

I raised my eyebrows and shrugged. "What are you talking about? Didn't that come from your capsule?"

"*Ne, Irkmaan.*"

I bent down and picked up the rod. Its surface was uncorroded and at one end were arabic numerals—a part number. For a moment a flood of hope washed over me, but it drained away when I realized it was a civilian part number. I threw the rod on the sand. "There's no telling how long that's been here, Jerry. It's a civilian part number and no civilian missions have been in this part of the galaxy since the war. Might be left over from an old seeding operation or exploratory mission..."

The Drac nudged it with the toe of his boot. "New, *gavey*?"

I looked up at it. "You *gavey* stainless steel?"

Jerry snorted and turned back toward the shack. "I stay, *nasesay* stay; where you want, you go, Davidge!"

With the black of the long night firmly bolted down on us, the wind picked up, shrieking and whistling in and through the holes in the walls. The plastic roof flapped, pushed in and sucked out with such violence it threatened to either tear or sail off into the night. Jerry sat on the sand floor, its back leaning against the *nasesay* as if to make clear that both Drac and capsule were staying put, although the way the sea was picking up seemed to weaken Jerry's argument.

"Sea rough now is, Davidge, *ne*?"

"It's too dark to see, but with this wind..." I shrugged more for my own benefit than the Drac's, since the only thing visible inside the shack was the pale light coming through the roof. Any minute we could be washed off that sandbar. "Jerry, you're being silly about that rod. You know that?"

"Surda." The Drac sounded contrite if not altogether miserable.

"Ess?"

"Ess eh 'Surda'?"

"Ae."

Jerry remained silent for a moment. "Davidge, *gavey* 'not certain not is'?"

I sorted out the negatives. "You mean 'possible,' 'maybe,' 'perhaps'?"

"Ae, possiblemaybeperhaps. Dracon fleet Irkmaan ships have. Before war buy; after war capture. Rod possiblemaybeperhaps Dracon is,"

"So, if there's a secret base on the big island, *surda* it's a Dracon base?"

"Possiblemaybeperhaps, Davidge."

"Jerry, does that mean you want to try it? The *nasesay?"*

"Ne."

"Ne? Why, Jerry? If it might be a Drac base—"

"Ne! *Ne* talk!" The Drac seemed to choke on the words.

"Jerry, we talk, and you better *believe* we talk! If I'm going to death it on this island, I have a right to know why."

The Drac was quiet for a long time. "Davidge."

"Ess?"

"Nasesay, you take. Half ration bars you leave. I stay."

I shook my head to clear it. "You want me to take the capsule alone?"

"What you want is, *ne?"*

"Ae, but why? You must realize by now there won't be any pickup."

"Possiblemaybeperhaps."

"Surda, nothing. You know there isn't going to be a pickup. What is it? You afraid of the water? If that's it, we have a better chance—"

"Davidge, up your mouth shut. *Nasesay* you have. Mc *ne* you need, *gavey?"*

I nodded in the dark. The capsule was mine for the taking; what did I need a grumpy Drac along for—especially since our truce could expire at any moment? The answer made me feel a little silly—human. Perhaps it's the same thing. The Drac was all that stood between me and utter aloneness. Still, there was the small matter of staying alive. "We should go together, Jerry."

"Why?"

I felt myself blush. If humans have this need for companionship, why are they also ashamed to admit it? "We just should. Our chances would be better."

"Alone your chances better are, Davidge. Your enemy I am."

I nodded again and grimaced in the dark. "Jerry, you *gavey* 'loneliness'?"

"Ne gavey."

"Lonely. Being alone, by myself."

"Gavey you alone. Take *nasesay*; I stay."

"That's it . . . See, *viga*, I don't want to."

"You want together go?" A low, dirty chuckle came from the other side of the shack. "You Dracon like? You me death, Irkmaan." Jerry chuckled some more. *"Irkmaan poorzhab* in head, *poorzhab."*

"Forget it!" I slid down from the wall, smoothed out the sand and curled up with my back toward the Drac. The wind seemed to die down a bit and I closed my eyes to try and sleep. In a bit, the snap-crack of the plastic roof blended in with the background of shrieks and whistles and I felt myself drifting off, when my eyes opened wide at the sound of footsteps in the sand. I tensed, ready to spring.

"Davidge?" Jerry's voice was very quiet.

"What?"

I heard the Drac sit on the sand next to me. "You loneliness, Davidge. About it hard you talk, *ne?"*

"So what?" The Drac mumbled something that was lost in the wind. "What?" I turned over and saw Jerry looking through a hole in the wall.

"Why I stay. Now, you I tell, *ne?"*

I shrugged. "Okay; why not?"

Jerry seemed to struggle with the words, then opened its mouth to speak. Its eyes opened wide. "Magasienna!"

I sat up. *"Ess?"*

Jerry pointed at the hole. "Soaker!"

I pushed it out of the way and looked through the hole. Steaming toward our island was an insane mountainous fury of whitecapped rollers. It was hard to tell in the dark, but the one in front looked taller than the one that had wet our feet a few days before. The ones following it were bigger. Jerry put a hand on my shoulder and I looked into the Drac's eyes. We broke and ran for the capsule. We heard the first wave rumbling up the slope as we felt around in the dark for the recessed doorlatch. I just got my finger on it when the wave smashed against the shack, collapsing the roof. In half a second we were underwater, the currents inside the shack agitating us like socks in a washing machine.

The water receded, and as I cleared my eyes, I saw that the windward wall of the shack had caved in. "Jerry!"

Through the collapsed wall, I saw the Drac staggering around outside. "Irkmaan?" Behind him I could see the second roller gathering speed.

"*Kizlode*, what'n the Hell you doing out there? Get in here!"

I turned to the capsule, still lodged firmly between the two rocks, and found the handle. As I opened the door, Jerry stumbled through the missing wall and fell against me. "Davidge...forever soakers go on! Forever!"

"Get in!" I helped the Drac through the door and didn't wait for it to get out of the way. I piled in on top of Jerry and latched the door just as the second wave hit. I could feel the capsule lift a bit and rattle against the overhang of the one rock.

"Davidge, we float?"

"No. The rocks are holding us. We'll be all right once the breakers stop."

"Over you move."

"Oh." I got off Jerry's chest and braced myself against one end of the capsule. After a bit, the capsule came to rest and we waited for the next one. "Jerry?"

"*Ess?*"

"What was it that you were about to say?"

"Why I stay?"

"Yeah."

"About it hard me talk, *gavey*?"

"I know, I know."

The next breaker hit and I could feel the capsule rise and rattle against the rock. "Davidge, *gavey 'vi nessa*'?"

"*Ne gavey.*"

"*Vi nessa* . . . little me, *gavey?*"

The capsule bumped down the rock and came to rest. "What about little you?"

"Little me . . . little Drac. From me, *gavey?*"

"Are you telling me you're *pregnant?*"

"Possiblemaybeperhaps."

I shook my head. "Hold on, Jerry. I don't want any misunderstandings. Pregnant . . . are you going to be a parent?"

"*Ae*, parent, two-zero-zero in line, very important is, *ne?*"

"Terrific. What's this got to do with you not wanting to go to the other island?"

"Before *vi nessa, gavey?* *Tean* death."

"Your child, it died?"

"*Ae!*" The Drac's sob was torn from the lips of the universal mother. "I in fall hurt. *Tean* death. *Nasesay* in sea us bang. *Tean* hurt, *gavey?*"

"*Ae*, I *gavey.*" So, Jerry was afraid of losing another child. It was almost certain that the capsule trip would bang us around a lot, but staying on the sandbar didn't appear to be improving our chances. The capsule had been at rest for quite a while, and I decided to risk a peek outside. The small canopy windows seemed to be covered with sand, and I opened the door. I looked around, and all of the walls had been smashed flat. I looked toward the sea, but could see nothing. "It looks safe, Jerry . . ." I looked up, toward the blackish sky, and above me towered the white plume of a descending breaker. "Maga damn sienna!" I slammed the hatch door.

"*Ess*, Davidge?"

"Hang on, Jerry!"

The sound of the water hitting the capsule was beyond hearing. We banged once, twice against the rock, then we could feel ourselves twisting, shooting upward. I made a grab to hang on, but missed as the capsule took a sickening lurch downward. I fell into Jerry then was flung to the opposite wall where I struck my head. Before I went blank, I heard Jerry cry "*Tean! Vi tean!*"

. . . *the lieutenant pressed his hand control and a figure—tall, humanoid, yellow—appeared on the screen.*

"Dracslime!" shouted the auditorium of seated recruits.

The lieutenant faced the recruits. "Correct. This is a Drac. Note that the Drac race is uniform as to color; they are all yellow." The recruits chuckled politely. The officer preened a bit, then with a light wand began pointing out various features. "The three-fingered hands are distinctive, of course, as is the almost noseless face, which gives the Drac a toad-like appearance. On average, eyesight is slightly better than human, hearing about the same, and smell..." The lieutenant paused. "The smell is terrible!" The officer beamed at the uproar from the recruits. When the auditorium quieted down, he pointed his light wand at a fold in the figure's belly. "This is where the Drac keeps its family jewels—all of them." Another chuckle. "That's right, Dracs are hermaphrodites, with both male and female reproductive organs contained in the same individual." The lieutenant faced the recruits. "You go tell a Drac to go boff himself, then watch out, because he can!" The laughter died down and the lieutenant held out a hand toward the screen. "You see one of these things, what do you do?"

"KILL IT..."

...I cleared the screen and computer-sighted on the next Drac fighter, looking like a double 'x' in the screen's display. The Drac shifted hard to the left, then right again. I felt the autopilot pull my ship after the fighter, sorting out and ignoring the false images, trying to lock its electronic crosshairs on the Drac. "Come on, toadface...a little bit to the left..." The double cross-image moved into the ranging rings on the display and I felt the missile attached to the belly of my fighter take off. "Gotcha!" Through my canopy I saw the flash as the missile detonated. My screen showed the Drac fighter out of control, spinning toward Fyrine IV's cloud-shrouded surface. I dived after it to confirm the kill... skin temperature increasing as my ship brushed the upper atmosphere. "Come on, damn it, blow!" I shifted the ship's systems over for atmospheric flight when it became obvious that I'd have to follow the Drac right to the ground. Still above the clouds, the Drac stopped spinning and turned. I hit the auto override and pulled the stick into my lap. The fighter wallowed as it tried to pull up. Everyone knows the

*Drac ships work better in atmosphere ... Heading toward me on
an interception course ... Why doesn't the slime fire? ... Just
before the collision, the Drac ejects ... Power gone; have to
deadstick it in. I track the capsule as it falls through the muck,
intending to find that Dracslime and finish the job ...*

It could have been for seconds or years that I groped into the
darkness around me. I felt touching, but the parts of me being
touched seemed far, far away. First chills, then fever, then chills
again, my head being cooled by a gentle hand. I opened my eyes
to narrow slits and saw Jerry hovering over me, blotting my
forehead with something cool. I managed a whisper. "Jerry."

The Drac looked into my eyes and smiled. "Good is,
Davidge. Good is."

The light on Jerry's face flickered and I smelled smoke.
"Fire."

Jerry got out of the way and pointed toward the center of the
room's sandy floor. I let my head roll over and realized that I was
lying on a bed of soft, springy branches. Opposite my bed was
another bed, and between them crackled a cheery campfire.
"Fire now we have, Davidge. And wood." Jerry pointed toward
the roof made of wooden poles thatched with broad leaves.

I turned and looked around, then let my throbbing head sink
down and closed my eyes. "Where are we?"

"Big island, Davidge. Soaker off sandbar us washed. Wind
and waves us here took. Right you were."

"I ... I don't understand; *ne gavey*. It'd take days to get to the
big island from the sandbar."

Jerry nodded and dropped what looked like a sponge into a
shell of some sort·filled with water. "Nine days. You I strap to
nasesay, then here on beach we land."

"Nine days? I've been out for nine days?"

Jerry shook his head. "Seventeen. Here we land eight
days..." The Drac waved its hand behind itself.

"Ago ... eight days ago."

"Ae."

Seventeen days on Fyrine IV was better than a month on
Earth. I opened my eyes again and looked at Jerry. The Drac
was almost bubbling with excitement. "What about *tean*, your
child?"

Jerry patted its swollen middle. "Good is, Davidge. You more *nasesay* hurt."

I overcame an urge to nod. "I'm happy for you." I closed my eyes and turned my face toward the wall, a combination of wood poles and leaves. "Jerry?"

"Ess?"

"You saved my life."

"Ae."

"Why?"

Jerry sat quietly for a long time. "Davidge. On sandbar you talk. Loneliness now *gavey*." The Drac shook my arm. "Here, now you eat."

I turned and looked into a shell filled with a steaming liquid. "What is it; chicken soup?"

"Ess?"

"Ess va?" I pointed at the bowl, realizing for the first time how weak I was.

Jerry frowned. "Like slug, but long."

"An eel?"

"Ae, but eel on land, *gavey?"*

"You mean 'snake'?"

"Possiblemaybeperhaps."

I nodded and put my lips to the edge of the shell. I sipped some of the broth, swallowed and let the broth's healing warmth seep through my body. "Good."

"You *custa* want?"

"Ess?"

"Custa." Jerry reached next to the fire and picked up a squareish chunk of clear rock. I looked at it, scratched it with my thumbnail, then touched it with my tongue.

"Halite! Salt!"

Jerry smile. *"Custa* you want?"

I laughed. "All the comforts. By all means, let's have *custa.*"

Jerry took the halite, knocked off a corner with a small stone, then used the stone to grind the pieces against another stone. He held out the palm of his hand with a tiny mountain of white granules in the center. I took two pinches, dropped them into my snake soup and stirred it with my finger. Then I took a long swallow of the delicious broth. I smacked my lips. "Fantastic."

"Good, *ne?"*

"Better than good; fantastic." I took another swallow making a big show of smacking my lips and rolling my eyes.

"Fantastic, Davidge, *ne*?"

"Ae." I nodded at the Drac. "I think that's enough. I want to sleep."

"Ae, Davidge, *gavey*." Jerry took the bowl and put it beside the fire. The Drac stood, walked to the door and turned back. Its yellow eyes studied me for an instant, then it nodded, turned and went outside. I closed my eyes and let the heat from the campfire coax the sleep over me.

In two days I was up in the shack trying my legs, and in two more days Jerry helped me outside. The shack was located at the top of a long, gentle rise in a scrub forest; none of the trees any taller than five or six meters. At the bottom of the slope, better than eight kilometers from the shack, was the still-rolling sea. The Drac had carried me. Our trusty *nasesay* had filled with water and had been dragged back into the sea soon after Jerry pulled me to dry land. With it went the remainder of the ration bars. Dracs are very fussy about what they eat, but hunger finally drove Jerry to sample some of the local flora and fauna—hunger and the human lump that was rapidly drifting away from lack of nourishment. The Drac had settled on a bland, starchy type of root, a green bushberry that when dried made an acceptable tea, and snakemeat. Exploring, Jerry had found a partly eroded salt dome. In the days that followed, I grew stronger, and added to our diet with several types of sea mollusk and a fruit resembling a cross between a pear and a plum.

As the days grew colder, the Drac and I were forced to realize that Fyrine IV had a winter. Given that, we had to face the possibility that the winter would be severe enough to prevent the gathering of food—and wood. When dried next to the fire, the berrybush and roots kept well, and we tried both salting and smoking snakemeat. With strips of fiber from the berrybush for thread, Jerry and I pieced together the snake skins for winter clothing. The design we settled on involved two layers of skins with the down from berrybush seed pods stuffed between and then held in place by quilting the layers.

We agreed that the house would never do. It took three days of searching to find our first cave, and another three days before we found one that suited us. The mouth opened onto a view of the eternally tormented sea, but was set in the face of a low cliff well above sea level. Around the cave's entrance we found great quantities of dead wood and loose stone. The wood we gathered for heat and the stone we used to wall up the entrance, leaving only space enough for a hinged door. The hinges were made of snake leather and the door of wooden poles tied together with berrybush fiber. The first night after completing the door, the sea winds blew it to pieces, and we decided to go back to the original door design we had used on the sandbar.

Deep inside the cave, we made our living quarters in a chamber with a wide, sandy floor. Still deeper, the cave had natural pools of water, which were fine for drinking but too cold for bathing. We used the pool chamber for our supply room. We lined the walls of our living quarters with piles of wood and made new beds out of snakeskins and seed-pod down. In the center of the chamber we built a respectable fireplace with a large flatstone over the coals for a griddle. The first night we spent in our new home, I discovered that, for the first time since ditching on that damned planet, I couldn't hear the wind.

During the long nights, we would sit at the fireplace making things—gloves, hats, pack bags—out of snake leather, and we would talk. To break the monotony, we alternated days between speaking Drac and English, and by the time the winter hit with its first ice storm, each of us was comfortable in the other's language.

We talked of Jerry's coming child:

"What are you going to name it, Jerry?"

"It already has a name. See, the Jeriba line has five names. My name is Shigan; before me came my parent, Gothig; before Gothig was Haesni; before Haesni was Ty, and before Ty was Zammis. The child is named Jeriba Zammis."

"Why only the five names? A human child can have just about any name its parents pick for it. In fact, once a human becomes an adult, he or she can pick any name he or she wants."

The Drac looked at me, its eyes filled with pity. "Davidge, how lost you must feel. You humans—how lost you must feel."

"Lost?"

Jerry nodded. "Where do you come from, Davidge?"

"You mean my parents?"

"Yes."

I shrugged. "I remember my parents."

"And their parents?"

"I remember my mother's father. When I was young we used to visit him."

"Davidge, what do you know about this grandparent?"

I rubbed my chin. "It's kind of vague . . . I think he was in some kind of agriculture—I don't know."

"And his parents?"

I shook my head. "The only thing I remember is that somewhere along the line, English and Germans figured. *Gavey* Germans and English?"

Jerry nodded. "Davidge, I can recite the history of my line back to the founding of my planet by Jeriba Ty, one of the original settlers, one hundred and ninety-nine generations ago. At our line's archives on Draco, there are the records that trace the line across space to the race-home planet, Sindie, and there back seventy generations to Jeriba Ty, the founder of the Jeriba line."

"How does one become a founder?"

"Only the firstborn carries the line. Products of second, third or fourth births must found their own lines."

I nodded, impressed. "Why only the five names? Just to make it easier to remember them?"

Jerry shook its head. "No. The names are things to which we add distinction; they are the same, commonplace five so that they do not overshadow the events that distinguish their bearers. The name I carry, Shigan, has been served by great soldiers, scholars, students of philosophy and several priests. The name my child will carry has been served by scientists, teachers and explorers."

"You remember all of your ancestor's occupations?"

Jerry nodded. "Yes, and what they each did and where they did it. You must recite your line before the line's archives to be admitted into adulthood, as I was twenty-two of my years ago. Zammis will do the same, except the child must begin its recitation..."—Jerry smiled—"with my name, Jeriba Shigan."

"You can recite almost two hundred biographies from memory?"

"Yes."

I went over to my bed and stretched out. As I stared up at the smoke being sucked through the crack in the chamber's ceiling, I began to understand what Jerry meant by feeling lost. A Drac with several dozens of generations under its belt knew who it was and what it had to live up to. "Jerry?"

"Yes, Davidge?"

"Will you recite them for me?" I turned my head and looked at the Drac in time to see an expression of utter surprise melt into joy. It was only after many months had passed that I learned I had done Jerry a great honor in requesting his line. Among the Dracs, it is a rare expression of respect, not only of the individual but of the line.

Jerry placed the hat he was sewing on the sand, stood and began.

"Before you here I stand, Shigan of the line of Jeriba, born of Gothig, the teacher of music. A musician of high merit, the students of Gothig included Datzizh of the Nem line, Perravane of the Tuscor line and many lesser musicians. Trained in music at the Shimuram, Gothig stood before the archives in the year 12,051 and spoke of its parent Haesni, the manufacturer of ships..."

As I listened to Jerry's singsong of formal Dracon, the backward biographies—beginning with death and ending with adulthood—I experienced a sense of time-binding, of being able to know and touch the past. Battles, empires built and destroyed, discoveries made, great things done—a tour through twelve thousand years of history, but perceived as a well-defined, living continuum.

Against this: I Willis of the Davidge line stand before you, born of Sybil the housewife and Nathan the second-rate civil engineer, one of them born of Grandpop, who probably had something to do with agriculture, born of nobody in particular... Hell, I wasn't even that! My older brother carried the line; not me. I listened and made up my mind to memorize the line of Jeriban.

*   *   *

We talked of war:

"That was a pretty neat trick, suckering me into the atmosphere, then ramming me."

Jerry shrugged. "Dracon fleet pilots are best; this is well known."

I raised my eyebrows. "That's why I shot your tail feathers off, huh?"

"Lucky shot."

"And ramming my ship with a crippled fighter at five times the speed of sound with no pilot wasn't a lucky shot, is that it?"

Jerry shrugged, frowned and continued sewing on the scraps of snake leather. "Why do the Earthmen invade this part of the galaxy, Davidge? We had thousands of years of peace before you came."

"Hah! Why do the Dracs invade? We were at peace, too. What are you doing here?"

"We settle these planets. It is the Drac tradition. We are explorers and founders."

"Well, toadface, what do you think we are, a bunch of homebodies? Humans have had space travel for less than a hundred years, but we've settled almost twice as many planets as the Dracs—"

Jerry held up a finger. "Exactly! You humans spread like a disease. Enough! We don't want you here!"

"Well, we're here, and here to stay. Now, what are you going to do about it?"

"You see what we do, *Irkmaan*, we fight!"

"Phooey! You call that little scrap we were in a fight? Hell, Jerry, we were kicking you junk jocks out of the sky—"

"Haw, Davidge! That's why you sit here sucking on smoked snakemeat!"

I pulled the little rascal out of my mouth and pointed it at the Drac. "I notice your breath has a snake flavor too, Drac!"

Jerry snorted and turned away from the fire. I felt stupid, first because we weren't going to settle an argument that had plagued a hundred worlds for almost a century. Second, I wanted to have

Jerry check my recitation. I had over a hundred generations memorized. The Drac's side was toward the fire, leaving enough light falling on its lap to see its sewing.

"Jerry, what are you working on?"

"We have nothing to talk about, Davidge."

"Come on, what is it?"

Jerry turned its head toward me, then looked back into its lap and picked up a tiny snakeskin suit. "For Zammis." Jerry smiled and I shook my head, then laughed.

We talked of philosophy:

"You studied Shizumaat, Jerry, why won't you tell me about its teachings?"

Jerry frowned. "No, Davidge."

"Are Shizumaat's teachings secret or something?"

Jerry shook its head. "No. But we honor Shizumaat too much for talk."

I rubbed my chin. "Do you mean too much to talk about it, or to talk about it with a human?"

"Not with humans, Davidge; just not with you."

"Why?"

Jerry lifted its head and narrowed its yellow eyes. "You know what you said . . . on the sandbar."

I scratched my head and vaguely recalled the curse I laid on the Drac about Shizumaat eating it. I held out my hands. "But, Jerry, I was mad, angry. You can't hold me accountable for what I said then."

"I do."

"Will it change anything if I apologize?"

"Not a thing."

I stopped myself from saying something nasty and thought back to that moment when Jerry and I stood ready to strangle each other. I remembered something about that meeting and screwed the corners of my mouth in place to keep from smiling. "Will you tell me Shizumaat's teachings if I forgive you . . . for what you said about Mickey Mouse?" I bowed my head in an appearance of reverence, although its chief purpose was to suppress a cackle.

Jerry looked up at me, its face pained with guilt. "I have felt bad about that, Davidge. If you forgive me, I will talk about Shizumaat."

"Then, I forgive you, Jerry."

"One more thing."

"What?"

"You must tell me of the teachings of Mickey Mouse."

"I'll . . . uh, do my best."

We talked of Zammis:

"Jerry, what do you want little Zammy to be?"

The Drac shrugged. "Zammis must live up to its own name. I want it to do that with honor. If Zammis does that, it is all I can ask."

"Zammy will pick its own trade?"

"Yes."

"Isn't there anything special you want, though?"

Jerry nodded. "Yes, there is."

"What's that?"

"That Zammis will, one day, find itself off this miserable planet."

I nodded. "Amen."

"Amen."

The winter dragged on until Jerry and I began wondering if we had gotten in on the beginning of an ice age. Outside the cave, everything was coated with a thick layer of ice, and the low temperature combined with the steady winds made venturing outside a temptation of death by falls or freezing. Still, by mutual agreement, we both went outside to relieve ourselves. There were several isolated chambers deep in the cave, but we feared polluting our water supply, not to mention the air inside the cave. The main risk outside was dropping one's drawers at a wind-chill factor that froze breath vapor before it could be blown through the thin face muffs we had made out of our flight suits. We learned not to dawdle.

One morning, Jerry was outside answering the call while I stayed by the fire, mashing up dried roots with water for griddle cakes. I heard Jerry call from the mouth of the cave. "Davidge!"

"What?"

"Davidge, come quick!"

A ship! It had to be! I put the shell bowl on the sand, put on my hat and gloves and ran through the passage. As I came close to the door, I untied the muff from around my neck and tied it over my mouth and nose to protect my lungs. Jerry, its head bundled in a similar manner, was looking through the door, waving me on. "What is it?"

Jerry stepped away from the door to let me through. "Come, look!"

Sunlight. Blue sky and sunlight. In the distance over the sea, new clouds were piling up, but above us the sky was clear. Neither of us could look at the sun directly, but we turned our faces to it and felt the rays of Fyrine on our skins. The light glared and sparkled off the ice-covered rocks and trees. "Beautiful."

"Yes." Jerry grabbed my sleeve with a gloved hand. "Davidge, you know what this means?"

"What?"

"Signal fires at night. On a clear night, a large fire could be seen from orbit, *ne*?"

I looked at Jerry, then back at the sky. "I don't know. If the fire were big enough, and we get a clear night, and if anybody picks that moment to look . . ." I let my head hang down. "That's always supposing there's someone in orbit up there to do the looking." I felt the pain begin in my fingers. "We better go back in."

"Davidge, it's a chance!"

"What are we going to use for wood, Jerry?" I held out an arm toward the trees above and around the cave. "Everything that can burn has at least fifteen centimeters of ice on it."

"In the cave—"

"Our firewood?" I shook my head. "How long is this winter going to last? Can you be sure that we have enough wood to waste on signal fires?"

"It's a chance, Davidge. It's a chance!"

Our survival riding on a toss of the dice. I shrugged. "Why not?"

We spent the next few hours hauling a quarter of our

carefully gathered firewood and dumping it outside the mouth of the cave. By the time we were finished, and long before night came, the sky was again a solid blanket of gray. Several times each night we would check the sky, waiting for stars to appear. During the days, we would frequently have to spend several hours beating the ice off the woodpile. Still, it gave both of us hope, until the wood in the cave ran out and we had to start borrowing from the signal pile.

That night, for the first time, the Drac looked absolutely defeated. Jerry sat at the fireplace, staring at the flames. Its hand reached inside its snakeskin jacket through the neck and pulled out a small golden cube suspended on a chain. Jerry held the cube clasped in both hands, shut its eyes and began mumbling in Drac. I watched from my bed until Jerry finished. The Drac sighed, nodded and replaced the object within its jacket.

"What's that thing?"

Jerry looked up at me, frowned, then touched the front of its jacket. "This? It is my *Talman*—what you call a Bible."

"A Bible is a book. You know, with pages that you read."

Jerry pulled the thing from its jacket, mumbled a phrase in Drac, then worked a small catch. Another gold cube dropped from the first and the Drac held it out to me. "Be very careful with it, Davidge."

I sat up, took the object and examined it in the light of the fire. Three hinged pieces of the golden metal formed the binding of a book two and a half centimeters on an edge. I opened the book in the middle and looked over the double columns of dots, lines and squiggles. "It's in Drac."

"Of course."

"But I can't read it."

Jerry's eyebrows went up. "You speak Drac so well, I didn't remember . . . Would you like me to teach you?"

"To read this?"

"Why not? You have an appointment you have to keep?"

I shrugged. "No." I touched my finger to the book and tried to turn one of the tiny pages. Perhaps fifty pages went at once. "I can't separate the pages."

Jerry pointed at a small bump at the top of the spine. "Pull out the pin. It's for turning the pages."

I pulled out the short needle, touched it against a page and it slid loose of its companion and flipped. "Who wrote your *Talman*, Jerry?"

"Many. All great teachers."

"Shizumaat?"

Jerry nodded. "Shizumaat is one of them."

I closed the book and held it in the palm of my hand. "Jerry, why did you bring this out now?"

"I needed its comfort." The Drac held out its arms. "This place. Maybe we will grow old here and die. Maybe we will never be found. I see this today as we brought in the signal firewood." Jerry placed its hands on its belly. "Zammis will be born here. The *Talman* helps me to accept what I cannot change."

"Zammis; how much longer?"

Jerry smiled. "Soon."

I looked at the tiny book. "I would like you to teach me to read this, Jerry."

The Drac took the chain and case from around its neck and handed it to me. "You must keep the *Talman* in this."

I held it for a moment, then shook my head. "I can't keep this, Jerry. It's obviously of great value to you. What if I lost it?"

"You won't. Keep it while you learn. The student must do this."

I put the chain around my neck. "This is quite an honor you do me."

Jerry shrugged. "Much less than the honor you do me by memorizing the Jeriban line. Your recitations have been accurate, and moving." Jerry took some charcoal from the fire, stood and walked to the wall of the chamber. That night I learned the thirty-one letters and sounds of the Drac alphabet, as well as the additional nine sounds and letters used in formal Drac writings.

The wood eventually ran out. Jerry was very heavy and very, very sick as Zammis prepared to make its appearance, and it was all the Drac could do to waddle outside with my help to relieve itself. Hence, wood-gathering, which involved taking our remaining stick and beating the ice off the dead standing trees, fell to me, as did cooking.

On a particularly blustery day, I noticed that the ice on the trees was thinner. Somewhere we had turned winter's corner and were heading for spring. I spent my ice-pounding time feelin, great at the thought of spring, and I knew Jerry would pick up some at the news. The winter was really getting the Drac down. I was working the woods above the cave, taking armloads of gathered wood and dropping them down below, when I heard a scream. I froze, then looked around. I could see nothing but the sea and the ice around me. Then, the scream again. "Davidge!" It was Jerry. I dropped the load I was carrying and ran to the cleft in the cliff's face that served as a path to the upper woods. Jerry screamed again, and I slipped, then rolled until I came to the shelf level with the cave's mouth. I rushed through the entrance, down the passageway, until I came to the chamber. Jerry writhed on its bed, digging its fingers into the sand.

I dropped on my knees next to the Drac. "I'm here, Jerry. What is it? What's wrong?"

"Davidge!" The Drac rolled its eyes, seeing nothing, its mouth worked silently, then exploded with another scream.

"Jerry, it's me!" I shook the Drac's shoulder. "It's me, Jerry. Davidge!"

Jerry turned its head toward me, grimaced, then clasped the fingers of one hand around my left wrist with the strength of pain. "Davidge! Zammis . . . something's gone wrong!"

"What? What can I do?"

Jerry screamed again, then its head fell back to the bed in a half-faint. The Drac fought back to consciousness and pulled my head down to its lips. "Davidge, you must swear."

"What, Jerry? Swear what?"

"Zammis . . . on Draco. To stand before the line's archives. Do this."

"What do you mean? You talk like you're dying."

"I am, Davidge. Zammis two hundredth generation . . . very important. Present my child, Davidge. Swear!"

I wiped the sweat from my face with my free hand. "You're not going to die, Jerry. Hang on!"

"Enough! . . . face truth, Davidge! I die! You must teach the line of Jeriba to Zammis . . . and the book, the *Talman*, *gavey*?"

"Stop it!" Panic stood over me almost as a physical presence.

"Stop talking like that! You aren't going to die, Jerry. Come on; fight, you *kizlode* sonofabitch..."

Jerry screamed. Its breathing was weak and the Drac drifted in and out of consciousness. "Davidge."

"What?" I realized I was sobbing like a kid.

"Davidge, you must help Zammis come out."

"What... how? What in the Hell are you talking about?"

Jerry turned its face to the wall of the cave. "Lift my jacket."

"What?"

"Lift my jacket, Davidge. Now!"

I pulled up the snakeskin jacket exposing Jerry's swollen belly. The fold down the center was bright red and oozing a clear liquid. "What... what should I do?"

Jerry breathed rapidly, then held its breath. "Tear it open! You must tear it open, Davidge!"

"No!"

"Do it! Do it, or Zammis dies!"

"What do I care about your goddamn child, Jerry? What do I have to do to save you?"

"Tear it open...," whispered the Drac. "Take care of my child, *Irkmaan*. Present Zammis before the Jeriba archives. Swear this to me."

"Oh, Jerry..."

"Swear this!"

I nodded, hot, fat tears dribbling down my cheeks. "I swear it..." Jerry relaxed its grip on my wrist and closed its eyes. I knelt next to the Drac, stunned. "No. No, no, no, no."

Tear it open! You must tear it open, Davidge!

I reached up a hand and gingerly touched the fold on Jerry's belly. I could feel life struggling beneath it, trying to escape the airless confines of the Drac's womb. I hated it; I hated the damned thing as I never hated anything before. Its struggles grew weaker, then stopped.

Present Zammis before the Jeriban archives. Swear this to me...

"I swear it..."

I lifted my other hand and inserted my thumbs into the fold and tugged gently. I increased the amount of force, then tore at Jerry's belly like a madman. The fold burst open, soaking the front of my jacket with the clear fluid. Holding the fold open, I could see the still form of Zammis huddled in a well of the fluid, motionless.

I vomited. When I had nothing more to throw up, I reached into the fluid and put my hands under the Drac infant. I lifted it, wiped my mouth on my upper left sleeve, and closed my mouth over Zammis' and pulled the child's mouth open with my right hand. Three times, four times, I inflated the child's lungs, then it coughed. Then it cried. I tied off the two umbilicals with berrybush fiber, then cut them. Jeriban Zammis was freed of the dead flesh of its parent.

I held the rock over my head, then brought it down with all of my force upon the ice. Shards splashed away from the point of impact exposing the dark green beneath. Again, I lifted the rock and brought it down, knocking loose another rock. I picked it up, stood and carried it to the half-covered corpse of the Drac. "The Drac," I whispered. *Good. Just call it 'the Drac.' Toadface. Dragger. The enemy. Call it anything to insulate those feelings against the pain.*

I looked at the pile of rocks I had gathered, decided it was sufficient to finish the job, then knelt next to the grave. As I placed the rocks on the pile, unmindful of the gale-blown sleet freezing on my snakeskins, I fought back the tears.

I smacked my hands together to help restore the circulation. Spring was coming, but it was still dangerous to stay outside too long. And I had been a long time building the Drac's grave. I picked up another rock and placed it into position. As the rock's weight leaned against the snakeskin mattress cover, I realized that the Drac was already frozen. I quickly placed the remainder of the rocks, then stood.

The wind rocked me and I almost lost my footing on the ice next to the grave. I looked toward the boiling sea, pulled my snakeskins around myself more tightly, then looked down at the pile of rocks. *There should be words. You don't just cover up the dead, then go to dinner. There should be words.* But what words? I was no religionist, and neither was the Drac. Its formal philosophy on the matter of death was the same as my informal rejection of Islamic delights, pagan Valhallas, and Judeo-Christian pies in the sky. Death is death; *finis*; the end; the worms crawl in, the worms crawl out... *Still, there should be words.*

I reached beneath my snakeskins and clasped my gloved hand around the golden cube of the *Talman*. I felt the sharp corners of the cube through my glove, closed my eyes and ran through the words of the great Drac philosophers. But there was nothing they had written for this moment.

The *Talman* was a book on life. *Talma* means life, and this occupies Drac philosophy. They spare nothing for death. Death is a fact; the end of life. The *Talman* had no words for me to say. The wind knifed through me, causing me to shiver. Already my fingers were numb and pains were beginning in my feet. Still, there should be words. But, the only words I could think of would open the gate, flooding my being with pain—with the realization that the Drac was gone. *Still... still, there should be words.*

"Jerry, I..." I had no words. I turned from the grave, my tears mixing with the sleet.

With the warmth and silence of the cave around me, I sat on my mattress, my back against the wall of the cave. I tried to lose myself in the shadows and flickers of light cast on the opposite wall by the fire. Images would half form, then dance away before I could move my mind to see something in them. As a child I used to watch clouds, and in them see faces, castles, animals, dragons and giants. It was a world of escape—fantasy; something to inject wonder and adventure into the mundane, regulated life of a middle-class boy leading a middle-class life. All I could see on the wall of the cave was a representation of Hell; flames licking at twisted, grotesque representations of condemned souls. I laughed at the thought. We think of Hell as fire, supervised by a cackling sadist in a red union suit. Fyrine IV taught me that much: Hell is loneliness, hunger and endless cold.

I heard a whimper, and I looked into the shadows toward the small mattress at the back of the cave. Jerry had made the snakeskin sack filled with seed-pod down for Zammis. It whimpered again, and I leaned forward, wondering if there was something it needed. A pang of fear tickled my guts. What does a Drac infant eat? Dracs aren't mammals. All they ever taught us in training was how to recognize Dracs—that, and how to kill them. Then real fear began working on me. "What in the Hell am I going to use for diapers?"

It whimpered again. I pushed myself to my feet, walked the sandy floor to the infant's side, then knelt beside it. Out of the bundle that was Jerry's old flight suit, two chubby, three-fingered arms waved. I picked up the bundle, carried it next to the fire, and sat on a rock. Balancing the bundle on my lap, I carefully unwrapped it. I could see the yellow glitter of Zammis' eyes beneath yellow, sleep-heavy lids. From the almost noseless face and solid teeth to its deep yellow color, Zammis was every bit a miniature of Jerry, except for the fat. Zammis fairly wallowed in rolls of fat. I looked, and was grateful to find that there was no mess.

I looked into Zammis' face. "You want something to eat?"

"Guh."

Its jaws were ready for business, and I assumed that Dracs must chew solid food from day one. I reached over the fire and picked up a twist of dried snake, then touched it against the infant's lips. Zammis turned its head. "C'mon, eat. You're not going to find anything better around here."

I pushed the snake against its lips again, and Zammis pulled back a chubby arm and pushed it away. I shrugged. "Well, whenever you get hungry enough, it's there."

"Guh meh!" Its head rocked back and forth on my lap, a tiny, three-fingered hand closed around my finger, and it whimpered again.

"You don't want to eat, you don't need to be cleaned up, so what do you want? *Kos va nu?*"

Zammis' face wrinkled, and its hand pulled at my finger. Its other hand waved in the direction of my chest. I picked Zammis up to arrange the flight suit, and the tiny hands reached out, grasped the front of my snakeskins, and held on as the chubby arms pulled the child next to my chest. I held it close, it placed its cheek against my chest and promptly fell asleep. "Well . . . I'll be damned."

Until the Drac was gone, I never realized how closely I had stood near the edge of madness. My loneliness was a cancer—a growth that I fed with hate: hate for the planet with its endless cold, endless winds and endless isolation; hate for the helpless yellow child with its clawing need for care, food and an affection that I couldn't give; and hate for myself. I found myself doing things that frightened and disgusted me. To break my solid wall of being alone, I would talk, shout and sing to myself—uttering curses, nonsense, or meaningless croaks.

Its eyes were open, and it waved a chubby arm and cooed. I picked up a large rock, staggered over to the child's side and held the weight over the tiny body. "I could drop this thing, kid. Where would you be then?" I felt laughter coming from my lips. I threw the rock aside. "Why should I mess up the cave? Outside. Put you outside for a minute, and you die! You hear me? Die!"

The child worked its three-fingered hands at the empty air, shut its eyes and cried. "Why don't you eat? Why don't you crap? Why don't you do anything right, but cry?" The child cried more loudly. "Bah! I ought to pick up that rock and finish it! That's what I ought..." A wave of revulsion stopped my words and I went to my mattress, picked up my cap, gloves and muff, then headed outside.

Before I came to the rocked-in entrance to the cave, I felt the bite of the wind. Outside, I stopped and looked at the sea and sky—a roiling panorama in glorious black and white, gray and gray. A gust of wind slapped against me, rocking me back toward the entrance. I regained my balance, walked to the edge of the cliff and shook my fist at the sea. "Go ahead! Go ahead and blow, you *kizlode* sonofabitch! You haven't killed me yet!"

I squeezed the windburned lids of my eyes shut, then opened them and looked down. A forty-meter drop to the next ledge, but if I took a running jump I could clear it. Then it would be a hundred and fifty meters to the rocks below. *Jump.* I backed away from the cliff's edge. "Jump! Sure, jump!" I shook my head at the sea. "I'm not going to do your job for you! You want me dead, you're going to have to do it yourself!"

I looked back and up, above the entrance to the cave. The sky was darkening, and in a few hours night would shroud the landscape. I turned toward the cleft in the rock that led to the scrub forest above the cave.

I squatted next to the Drac's grave and studied the rocks I had placed there, already fused together with a layer of ice.

"Jerry. What am I going to do?"

The Drac would sit by the fire, both of us sewing. And we talked.

"You know, Jerry, all this,"—I held up the Talman—*"I've heard it all before. I expected something different."*

The Drac lowered its sewing to its lap and studied me for an instant. Then it shook its head and resumed its sewing. "You are not a terribly profound creature, Davidge."

"What's that supposed to mean?"

Jerry held out a three-fingered hand. "A universe, Davidge— there is a universe out there, a universe of life, objects and events. There are differences, but it is all the same universe, and we all must obey the same universal laws. Did you ever think of that?"

"No."

"That is what I mean, Davidge. Not terribly profound."

I snorted. "I told you, I'd heard this stuff before. So, I imagine that shows humans to be just as profound as Dracs."

Jerry laughed. "You always insist on making something racial out of my observations. What I said applied to you, not to the race of humans . . ."

I spat on the frozen ground. "You Dracs think you're so damned smart." The wind picked up, and I could taste the sea salt in it. One of the big blows was coming. The sky was changing to that curious darkness that tricked me into thinking it was midnight blue, rather than black. A trickle of ice found its way under my collar.

"What's wrong with me just being me? Everybody in the universe doesn't have to be a damned philosopher, toadface!" There were millions—billions—like me. More, maybe. "What difference does it make to anything whether I ponder existence or not? It's here; that's all I have to know."

"Davidge, you don't even know your family line beyond your parents, and now you say you refuse to know that of your universe that you can know. How will you know your place in this existence, Davidge? Where are you? Who are you?"

I shook my head and stared at the grave, then I turned and faced the sea. In another hour, or less, it would be too dark to see the whitecaps. "I'm me, that's who." But, was *that* "me" who held the rock over Zammis, threatening a helpless infant with death? I felt my guts curdle as the loneliness I thought I felt grew claws and fangs and began gnawing and slashing at the remains of my sanity. I turned back to the grave, closed my eyes, then opened them. "I'm a fighter pilot, Jerry. Isn't that something?"

"That is what you do, Davidge; that is not who nor what you are."

I knelt next to the grave and clawed at the ice-sheathed rocks with my hands. "You don't talk to me now, Drac! *You're dead*!" I stopped, realizing that the words I had heard were from the *Talman*, processed into my own context. I slumped against the rocks, felt the wind, then pushed myself to my feet. "Jerry, Zammis won't eat. It's been three days. What do I do? Why didn't you tell me anything about Drac brats before you?..." I held my hands to my face. "Steady, boy. Keep it up, and they'll stick you in a home." The wind pressed against my back, I lowered my hands, then walked from the grave.

I sat in the cave, staring at the fire. I couldn't hear the wind through the rock and the wood was dry, making the fire hot and quiet. I tapped my fingers against my knees, then began humming. Noise, any kind, helped to drive off the oppressing loneliness. "Sonofabitch." I laughed and nodded. "Yea, verily, and *kizlode va nu, dutshaat*." I chuckled, trying to think of all the curses and obscenities in Drac that I had learned from Jerry. There were quite a few. My toe tapped against the sand and my humming started up again. I stopped, frowned, then remembered the song.

> "Highty tighty Christ Almighty,
> Who the Hell are we?
> Zim zam, Gawd damn,
> We're in Squadron B."

I leaned back against the wall of the cave, trying to remember another verse. *A pilot's got a rotten life/ No crumpets with our tea/ We have to service the general's wife/ And pick fleas from her knee.* "Damn!" I slapped my knee, trying to see the faces of the other pilots in the squadron lounge. I could almost feel the whiskey fumes tickling the inside of my nose. Vadik, Wooster,

Arnold...the one with the broken nose—Demerest, Kadiz. I
hummed again, swinging an imaginary mug of issue grog by its
imaginary handle.

> "And if he doesn't like it,
> I'll tell you what we'll do:
> We'll fill his ass with broken glass,
> And seal it up with glue."

The cave echoed with the song. I stood, threw up my arms
and screamed. "Yaaaaahoooooo!"

Zammis began crying. I bit my lip and walked over to to the
bundle on the mattress. "Well? You ready to eat?"

"Unh, unh, weh." The infant rocked its head back and forth. I
went to the fire, picked up a twist of snake, then returned. I knelt
next to Zammis and held the snake to its lips. Again the child
pushed it away. "Come on, you. You have to eat." I tried again
with the same results. I took the wraps off the child and looked
at its body. I could tell it was losing weight, although Zammis
didn't appear to be getting weak. I shrugged, wrapped it up
again, stood and began walking back to my mattress.

"Guh, weh."

I turned. "What?"

"Ah, guh, guh."

I went back, stooped over and picked the child up. Its eyes
were open and it looked into my face, then smiled.

"What're you laughing at, ugly? You should get a load of
your own face."

Zammis barked out a short laugh, then gurgled. I went to my
mattress, sat down and arranged Zammis in my lap. "Gumma,
buh, buh." Its hand grabbed a loose flap of snakeskin on my
shirt and pulled on it.

"Gumma buh buh to you, too. So, what do we do now? How
about I start teaching you the line of Jeriba? You're going to
have to learn it sometime, and it might as well be now." I looked
into Zammis' eyes. "When I bring you to stand before the Jeriba
archives, you will say this: 'Before you here I stand, Zammis of
the line of Jeriba, born of Shigan, the fighter pilot.'" I smiled,
thinking of the upraised yellow brows if Zammis continued:

"And, by damn, Shigan was a helluva good pilot, too. Why, I was once told he took a smart round in his tail feathers, then pulled around and rammed the kizlode *sonofabitch, known to one and all us Willis E. Davidge...* I shook my head. "You're not going to get your wings by doing the line in English, Zammis." I began again:

"Naatha nu enta va Zammis zea dos Jeriba, estay va Shigan, asaam naa denvadar..."

For eight of those long days and nights, I feared the child would die. I tried everything—roots, dried berries, dried plumfruit, snakemeat dried, boiled, chewed and ground. Zammis refused it all. I checked frequently, but each time I looked through the child's wraps, they were as clean as when I had put them on. Zammis lost weight, but seemed to grow stronger. By the ninth day it was crawling the floor of the cave. Even with the fire, the cave wasn't really warm. I feared that the kid would get sick crawling around naked, and I dressed it in the tiny snakeskin suit and cap Jerry had made for it. After dressing it, I stood Zammis up and looked at it. The kid had already developed a smile full of mischief that, combined with the twinkle in its yellow eyes, suit and cap, made it look like a elf. I was holding Zammis up in a standing position. The kid seemed pretty steady on its legs, and I let go. Zammis smiled, waved its thinning arms about, then the child laughed and took a faltering step toward me. I caught it as it fell, and the little Drac squealed.

In two more days Zammis was walking and getting into everything that could be gotten into. I spent many an anxious moment searching the chambers at the back of the cave for the kid after coming in from outside. Finally, when I caught him at the mouth of the cave heading full steam for the outside, I had had enough. I made a harness out of snakeskin, attached it to a snake-leather leash, and tied the other end to a projection of rock above my head. Zammis still got into everything, but at least I could find it.

Four days after it learned to walk, it wanted to eat. Drac babies are probably the most convenient and considerate infants in the universe. They live off their fat for about three or four Earth weeks, and don't make a mess the entire time. After they learn to walk, and can therefore make it to a mutually agreed-upon spot, then they want food and begin discharging wastes. I showed the kid once how to use the litter box I had made, and never had to again. After five or six lessons, Zammis was handling its own drawers. Watching the little Drac learn and grow, I began to understand those pilots in my squadron who used to bore each other—and everyone else—with countless pictures of ugly children, accompanied by thirty-minute narratives for each snapshot. Before the ice melted, Zammis was talking. I taught it to call me "Uncle."

For lack of a better term, I called the ice-melting season "spring." It would be a long time before the scrub forest showed any green, or the snakes would venture forth from their icy holes. The sky maintained its eternal cover of dark, angry clouds, and still the sleet would come and coat everything with a hard, slippery glaze. But the next day the glaze would melt, and the warmer air would push another millimeter into the soil.

I realized that this was the time to be gathering wood. Before the winter hit, Jerry and I working together hadn't gathered enough wood. The short summer would have to be spent putting up food for the next winter. I was hoping to build a tighter door over the mouth of the cave, and I swore that I would figure out some kind of indoor plumbing. Dropping your drawers outside in the middle of winter was dangerous. My mind was full of these things as I stretched out on my mattress watching the smoke curl through a crack in the roof of the cave. Zammis was off in the back of the cave playing with some rocks that it had found, and I must have fallen asleep. I awoke with the kid shaking my arm.

"Uncle?"

"Huh? Zammis?"

"Uncle. Look."

I rolled over on my left side and faced the Drac. Zammis was holding up his right hand, fingers spread out. "What is it, Zammis?"

"Look." It pointed at each of its three fingers in turn. "One, two, three."

"So?"

"Look." Zammis grabbed my right hand and spread out the fingers. "One, two, three, *four, five!*"

I nodded. "So, you can count to five."

The Drac frowned and made an impatient gesture with its tiny fists. "Look." It took my outstretched hand and placed its own on top of it. With its other hand, Zammis pointed first at one of its own fingers, then at one of mine. "One, one." The child's yellow eyes studied me to see if I understood.

"Yes."

The child pointed again. "Two, two." It looked at me, then looked back at my hand and pointed. "Three, three." Then he grabbed my two remaining fingers. *"Four, Five!"* It dropped my hand, then pointed to the side of its own hand. "Four, five?"

I shook my head. Zammis, at less than four Earth months old, had detected part of the difference between Dracs and humans. A human child would be—what?—five, six or seven years old before asking questions like that. I sighed. "Zammis."

"Yes, Uncle?"

"Zammis, you are a Drac. Dracs only have three fingers on a hand." I held up my right hand and wiggled the fingers. "I'm a human. I have five."

I swear that tears welled in the child's eyes. Zammis held out its hands, looked at them, then shook its head. "Grow four, five?"

I sat up and faced the kid. Zammis was wondering where its other four fingers had gone. "Look, Zammis. You and I are different . . . different kinds of beings, understand?"

Zammis shook his head. "Grow four, five?"

"You won't. You're a Drac." I pointed at my chest. "I'm human." This was getting me nowhere. "Your parent, where you came from, was a Drac. Do you understand?"

Zammis frowned. "Drac. What Drac?"

The urge to resort to the timeless standby of "you'll understand when you get older" pounded at the back of my mind. I shook my head. "Dracs have three fingers on each hand. Your parent had three fingers on each hand." I rubbed my beard. "My parent was a human and had five fingers on each hand. That's why I have five fingers on each hand."

Zammis knelt on the sand and studied its fingers. It looked up at me, back to its hands, then back at me. "What parent?"

I studied the kid. It must be having an identity crisis of some kind. I was the only person it had ever seen, and I had five fingers per hand. "A parent is . . . the thing . . ." I scratched my beard again. "Look . . . we all come from someplace. I had a mother and father—two different kinds of humans—that gave me life, that made me. Understand?" Zammis gave me a look that could be interpreted as "Mac, you are full of it." I shrugged. "I don't know if I can explain it."

Zammis pointed at its own chest. "My mother? My father?"

I held out my hands, dropped them into my lap, pursed my lips, scratched my beard and generally stalled for time. Zammis held an unblinking gaze on me the entire time. "Look, Zammis. You don't have a mother and a father. I'm a human, so I have them; you're a Drac. You have a parent—just one, see?"

Zammis shook its head. It looked at me, then pointed at its own chest. "Drac."

"Right."

Zammis pointed at my chest. "Human."

"Right again."

Zammis removed its hand and dropped it in its lap. "Where Drac come from?"

Sweet Jesus! Trying to explain hermaphroditic reproduction to a kid who shouldn't even be crawling yet! "Zammis . . ." I held up my hands, then dropped them into my lap. "Look. You see how much bigger I am than you?"

"Yes, Uncle."

"Good." I ran my fingers through my hair, fighting for time and inspiration. "Your parent was big, like me. Its name was . . . Jeriba Shigan." Funny how just saying the name was painful. "Jeriba Shigan was like you. It only had three fingers on each hand. It grew you in its tummy." I poked Zammis' middle. "Understand?"

Zammis giggled and held its hands over its stomach. "Uncle, how Dracs grow there?"

I lifted my legs onto the mattress and stretched out. Where do little Dracs come from? I looked over to Zammis and saw the child hanging upon my every word. I grimaced and told the truth. "Damned if I know, Zammis. Damned if I know." Thirty seconds later, Zammis was back playing with its rocks.

Summer, and I taught Zammis how to capture and skin the long gray snakes, and then how to smoke the meat. The child would squat on the shallow bank above a mudpool, its yellow eyes fixed on the snake holes in the bank, waiting for one of the occupants to poke out its head. The wind would blow, but Zammis wouldn't move. Then a flat, triangular head set with tiny blue eyes would appear. The snake would check the pool, turn and check the bank, then check the sky. It would advance out of the hole a bit, then check it all again. Often the snakes would look directly at Zammis, but the Drac could have been carved from rock. Zammis wouldn't move until the snake was too far out of the hole to pull itself back in tail first. Then Zammis would strike, grabbing the snake with both hands just behind the head. The snakes had no fangs and weren't poisonous, but they were lively enough to toss Zammis into the mudpool on occasion.

The skins were spread and wrapped around tree trunks and pegged in place to dry. The tree trunks were kept in an open place near the entrance to the cave, but under an overhang that faced away from the ocean. About two-thirds of the skins put up in this manner cured; the remaining third would rot.

Beyond the skin room was the smokehouse, a rock-walled chamber that we would hang with rows of snakemeat. A greenwood fire would be set in a pit in the chamber's floor, then we would fill in the small opening with rocks and dirt.

"Uncle, why doesn't the meat rot after it's smoked?"

I thought upon it. "I'm not sure; I just know it doesn't."

"Why do you know?"

I shrugged. "I just do. I read about it probably."

"What's read?"

"Reading. Like when I sit down and read the *Talman*."

"Does the *Talman* say why the meat doesn't rot?"

"No. I meant that I probably read it in another book."

"Do we have more books?"

I shook my head. "I meant before I came to this planet."

"Why did you come to this planet?"

"I told you. Your parent and I were stranded here during the battle."

"Why do the humans and Dracs fight?"

"It's very complicated." I waved my hands about for a bit. The human line was that the Dracs were aggressors invading our space. The Drac line was that the humans were aggressors invading their space. The truth? "Zammis, it has to do with the colonization of new planets. Both races are expanding and both races have a tradition of exploring and colonizing new planets. I guess we just expanded into each other. Understand?"

Zammis nodded, then became mercifully silent as it fell into deep thought. The main thing I learned from the Drac child was all of the questions I didn't have answers to. I was feeling very smug, however, at having gotten Zammis to understand about the war, thereby avoiding my ignorance on the subject of preserving meat. "Uncle?"

"Yes, Zammis?"

"What's a planet?"

As the cold, wet summer came to an end, we had the cave jammed with firewood and preserved food. With that out of the way, I concentrated my efforts on making some kind of indoor plumbing out of the natural pools in the chambers deep within the cave. The bathtub was no problem. By dropping heated rocks into one of the pools, the water could be brought up to a bearable—even comfortable—temperature. After bathing, the hollow stems of a bamboo-like plant could be used to siphon out the dirty water. The tub could then be refilled from the pool above. The problem was where to siphon the water. Several of the chambers had holes in their floors. The first three holes we tried drained into our main chamber, wetting the low edge near the entrance. The previous winter, Jerry and I had considered using one of those holes for a toilet that we would flush with water from the pools. Since we didn't know where the goodies would come out, we decided against it.

The fourth hole Zammis and I tried drained out below the entrance to the cave in the face of the cliff. Not ideal, but better than answering the call of nature in the middle of a combination ice storm and blizzard. We rigged up the hole as a drain for both the tub and toilet. As Zammis and I prepared to enjoy our first hot bath, I removed my snakeskins, tested the water with my toe, then stepped in. "Great!" I turned to Zammis, the child still half-dressed. "Come on in, Zammis. The water's fine." Zammis was staring at me, its mouth hanging open. "What's the matter?"

The child stared wide-eyed, then pointed at me with a three-fingered hand. "Uncle . . . what's that?"

I looked down. "Oh." I shook my head, then looked up at the child. "Zammis, I explained all that, remember? I'm a human."

"But, what's it *for*?"

I sat down in the warm water, removing the object of discussion from sight. "It's for the elimination of liquid wastes...among other things. Now, hop in and get washed."

Zammis shucked its snakeskins, looked down at its own smooth-surfaced, combined system, then climbed into the tub. The child settled into the water up to its neck, its yellow eyes studying me. "Uncle?"

"Yes?"

"What *other things*?"

Well, I told Zammis. For the first time, the Drac appeared to be trying to decide whether my response was truthful or not, rather than its usual acceptance of my every assertion. In fact, I was convinced that Zammis thought I was lying—probably because I was.

Winter began with a sprinkle of snowflakes carried on a gentle breeze. I took Zammis above the cave to the scrub forest. I held the child's hand as we stood before the pile of rocks that served as Jerry's grave. Zammis pulled its snakeskins against the wind, bowed its head, then turned and looked up into my face. "Uncle, this is the grave of my parent?"

I nodded. "Yes."

Zammis turned back to the grave, then shook its head. "Uncle, how should I feel?"

"I don't understand, Zammis."

The child nodded at the grave. "I can see that you are sad being here. I think you want me to feel the same. Do you?"

I frowned, then shook my head. "No. I don't want you to be sad. I just wanted you to know where it is."

"May I go now?"

"Sure. Are you certain you know the way back to the cave?"

"Yes. I just want to make sure my soap doesn't burn again."

I watched as the child turned and scurried off into the naked trees, then I turned back to the grave. "Well, Jerry, what do you think of your kid? Zammis was using wood ashes to clean the grease off the shells, then it put a shell back on the fire and put water in it to boil off the burnt-on food. Fat and ashes. The next thing, Jerry, we were making soap. Zammis' first batch almost took the hide off us, but the kid's getting better..."

I looked up at the clouds, then brought my glance down to the sea. In the distance, low, dark clouds were building up. "See that? You know what that means, don't you? Ice storm number one." The wind picked up and I squatted next to the grave to replace a rock that had rolled from the pile. "Zammis is a good kid, Jerry. I wanted to hate it... after you died. I wanted to hate it." I replaced the rock, then looked back toward the sea.

"I don't know how we're going to make it off planet, Jerry." I caught a flash of movement out of the corner of my vision. I turned to the right and looked over the tops of the trees. Against the gray sky, a black speck streaked away. I followed it with my eyes until it went above the clouds.

I listened, hoping to hear an exhaust roar, but my heart was pounding so hard all I could hear was the wind. Was it a ship? I stood, took a few steps in the direction the speck was going, then stopped. Turning my head, I saw that the rocks on Jerry's grave were already capped with thin layers of fine snow. I shrugged and headed for the cave. "Probably just a bird."

Zammis sat on its mattress, stabbing several pieces of snakeskin with a bone needle. I stretched out on my own mattress and watched the smoke curl up toward the crack in the ceiling. Was it a bird? Or was it a ship? Damn, but it worked on me. Escape from the planet had been out of my thoughts, had been buried, hidden for all that summer. But again, it twisted at me. To walk where a sun shined, to wear cloth again, experience central heating, eat food prepared by a chef, to be among... people again.

I rolled over on my right side and stared at the wall next to my mattress. People. Human people. I closed my eyes and swallowed. Girl human people. Female persons. Images drifted before my eyes—faces, bodies, laughing couples, the dance after flight training... What was her name? Dolora? Dora?

I shook my head, rolled over and sat up, facing the fire. Why did I have to see whatever it was? All those things I had been able to bury—to forget—boiling over.

"Uncle?"

I looked up at Zammis. Yellow skin, yellow eyes, noseless toadface. I shook my head. "What?"

"Is something wrong?"

Is something wrong, hah. "No. I just thought I saw something today. It probably wasn't anything." I reached to the fire and took a piece of dried snake from the griddle. I blew on it, then gnawed on the stringy strip.

"What did it look like?"

"I don't know. The way it moved, I thought it might be a ship. It went away so fast, I couldn't be sure. Might have been a bird."

"Bird?"

I studied Zammis. It'd never seen a bird; neither had I on Fyrine IV. "An animal that flies."

Zammis nodded. "Uncle, when we were gathering wood up in the scrub forest, I saw something fly."

"What? Why didn't you tell me?"

"I meant to, but I forgot."

"Forgot!" I frowned. "In which direction was it going?"

Zammis pointed to the back of the cave. "That way. Away from the sea." Zammis put down its sewing. "Can we go see where it went?"

I shook my head. "The winter is just beginning. You don't know what it's like. We'd die in only a few days."

Zammis went back to poking holes in the snakeskin. The winter would kill us. But spring would be something else. We could survive with double-layered snakeskins stuffed with seed-pod down, and a tent. We had to have a tent. Zammis and I could spend the winter making it, and packs. Boots. We'd need sturdy walking boots. Have to think on that...

It's strange how a spark of hope can ignite, and spread, until all desperation is consumed. Was it a ship? I didn't know. If it was, was it taking off, or landing? I didn't know. If it was taking off, we'd be heading in the wrong direction. But, the opposite direction meant crossing the sea. Whatever. Come spring we would head beyond the scrub forest and see what was there.

The winter seemed to pass quickly, with Zammis occupied with the tent and my time devoted to rediscovering the art of boot-making. I made tracings of both of our feet on snakeskin, and after some experimentation I found that boiling the snake leather with plumfruit made it soft and gummy. By taking several of the gummy layers, weighting them, then setting them aside to dry, the result was a tough, flexible sole. By the time I finished Zammis' boots, the Drac needed a new pair.

"They're too small, Uncle."

"Waddaya mean, too small?"

Zammis pointed down. "They hurt. My toes are all crippled up."

I squatted down and felt the tops over the child's toes. "I don't understand. It's only been twenty, twenty-five days since I made the tracings. You sure you didn't move when I made them?"

Zammis shook its head. "I didn't move."

I frowned, then stood. "Stand up, Zammis." The Drac stood and I moved next to it. The top of Zammis' head came to the middle of my chest. Another sixty centimeters and it'd be as tall as Jerry. "Take them off, Zammis. I'll make a bigger pair. Try not to grow so fast."

Zammis pitched the tent inside the cave, put glowing coals inside, then rubbed fat into the leather to waterproof it. It had grown taller, and I had held off making the Drac's boots until I could be sure of the size it would need. I tried to do a projection by measuring Zammis' feet every ten days, then extending the curve into spring. According to my fingers, the kid would have been resembling a pair of attack transports by the time the snow melted. By spring, Zammis would be full-grown. Jerry's old flight boots had fallen apart before Zammis had been born, but I had saved the pieces. I used the soles to make my tracings and hoped for the best.

I was busy with the new boots and Zammis was keeping an eye on the tent treatment. The Drac looked back at me.

"Uncle?"

"What?"

"Existence is the first given?"

I shrugged. "That's what Shizumaat says; I'll buy it."

"But, Uncle, how do we *know* that existence is real?"

I lowered my work, looked at Zammis, shook my head, then

resumed stitching the boots. "Take my word for it."

The Drac grimaced. "But, Uncle, that is not knowledge; that is faith."

I sighed, thinking back to my sophomore year at the University of Nations—a bunch of adolescents lounging around a cheap flat experimenting with booze, powders and philosophy. At a little more than one Earth year old, Zammis was developing into an intellectual bore. "So, what's wrong with faith?"

Zammis snickered. "Come now, Uncle. *Faith*?"

"It helps some of us along this drizzle-soaked coil."

"Coil?"

I scratched my head. "This mortal coil; life. Shakespeare, I think."

Zammis frowned. "It is not in the *Talman*."

"He, not it. Shakespeare was a human."

Zammis stood, walked to the fire and sat across from me. "Was he a philosopher, like Mistan or Shizumaat?"

"No. He wrote plays—like stories, acted out."

Zammis rubbed its chin. "Do you remember any of Shakespeare?"

I held up a finger. "'To be, or not to be; that is the question.'"

The Drac's mouth dropped open, then it nodded its head. "Yes. Yes! To be or not to be; that *is* the question!" Zammis held out its hands. "How do we *know* the wind blows outside the cave when we are not there to see it? Does the sea still boil if we are not there to feel it?"

I nodded. "Yes."

"But, Uncle, how do we *know*?"

I squinted at the Drac. "Zammis, I have a question for you. Is the following statement true or false?: What I am saying right now is false."

Zammis blinked. "If it is false, then the statement is true. But...if it's true...the statement is false, but..." Zammis blinked again, then turned and went back to rubbing fat into the tent. "I'll think upon it, Uncle."

"You do that, Zammis."

The Drac thought upon it for about ten minutes, then turned back. "The statement is false."

I smiled. "But that's what the statement said, hence it is true, but..." I let the puzzle trail off. Oh, smugness, thou temptest even saints.

"No, Uncle. The statement is meaningless in its present context." I shrugged. "You see, Uncle, the statement assumes the existence of truth values that can comment upon themselves devoid of any other reference. I think Lurrvena's logic in the *Talman* is clear on this, and if meaninglessness is equated with falsehood..."

I sighed. "Yeah, well—"

"You see, Uncle, you must, first, establish a context in which your statement has meaning."

I leaned forward, frowned and scratched my beard. "I see. You mean I was putting Descartes before the horse?"

Zammis looked at me strangely, and even more so when I collapsed on my mattress cackling like a fool.

"Uncle, why does the line of Jeriba have only five names? You say that human lines have many names."

I nodded. "The five names of the Jeriba line are things to which their bearers must add deeds. The deeds are important—not the names."

"Gothig is Shigan's parent as Shigan is my parent."

"Of course. You know that from your recitations."

Zammis frowned. "Then, I *must* name my child Ty when I become a parent?"

"Yes. And Ty must name its child Haesni. Do you see something wrong with that?"

"I would like to name my child Davidge, after you."

I smiled and shook my head. "The Ty name has been served by great bankers, merchants, inventors and—well, you know your recitation. The name Davidge hasn't been served by much. Think of what Ty would miss by not being Ty."

Zammis thought awhile, then nodded. "Uncle, do you think Gothig is alive?"

"As far as I know."

"What is Gothig like?"

I thought back to Jerry talking about its parent, Gothig. "It taught music, and is very strong. Jerry... Shigan said that its parent could bend metal bars with its fingers. Gothig is also very dignified. I imagine that right now Gothig is also very sad. Gothig must think that the line of Jeriban has ended."

Zammis frowned and its yellow brow furrowed. "Uncle, we must make it to Draco. We must tell Gothig the line continues."

"We will."

The winter's ice began thinning, and boots, tent and packs were ready. We were putting the finishing touches on our new insulated suits. As Jerry had given the *Talman* to me to learn, the golden cube now hung around Zammis' neck. The Drac would drop the tiny golden book from the cube and study it for hours at a time.

"Uncle?"

"What?"

"Why do Dracs speak and write in one language and the humans in another?"

I laughed. "Zammis, the humans speak and write in many languages. English is just one of them."

"How do the humans speak among themselves?"

I shrugged. "They don't always; when they do, they use interpreters—people who can speak both languages."

"You and I speak both English and Drac; does that make us interpreters?"

"I suppose we could be, if you could ever find a human and a Drac who want to talk to each other. Remember, there's a war going on."

"How will the war stop if they do not talk?"

"I suppose they will talk, eventually."

Zammis smiled. "I think I would like to be an interpreter and help end the war." The Drac put its sewing aside and stretched out on its new mattress. Zammis had outgrown even its old mattress, which it now used for a pillow. "Uncle, do you think that we will find anybody beyond the scrub forest?"

"I hope so."

"If we do, will you go with me to Draco?"

"I promised your parent that I would."

"I mean after. After I make my recitation, what will you do?"

I stared at the fire. "I don't know." I shrugged. "The war

might keep us from getting to Draco for a long time."

"After that, what?"

"I suppose I'll go back into the service."

Zammis propped itself up on an elbow. "Go back to being a fighter pilot?"

"Sure. That's about all I know how to do."

"And kill Dracs?"

I put my own sewing down and studied the Drac. Things had changed since Jerry and I had slugged it out—more things than I had realized. I shook my head. "No. I probably won't be a pilot—not a service one. Maybe I can land a job flying commercial ships." I shrugged. "Maybe the service won't give me any choice."

Zammis sat up, was still for a moment, then it stood, walked over to my mattress and knelt before me on the sand. "Uncle, I don't want to leave you."

"Don't be silly. You'll have your own kind around you. Your grandparent, Gothig, Shigan's siblings, their children—you'll forget all about me."

"Will you forget about me?"

I looked into those yellow eyes, then reached out my hand and touched Zammis' cheek. "No. I won't forget about you. But remember this, Zammis: you're a Drac and I'm a human, and that's how this part of the universe is divided."

Zammis took my hand from his cheek, spreak the fingers and studied them. "Whatever happens, Uncle, I will never forget you."

The ice was gone, and the Drac and I stood in the windblown drizzle, packs on our backs, before the grave. Zammis was as tall as I was, which made it a little taller than Jerry. To my relief, the boots fit. Zammis hefted its pack up higher on its shoulders, then turned from the grave and looked out at the sea. I followed Zammis' glance and watched the rollers steam in and smash on the rocks. I looked at the Drac. "What are you thinking about?"

Zammis looked down, then turned toward me. "Uncle, I didn't think of it before, but... I will miss this place."

I laughed. "Nonsense! This place?" I slapped the Drac on the shoulder. "Why would you miss this place?"

Zammis looked back out to sea. "I have learned many things here. You have taught me many things here, Uncle. My life happened here."

"Only the beginning, Zammis. You have a life ahead of you." I nodded my head at the grave. "Say good-bye."

Zammis turned toward the grave, stood over it, then knelt to one side and began removing the rocks. After a few moments, it had exposed the hand of a skeleton with three fingers. Zammis nodded, then wept. "I am sorry, Uncle, but I had to do that. This has been nothing but a pile of rocks to me. Now it is more." Zammis replaced the rocks, then stood.

I cocked my head toward the scrub forest. "Go on ahead. I'll catch up in a minute."

"Yes, Uncle."

Zammis moved off toward the naked trees, and I looked down at the grave. "What do you think of Zammis, Jerry? It's bigger than you were. I guess snake agrees with the kid." I squatted next to the grave, picked up a small rock and added it to the pile. "I guess this is it. We're either going to make it to Draco, or die trying." I stood and looked at the sea. "Yeah, I guess I learned a few things here. I'll miss it, in a way." I turned back to the grave and hefted my pack up. "*Ehdevva sahn, Jeriba Shigan.* So long, Jerry."

I turned and followed Zammis into the forest.

The days that followed were full of wonder for Zammis. For me, the sky was still the same, dull gray, and the few variations in plant and animal life that we found were nothing remarkable. Once we got beyond the scrub forest, we climbed a gentle rise for a day, and then found ourselves on a wide, flat, endless plain. It was ankle deep in a purple weed that stained our boots the same color. The nights were still too cold for hiking, and we would hole up in the tent. Both the greased tent and suits worked well, keeping out the almost constant rain.

We had been out perhaps two of Fyrine IV's long weeks, when we saw it. It screamed overhead, then disappeared over the horizon before either of us could say a word. I had no doubt that the craft I had seen was in landing attitude.

"Uncle! Did it see us?"

I shook my head. "No. I doubt it. But it was landing. Do you hear? It was landing somewhere ahead."

"Uncle?"

"Let's get moving! What is it?"

"Was it a Drac ship, or a human ship?"

I cooled in my tracks. I had never stopped to think about it. I waved my hand. "Come on. It doesn't matter. Either way, you go to Draco. You're a noncombatant, so the USE forces couldn't do anything, and if they're Dracs you're home free."

We began walking. "But, Uncle, if it's a Drac ship what will happen to you?"

I shrugged. "Prisoner of war. The Dracs say they abide by the interplanetary war accords, so I should be all right." *Fat chance*, said the back of my head to the front of my head. The big question was whether I preferred being a Drac POW or a permanent resident of Fyrine IV. I had figured out that long ago. "Come on, let's pick up the pace. We don't know how long it will take to get there, or how long it will be on the ground."

Pick 'em up; put 'em down. Except for a few breaks, we didn't stop—even when night came. Our exertion kept us warm. The horizon never seemed to grow nearer. The longer we slogged at it, the duller my mind grew. It must have been days, my mind as numb as my feet, when I fell through the purple weed into a hole. Immediately, everything grew dark, and I felt a pain in my right leg. I felt the blackout coming, and I welcomed its warmth, its rest, its peace.

"Uncle? Uncle? Wake up! Please wake up!"

I felt slapping against my face, although my face was somehow detached. Agony thundered into my brain, bringing me wide awake. Damned if I didn't break my leg. I looked up and saw the weedy edges of the hole. My rear end was seated in a trickle of water. Zammis squatted next to me. "What happened?

Zammis nodded up. "This hole was only covered by a thin crust of dirt and plants. The water must have taken the ground away. Are you all right?"

"My leg. I think I broke it." I leaned my back against the muddy wall. "Zammis, you're going to have to go on by yourself."

"I can't leave you, Uncle!"

"Look, if you find anyone, you can send them back for me."

"What if the water in here comes up?" Zammis felt along my leg until I winced. "I must carry you out of here. What must I do for the leg?"

The kid had a point. Drowning wasn't in my schedule. "We need something stiff. Bind the leg so it doesn't move."

Zammis pulled off its pack, and kneeling in the water and mud the Drac went through its pack, then through the tent roll. Using the tent poles, he wrapped my leg with snakeskins torn from the tent. Then, using more snakeskins, Zammis made two loops, slipped one over each of my legs, then propped me up and slipped the loops over its shoulders. It lifted, and I blacked out.

On the ground, covered with the remains of the tent, Zammis shaking my arm. "Uncle? Uncle?"

"Yes?" I whispered.

"Uncle, I'm ready to go." I pointed to my side. "Your food is here, and when it rains just pull the tent over your face. I'll mark the trail I make so I can find my way back."

I nodded. "Take care of yourself."

Zammis shook its head. "Uncle, I can carry you. We shouldn't separate."

I weakly shook my head. "Give me a break, kid. I couldn't make it. Find somebody and bring 'em back." I felt my stomach flip, and cold sweat drenched my snakeskins. "Go on; get going."

Zammis reached out, grabbed its pack and stood. The pack shouldered, Zammis turned and began running in the direction that the craft had been going. I watched until I couldn't see it. I faced up and looked at the clouds. "You almost got me that time, you *kizlode* sonofabitch, but you didn't figure on the Drac . . . You keep forgetting . . . there's two of us . . ." I drifted and and out of consciousness, felt rain on my face, then pulled up the tent and covered my head. In seconds, the blackout returned.

"Davidge? Lieutenant Davidge?"

I opened my eyes and saw something I hadn't seen for four Earth years: a human face. "Who are you?"

The face, young, long and capped by short blond hair, smiled. "I'm Captain Steerman, the medical officer. How do you feel?"

I pondered the question and smiled. "Like I've been shot full of very high-grade junk."

"You have. You were in pretty bad shape by the time the survey team brought you in."

"Survey team?"

"I guess you don't know. The United States of Earth and the Dracon Chamber have established a joint commission to supervise the colonization of new planets. The war is over."

"Over?"

"Yes."

Something heavy lifted from my chest. "Where's Zammis?"

"Who?"

"Jeriban Zammis; the Drac that I was with."

The doctor shrugged. "I don't know anything about it, but I suppose the Draggers are taking care of it."

Draggers. I'd once used the term myself. As I listened to it coming out of Steerman's mouth, it seemed foreign, alien, repulsive. "Zammis is a Drac, not a Dragger."

The doctor's brows furrowed, then he shrugged. "Of course. Whatever you say. Just you get some rest, and I'll check back on you in a few hours."

"May I see Zammis?"

The doctor smiled. "Dear, no. You're on your way back to the Delphi USEB. The . . . Drac is probably on its way to Draco." He nodded, then turned and left. God, I felt lost. I looked around and saw that I was in the ward of a ship's sick bay. The beds on either side of me were occupied. The man on my right shook his head and went back to reading a magazine. The one on my left looked angry.

"You damned dragger suck!" He turned on his left side and presented me his back.

Alien Earth. As I stepped down the ramp onto the USE field in Orleans, those were the first two words that popped into my head. Alien Earth. I looked at the crowds of USE Force personnel bustling around like so many ants, inhaled the smell of industrial man, then spat on the ramp.

"How you like, put in stockade time?"

I looked down and saw a white-capped Force Police private glaring up at me. I continued down the ramp. "Get bent."

"Quoi?" The FP marched over and met me at the end of the ramp.

"Get bent." I pulled my discharge papers from my breast pocket and waved them. *"Gavey* shorttimer, *kizlode*?"

The FP took my papers, frowned at them, then pointed at a long, low building at the edge of the field. *"Continuez tout droit."*

I smiled, turned and headed across the field, thinking of Zammis asking about how humans talk together. And where was Zammis? I shook my head, then entered the building. Most of the people inside the low building were crowding the in-processing or transportation-exchange aisles. I saw two bored officials behind two long tables and figured that they were the local customs clerks. A multilingual sign above their stations confirmed the hunch. I stopped in front of one of them. She glanced up at me, then held out her hand. *"Vôtre passeport?"*

I pulled out the blue and white booklet, handed it over, then stood holding my hands as I waited. I could feel the muscles at the back of my neck knot as I observed an old anti-Drac propaganda poster on the wall behind her. It showed two yellow, clawed hands holding a miniature Earth before a fanged mouth. Fangs and claws. The caption read: "They would call this victory" in seven languages.

"Avez-vous quelque chose à déclarer?"

I frowned at her. *"Ess?"*

She frowned back. *"Avez-vous quelque chose à déclarer?"*

I felt a tap on my back. "Do you speak English?"

I turned and saw the other customs clerk. My upper lip curled. *"Surda; ne surda. Adze Dracon?"*

His eyebrows went up as he mouthed the word "Drac." He turned to the other clerk, took my passport from her, then looked back at me. He tapped the booklet against his fingertips, then opened it, read the ident page, and looked back at me. "Come with me, Mister Davidge. We must have a talk." He turned and headed into a small office. I shrugged and followed. When I entered, he pointed toward a chair. As I lowered myself into it, he sat down behind a desk. "Why do you pretend not to speak English?"

"Why do you have that poster on the wall? The war is over."

The customs clerk clasped his hands, rested them on the desk, then shook his head. "The fighting is over, Mister Davidge, but for many the war is not. The Draggers killed many humans."

I cocked my head to one side. "A few Dracs died, too." I stood up. "May I go now?"

The customs clerk leaned back in his chair. "That chip on your shoulder you will find to be a considerable weight to bear on this planet."

"I'm the one who has to carry it."

The customs clerk shrugged, then nodded toward the door. "You may go. And good luck, Mister Davidge. You'll need it."

"Dragger suck." As an invective the term had all of the impact of several historical terms—Quisling, heretic, fag, nigger-lover, all rolled into one. Ex-Force pilots were a drag on the employment market, with no commercial positions open, especially not to a pilot who hadn't flown in four years, who had a gimpy leg, and who was a Dragger suck. Transportation to North America, and after a period of lonely wandering, to Dallas. Mistan's eight-hundred-year-old words from the *Talman* would haunt me: *Misnuuram va siddeth*; Your thought is loneliness. Loneliness is a thing one does to oneself. *Jerry shook his head that one time, then pointed a yellow finger at me as the words it wanted to say came together.* "Davidge . . . to me loneliness is a discomfort—unpleasant, and a thing to be avoided, but not a thing to be feared. I think you would prefer death to being alone with yourself."

Mistan observed: "If you are alone with yourself, you will forever be alone with others." A contradiction? The test of reality proves it true. I was out of place on my own planet, and it was more than a hate that I didn't share or a love that, to others, seemed impossible—perverse. Deep inside of myself, I had no use for the creature called "Davidge." Before Fyrine IV there had been other reasons—reasons that I could not identify; but now, my reason was known. My fault or not, I had betrayed an ugly, yellow thing called Zammis, as well as the creature's parent. *"Present Zammis before the Jeriba archives. Swear this to me."*

Oh, Jerry...

Swear this!

I swear it...

I had forty-eight thousand credits in back pay, and so money wasn't a problem. The problem was what to do with myself. Finally, in Dallas, I landed a job in a small book house translating manuscripts into Drac. It seemed that there was a craving among Dracs for westerns: "Stick 'em up, *naagusaat*!"

"Nu geph, lawman!" Thang! Thang! The guns flashed and another *kizlode shaddsaat* bit the dust.

I quit.

I finally called my parents. *Why didn't you call before, Willy? We've been worried sick... Had a few things I had to straighten out, Dad... No, not really... Well, we understand, son... it must have been awful... Dad, I'd like to come home for awhile...*

Even before I put down the money on the used Dearman Electric, I knew I was making a mistake going home. I felt the need of a home, but the one I had left at the age of eighteen wasn't it. But, I headed there because there was nowhere else to go.

I drove alone in the dark, using only the old roads, the quiet hum of the Dearman's motor the only sound. The December midnight was clear, and I could see the stars through the car's bubble canopy. Fyrine IV drifted into my thoughts, the raging ocean, the endless winds. I pulled off the road onto the shoulder and killed the lights. In a few minutes, my eyes adjusted to the dark and I stepped outside and shut the door. Kansas has a big sky, and the stars seemed close enough to touch. Snow crunched under my feet as I looked up, trying to pick Fyrine out of the thousands of visible stars.

Fyrine is in the constellation Pegasus, but my eyes were not practiced enough to pick the winged horse out from the surrounding stars. I shrugged, felt a chill, and decided to get back in the car. As I put my hand on the doorlatch, I saw a constellation that I did recognize, north, hanging just above the horizon: Draco. The Dragon, its tail twisted around Ursa Minor, hung upside down in the sky. Eltanin, the Dragon's nose, is the homestar of the Dracs. Its second planet, Draco, was Zammis' home.

Headlights from an approaching car blinded me, and I turned toward the car as it pulled to a stop. The window on the driver's side opened and someone spoke from the darkness.

"You need some help?"

I shook my head. "No, thank you." I held up a hand. "I was just looking at the stars."

"Quite a night, isn't it?"

"Sure is."

"Sure you don't need any help?"

I shook my head. "Thanks... Wait. Where is the nearest commercial spaceport?"

"About an hour ahead in Salina."

"Thanks." I saw a hand wave from the window, then the other car pulled away. I took another look at Eltanin, then got back in my car.

Nine weeks later I stood before the little gray man who ran Lone Star Publishing, Inc. He looked up at me and frowned. "So, what do you want? I thought you quit."

I threw a thousand-page manuscript on his desk. "This."

He poked it with a finger. "What is it?"

"The Drac bible; it's called the *Talman*."

"So what?"

"So it's the only book translated from Drac into English; so it's the explanation for how every Drac conducts itself; so it'll make you a bundle of credits."

He leaned forward, scanned several pages, then looked up at me. "You know, Davidge, I don't like you worth a damn."

I shrugged. "I don't like you either."

He returned to the manuscript. "Why now?"

"Now is when I need money."

He shrugged. "The best I can offer would be around eight or ten thousand. This is untried stuff."

"I need twenty-four thousand. You want to go for less than that, I'll take it to someone else."

He looked at me and frowned. "What makes you think that anyone else would be interested?"

"Let's quit playing around. There are a lot of survivors of the war—both military and civilian—who would like to understand what happened." I leaned forward and tapped the manuscript. "That's what's in there."

"Twenty-four thousand is a lot for a first manuscript."

I gathered up the pages. "I'll find someone who has some coin to invest in a sure thing."

He placed his hand on the manuscript. "Hold on, Davidge." He frowned. "Twenty-four thousand?"

"Not a quarter-note less."

He pursed his lips, then glanced at me. "I suppose you'll be Hell on wheels regarding final approval."

I shook my head. "All I want is the money. You can do whatever you want with the manuscript."

He leaned back in his chair, looked at the manuscript, then back at me. "The money. What're you going to do with it?"

"None of your business."

He leaned forward, then leafed through a few more pages. His eyebrows notched up, then he looked back at me. "You aren't picky about the contract?"

"As long as I get the money, you can turn that into *Mein Kampf* if you want to."

He leafed through a few more pages. "This is some pretty radical stuff."

"It sure is. And you can find the same stuff in Plato, Aristotle, Augustine, James, Freud, Szasz, Nortmyer, and the Declaration of Independence."

He leaned back in his chair. "What does this mean to you?"

"Twenty-four thousand credits."

He leafed through a few more pages, then a few more. In twelve hours I had purchased passage to Draco.

Six months later, I stood in front of an ancient cut-stone gate wondering what in the Hell I was doing. The trip to Draco, with nothing but Dracs as companions on the last leg, showed me the truth in Namvaac's words: "Peace is often only war without fighting." The accords, on paper, gave me the right to travel to the planet, but the Drac bureaucrats and their paperwork wizards had perfected the big stall long before the first human step into space. It took threats, bribes, and long days of filling out forms, being checked, and rechecked for disease, contraband, reason for visit, filling out more forms, refilling out the forms I had already filled out, more bribes, waiting, waiting, waiting...

On the ship, I spent most of my time in my cabin, but since the Drac stewards refused to serve me, I went to the ship's lounge for my meals. I sat alone, listening to the comments about me from other booths. I figured the path of least resistance was to pretend I didn't understand what they were saying. It is always assumed that humans do not speak Drac.

"Must we eat in the same compartment with the *Irkmaan* slime?"

"Look at it, how its pale skin blotches—and that evil-smelling thatch on top. Feh! The smell!"

I would grind my teeth a little and keep my glance riveted to my plate.

"It defies the *Talman* that the universe's laws could be so corrupt as to produce a creature such as that."

I turned and faced the three Dracs sitting in the booth across the aisle from mine. In Drac, I replied: "If your line's elders had seen fit to teach the village *kiz* to use contraceptives, you wouldn't even exist." I returned to my food while the two Dracs struggled to hold the third Drac down.

On Draco, it was no problem finding the Jeriba estate. The problem was getting in. A high stone wall enclosed the property, and from the gate I could see the huge stone mansion that Jerry had described to me. I told the guard at the gate that I wanted to see Jeriba Zammis. The guard stared at me, then went into an alcove behind the gate. In a few moments, another Drac emerged from the mansion and walked quickly across the wide lawn to the gate. The Drac nodded at the guard, then stopped and faced me. It was a dead ringer for Jerry.

"You are the *Irkmaan* that asked to see Jeriba Zammis?"

I nodded. "Yes. Zammis must have told you about me. I'm Willis Davidge."

The Drac studied me. "I am Estone Nev, Jeriban Shigan's sibling. My parent, Jeriba Gothig, wishes to see you." The Drac

turned abruptly and walked back to the mansion. I followed,
feeling heady at the thought of seeing Zammis again. I paid little
attention to my surroundings until I was ushered into a large
room with a vaulted stone ceiling. Jerry had told me that the
house was four thousand years old. I believed it. As I entered,
another Drac stood and walked over to me. It was old, but I
knew who it was.

"You are Gothig, Shigan's parent."

The yellow eyes studied me. "Who are you, *Irkmaan*?" It held
out a wrinkled, three-fingered hand. "What do you know of
Jeriba Zammis, and why do you speak the Drac tongue with the
style and accent of my child Shigan? What are you here for?"

"I speak Drac in this manner because that is the way Jeriban
Shigan taught me to speak it."

The old Drac cocked its head to one side and narrowed its
yellow eyes. "You knew my child? How?"

"Didn't the survey commission tell you?"

"It was reported to me that my child, Shigan, was killed in the
battle of Fyrine IV. That was over six of our years ago. What is
your game, *Irkmaan*?"

I turned from Gothig to Nev. The younger Drac was
examining me with the same look of suspicion. I turned back to
Gothig. "Shigan wasn't killed in the battle. We were stranded
together on the surface of Fyrine IV and lived there for a year.
Shigan died giving birth to Jeriba Zammis. A year later the joint
survey commission found us and—"

"Enough! Enough of this, *Irkmaan*! Are you here for money,
to use my influence for trade concessions—what?"

I frowned. "Where is Zammis?"

Tears of anger came to the old Drac's eyes. "There is no
Zammis, *Irkmaan*! The Jeriban line ended with the death of
Shigan!"

My eyes grew wide as I shook my head. "That's not true. I
know. I took care of Zammis—you heard nothing from the
commission?"

"Get to the point of your scheme, *Irkmaan*. I haven't all day."

I studied Gothig. The old Drac had heard nothing from the
commission. The Drac authorities took Zammis, and the child
had evaporated. Gothig had been told nothing. Why? "I was

with Shigan, Gothig. That is how I learned your language. When Shigan died giving birth to Zammis, I—"

"*Irkmaan*, if you cannot get to your scheme, I will have to ask Nev to throw you out. Shigan died in the battle of Fyrine IV. The Drac Fleet notified us only days later."

I nodded. "Then, Gothig, tell me how I came to know the line of Jeriba? Do you wish me to recite it for you?"

Gothig snorted. "You say you know the Jeriba line?"

"Yes."

Gothig flipped a hand at me. "Then recite."

I took a breath, then began. By the time I had reached the hundred and seventy-third generation, Gothig had knelt on the stone floor next to Nev. The Dracs remained that way for the three hours of the recital. When I concluded, Gothig bowed its head and wept. "Yes, *Irkmaan*, yes. You must have known Shigan. Yes." The old Drac looked up into my face, its eyes wide with hope. "And, you say Shigan continued the line—that Zammis was born?"

I nodded. "I don't know why the commission didn't notify you."

Gothig got to its feet and frowned. "We will find out, *Irkmaan*—what is your name?"

"Davidge. Willis Davidge."

"We will find out, Davidge."

Gothig arranged quarters for me in its house, which was fortunate, since I had little more than eleven hundred credits left. After making a host of inquiries, Gothig sent Nev and I to the Chamber Center in Sendievu, Draco's capital city. The Jeriba line, I found, was influential, and the big stall was held down to a minimum. Eventually, we were directed to the Joint Survey Commission representative, a Drac named Jozzdn Vrule. It looked up from the letter Gothig had given me and frowned. "Where did you get this, *Irkmaan*?"

"I believe the signature is on it."

The Drac looked at the paper, then back at me. "The Jeriba line is one of the most respected on Draco. You say that Jeriba Gothig gave you this?"

"I felt certain I said that; I could feel my lips moving—"

Nev stepped in. "You have the dates and the information concerning the Fyrine IV survey mission. We want to know what happened to Jeriba Zammis."

Jozzdn Vrule frowned and looked back at the paper. "Estone Nev, you are the founder of your line, is this not true?"

"It is true."

"Would you found your line in shame? Why do I see you with this *Irkmaan*?"

Nev curled its upper lip and folded its arms. "Jozzdn Vrule, if you contemplate walking this planet in the forseeable future as a free being, it would be to your profit to stop working your mouth and to start finding Jeriba Zammis."

Jozzdn Vrule looked down and studied its fingers, then returned its glance to Nev. "Very well, Estone Nev. You threaten me if I fail to hand you the truth. I think you will find the truth the greater threat." The Drac scribbled on a piece of paper, then handed it to Nev. "You will find Jeriba Zammis at this address, and you will curse the day that I gave you this."

We entered the retard colony feeling sick. All around us, Dracs stared with vacant eyes, or screamed, or foamed at the mouth, or behaved as lower-order creatures. After we had arrived, Gothig joined us. The Drac director of the colony frowned at me and shook its head at Gothig. "Turn back now, while it is still possible, Jeriba Gothig. Beyond this room lies nothing but pain and sorrow."

Gothig grabbed the director by the front of its wraps. "Hear me, insect: If Jeriba Zammis is within these walls, bring my grandchild forth! Else, I shall bring the might of the Jeriban line down upon your pointed head!"

The director lifted its head, twitched its lips, then nodded. "Very well. Very well, you pompous *Kazzmidth*! We tried to protect the Jeriba reputation. We tried! But now you shall see." The director nodded and pursed its lips. "Yes, you overwealthy fashion follower, now you shall see." The director scribbled on a piece of paper, then handed it to Nev. "By giving you that, I will lose my position, but take it! Yes, take it! See this being you call Jeriba Zammis. See it, and weep!"

*   *   *

Among trees and grass, Jeriba Zammis sat upon a stone bench, staring at the ground. Its eyes never blinked, its hands never moved. Gothig frowned at me, but I could spare nothing for Shigan's parent. I walked to Zammis. "Zammis, do you know me?"

The Drac retrieved its thoughts from a million warrens and raised its yellow eyes to me. I saw no sign of recognition. "Who are you?"

I squatted down, placed my hands on its arms and shook them. "Damn it, Zammis, don't you know me? I'm your Uncle. Remember that? Uncle Davidge?"

The Drac weaved on the bench, then shook its head. It lifted an arm and waved to an orderly. "I want to go to my room. Please, let me go to my room."

I stood and grabbed Zammis by the front of its hospital gown. "Zammis, it's me!"

The yellow eyes, dull and lifeless, stared back at me. The orderly placed a yellow hand upon my shoulder. "Let it go, *Irkmaan*."

"Zammis!" I turned to Nev and Gothig. "Say something!"

The Drac orderly pulled a sap from its pocket, then slapped it suggestively against the palm of its hand. "Let it go, *Irkmaan*."

Gothig stepped forward. "Explain this!"

The orderly looked at Gothig, Nev, me, and then Zammis. "This one—this creature—came to us professing a love, a *love*, mind you, of humans! This is no small perversion, Jeriba Gothig. The government would protect you from this scandal. Would you wish the line of Jeriba dragged into this?"

I looked at Zammis. "What have you done to Zammis, you *kizlode* sonofabitch? A little shock? A little drug? Rot out its mind?"

The orderly sneered at me, then shook its head. "You, *Irkmaan*, do not understand. This one would not be happy as an *Irkmaan vul*—a human lover. We are making it possible for this one to function in Drac society. You think this is wrong?"

I looked at Zammis and shook my head. I remembered too well my treatment at the hands of my fellow humans. "No. I don't think it's wrong . . . I just don't know."

The orderly turned to Gothig. "Please understand, Jeriba Gothig. We could not subject the Jeriba line to this disgrace. Your grandchild is almost well and will soon enter a reeducation program. In no more than two years, you will have a grandchild worthy of carrying on the Jeriba line. Is this wrong?"

Gothig only shook its head. I squatted down in front of Zammis and looked up into its yellow eyes. I reached up and took its right hand in both of mine. "Zammis?"

Zammis looked down, moved its left hand over and picked up my left hand and spread the fingers. One at a time Zammis pointed at the fingers of my hand, then it looked into my eyes, then examined the hand again. "Yes . . ." Zammis pointed again. "One, two, three, *four, five!*" Zammis looked into my eyes. "Four, five!"

I nodded. "Yes. Yes."

Zammis pulled my hand to its cheek and held it close. "Uncle . . . Uncle. I told you I'd never forget you."

I never counted the years that passed. Mistaan had words for those who count time as though their recognition of its passing marked their place in the Universe. Mornings, the weather as clear as weather gets on Fyrine IV, I would visit my friend's grave. Next to it, Estone Nev, Zammis, Ty and I buried Gothig. Shigan's parent had taken the healing Zammis, liquidated the Jeriba line's estate, then moved the whole shebang to Fyrine IV. When told the story, it was Ty who named the planet "Friendship."

One blustery day I knelt between the graves, replaced some rocks, then added a few more. I pulled my snakeskins tight against the wind, then sat down and looked out to sea. Still the rollers steamed in under the gray-black cover of clouds. Soon the ice would come. I looked at my scarred, wrinkled hands, then at the grave.

"I couldn't stay in the colony with them, Jerry. Don't get me wrong: it's nice. Damned nice. But, I kept looking out my window, seeing the ocean, thinking of the cave. I'm alone, in a way. But it's good. I know what and who I am, Jerry, and that's all there is to it, right?"

I heard a noise. I crouched over, placed my hands upon my withered knees and pushed myself to my feet. The Drac was coming from the colony compound, a child in its arms.

I rubbed my beard. "Eh, Ty, so that is your first child?"

The Drac nodded. "I would be pleased, Uncle, if you would teach it what it must be taught: the line, the *Talman*, and about life on Friendship."

I took the bundle into my arms. Chubby three-fingered arms waved at the air, then grasped my snakeskins. "Yes, Ty, this one is a Jeriban." I looked up at Ty. "And how is your parent, Zammis?"

Ty shrugged. "It is as well as can be expected. My parent wishes you well."

I nodded. "And the same to it, Ty. Zammis ought to get out of that air-conditioned capsule and come back to live in the cave. It'll do it good."

Ty grinned and nodded its head. "I will tell my parent, Uncle."

I stabbed my thumb into my chest. "Look at me! You don't see me sick, do you?"

"No, Uncle."

"You tell Zammis to kick that doctor out of there and to come back to the cave, hear?"

"Yes, Uncle." Ty smiled. "Is there anything you need?"

I nodded and scratched the back of my neck. "Toilet paper. Just a couple of packs. Maybe a couple of bottles of whiskey—no, forget the whiskey. I'll wait until Haesni, here, puts in its first year. Just the toilet paper."

Ty bowed. "Yes, Uncle, and may the many mornings find you well."

I waved my hand impatiently. "They will, they will. Just don't forget the toilet paper."

Ty bowed again. "I won't, Uncle."

Ty turned and walked through the scrub forest back to the colony. I lived with them for a year, but I moved out and went back to the cave. I gathered the wood, smoked the snake, and withstood the winter. Zammis gave me the young Ty to rear in the cave, and now Ty had handed me Haesni. I nodded at the child. "Your child will be called Gothig, and then . . ." I looked at the sky and felt the tears drying on my face. ". . . And then, Gothig's child will be called Shigan." I nodded and headed for the cleft that would bring us down to the level of the cave.

Legislative Assembly

of the

UNITED STATE OF EARTH

LEGISLATIVE REPORT

January 12, 2095

*Speaker.*It having been one legislative day since the tabling of Mister Vouch's motion to accept the committee's Ought to Pass report of L.D. 1906, "An Act Accepting the Savage Planet Regulations of the Ninth Quadrant Federation of Habitable Planets," it is our first order of business this morning. The chair recognizes Mister Chu of the East Asian Union.

*Mister Chu.*Mister Speaker, most honorable members of the Assembly. Never in my wildest imaginings did I ever dream of the moment when I would have to rise before this body to urge it not to disgrace and dishonor itself. Observe, however, that I have risen and I am so urging.

Neither the United States of Earth nor the USE planets are signatories to the Ninth Quadrant Charter, yet here we are actually considering adopting regulations promulgated by that body, and ordered by it to be forced down our throats. The Ninth Quadrant has issued us an ultimatum: accept these regulations and abide by them, else we shall destroy you.

I would remind the Assembly of Resolution 991, adopted without dissent by this body over sixty years ago. "Resolved: that the Legislative Assembly of the Government of the United States of Earth, in all related matters that shall come before it, will decide all such matters in accordance with the Manifest Destiny of Man, that He shall reign supreme in this and in any and all other galaxies of the Universe."

Can the adoption of these regulations, under blatant threats from the Ninth Quadrant, possibly be construed as serving the intent of Resolution 991? I think not. Instead, I think it subverts the intent of 991, and therefore our race.

Speaker. The chair recognizes Mister Vouch of the United States of Europe.

Mister Vouch. Mister Speaker, members of the Assembly, I hardly need point out that Eastern Mineral Resources, Incorporated, is headquartered in my distinguished colleague's district. I do not, however, impugn Mister Chu's honor. Nevertheless, every member of this body has been witness to the incredible lobbying effort mounted by various resource-extraction associations. I have been led to understand that the price tag on this effort is well into the hundreds of millions of credits. Despite this effort, the adoption of the Savage Planet regulations appears to be assured. And why is that? It is because the majority of the members of this body knows the regulations to be fair, necessary, and in service of worthwhile goals—human goals.

The Ninth Quadrant has undertaken the responsibility for the protection of savage populations. To raise them from brutality that they, too, may join the society of creatures ruled by law. Does this goal subvert the destiny of man? No.

The Ninth Quadrant requires that in exchange for the wealth extracted from savage planets, the companies or governments concerned establish affirmative civilization programs for such planets, and set aside a small percentage of their profits to finance such programs. Is this too high a price to pay to bring light to barbarian minds? Again, no.

In addition—and it is this that makes me wonder at the resistance of the resource-extraction lobby—the Ninth Quadrant Forces, under the Savage Planet Regulations, will protect companies engaged in operations on such planets. This is a service that we could never provide at an acceptable cost, and we get it for nothing more than enacting the regulations into our own law. What could be more fair? Nothing.

Simply because two powers with opposing interests find the same law a service to them does not make the law suspect. We already have many laws in conformance with the Ninth Quadrant Code, and again in conformance with the Great Code of the United Quadrants. Are they suspect? Do we repeal our sanctions against murder because the Ninth Quadrant, too, has sanctions against this crime? Ladies and gentlemen of the Assembly, I think not.

Speaker. Is there more discussion on the motion? Then we shall proceed to the vote.

(361 yea; 139 nay.)

A majority of those voting representatives voting in favor of the motion, the committee's Ought to Pass report is adopted, and upon the signature of the President-General, the Savage Planet Regulations of the Ninth Quadrant Federation of Habitable Planets will be enacted into the statutes of the United States of Earth. Now, to the next order of business . . .

Armath squatted in the snow as his deep red eyes studied the two-tracked vehicles in the valley below. The wind gusted, causing a light rain of fine snow to fall upon his broad, hairy back. As two creatures emerged from one of the vehicles, Armath drew back his lips, exposing gleaming white fangs. A low growl issued from his throat and he pawed the snow with dagger-tipped fingers.

"Hey, Charlie! Bring the caps!"

A third creature emerged from one of the vehicles, it walked over to the other two and handed something to them. The first two stooped over and dug at the snow while the third watched them. Armath looked at the marks the vehicles had made over the floor of the valley. Twenty times the vehicles had stopped, and as many times the creatures had emerged, buried something, then climbed back into the roaring metal carts. The two stood, waved at the one vehicle, then the three of them climbed into the second. The carts roared to life, then moved away.

Armath's heavy black brows wrinkled as the carts kept going

141

instead of following the pattern that had been established. He waited a moment longer, then rose on his four walking legs, shook his heavy mane to free it from the accumulation of snow, and began walking toward the most recent burial site. His eyes darted left and right, instinctively searching for darkness against the snow. Halfway down the slope, he spotted another male. Armath reared up, bellowed and held out his arms, fingers and claws extended. The other male reared up and returned the bellow. They both came down together and altered their paths slightly to avoid meeting.

Armath's new course took him away from the nearest burial site, and he chose another. As he approached it, he saw the other male squatting at one of the first sites, and clawing at the snow. He turned back to see the disturbed area, marked with a tiny orange flag. Five paces from the flag, the snow around Armath seemed to erupt with an ear-shattering slam. He fell to the shaking snow, covered his eyes, and howled as lumps of ice struck his back. When the ice stopped falling, Armath uncovered his eyes and stood, his ears ringing.

The tiny orange flag was gone. Cautiously he approached the site and saw a hole that extended deep into the snow, through the frozen soil, into the hard rock beneath. He frowned and looked toward another site. It too was nothing but a hole. Armath turned to look at the other male and saw him crumpled next to the site he had been investigating. Armath growled, then fell silent as he padded toward the other male. He was lying on the snow, his back toward Armath, the wind blowing back his long black hair, showing the gray skin beneath.

Armath halted the customary four paces away. "You!" The male did not move. "You!" Armath bellowed. Still nothing. Armath traversed a circle, four paces from the reclining figure, until he came to the male's other side. Armath looked down at the hole in the snow. It too went all the way to the rock of the valley floor. He looked up at the other male and howled. His face was missing.

On the liner to Bendadn to accept his post of chair of the Bendadn School Department of History, Michael studied two texts on the planet and its population. The Benda had evolved to dominate other lifeforms, and had been at the brink of their Iron Age, when RMI put down its ships and missionaries preaching the creed of the bountiful god of multiplanetary corporate domination. Earth was signatory to neither the Ninth Quadrant Council of Planets, nor the United Quadrants. However, both bodies had made clear to RMI that invading Bendadn with a combination of money and mercenaries would incur opposition by the combined armed forces of both organizations. Michael picked up the senior high-school text that was RMI's secret weapon: *Manifest Destiny—A History of Human Expansionism.*

Michael again opened the text and leafed through it. He had finished reading the thing eight days before, and it still hadn't changed. Michael shook his head. Some fantasy writer must have collaborated with an advertising copywriter to produce *Manifest*. Certainly no historian had anything to do with it. It was a simplistic, highly romanticized, overblown account of the human expansion into space, ignoring the warts and highlighting the invincible, inevitable nature of human force. The message was clear: humanity, because of its nature and tradition, was meant to rule. Willing subjugation meant peace and prosperity; resistance meant destruction. Michael closed the text with a snap. "What drivel."

He leaned back on his couch and closed his eyes. At first he'd refused to take the top history post, but as the good Mr. Sabin had pointed out, "you're selling your professional soul for eleven hundred a month; why not sell for twenty-five hundred? It's the same soul in either case." A good point, thought Michael. Whether or not my soul is for sale is the concern of principle; how much is only the concern of economics and bargaining. The crime is no more severe by being a high-ranked flunky rather than a middle- or low-ranked flunky. Michael nodded. The good Mr. Sabin had a definite way with words.

Michael closed his eyes and clenched his jaw. Then he shook his head. Opening his eyes, he leaned his head against the back of the seat. *No one who has sold out has a right to be bitter*, he thought. *Why am I doing this? As the good Mr. Sutton replied*

when asked why he robbed banks: "That's where the money is."
He nodded and tried to sleep. *Recognize it, accept it, and to Hell with it.*

A week to Bendadn, and Michael Fellman parked his water wagon and headed toward the ship's lounge for the first time. He had played with a vague thought of using his experience on Bendadn as an excuse for turning over a new leaf, but as the trip and his studies of *Manifest* dragged on, his resolve wore as thin as the cliché. As he slouched in an overpadded booth sipping his fifth Martini, he had to admit that Rolf Mineral Industries allowed one to sell out in style.

"Mind if I join you?"

Michael looked up and made out the face of Jacob Lynn, RMI's Project Manager for Bendadn. The man who would be the top RMI man on the planet. Michael held out a hand. "Be my guest, *sahib*."

Lynn raised his eyebrows, then laughed as he sat and placed his drink on the table. "You ivory-tower hypocrites really kill me." He sipped at his drink, then laughed again as he lowered it to the table.

"Perhaps you could share the cause of your amusement, Mr. Lynn."

His face in smiles, but his eyes colder than RMI steel, Lynn leaned back and studied Michael. "I've been wandering around the lounge listening to some of you old mossbacks bitching and whining about life in general, and their own places in it in particular."

Michael nodded. "And, Mr. Lynn, you are pleased with your place in this universe?"

"Yes." He nodded and sipped again from his drink. "There are still things that I want, but now that I've made my peace with reality, I know I'll get most of them." He smiled and waved a hand in the direction of a booth full of graying instructors working hard with the free booze, trying to forget its price. "Look at them. For the first time in their lives they are being practical. But all they can do is pickle their heads to try and ease the pain of growing up."

"You seem to take a perverse pleasure in their distress, Mr.

Lynn." Michael sipped again at his Martini. "Particularly when they in all likelihood don't even understand why they are unhappy."

Lynn nodded, then faced Michael. "But you understand it, Fellman. That's why you're the biggest hypocrite in the bunch. And, yes, I do enjoy it." Lynn finished off his drink and motioned to a steward for a refill. "The reason isn't too hard to understand, Fellman. When I left the university, after having you dream merchants stuff my head with nonsense for four years, reality slammed me right in the face. Every ideal you people implanted in my skull was a program for disaster. You didn't teach me what I had to do to survive in reality as it is. No, you and your fuzzy-headed colleagues taught me what you thought really *should* be." Lynn laughed, then took his fresh drink from the steward. "And here you all are, putting should be on the back burner while dancing to the tune of what is—if you'll pardon the mixed metaphor." He nodded and grinned. "I once had an instructor who was very picky about mixed metaphors. Now she's working for me as a secretary."

Michael raised his eyebrows, then finished off his drink. He lowered the glass, then frowned. "Tell me, Mr. Lynn. Why do I get the feeling that you want me to argue with you; to tell you that ideals are still important?"

"You're drunk."

"Which does not answer the question."

Lynn looked for a moment at the overhead, then brought his glance down to look at Michael. "Maybe I'd like to see you put up at least a little fight; something to tell me that those years I wasted in and after college were worth something. You know, when I finally made my peace with reality and got with the program, I felt guilty—like I was betraying myself. I didn't stop feeling guilty until I saw you characters being frozen out of teaching positions, and finally hopping on the RMI bandwagon." He shook his head. "And all the time the truth was staring me right in the face."

"Truth?"

"Biology. Any lifeform faced with the circumstances of its environment must either adapt to those circumstances, or perish."

"And you have adapted?"

Lynn nodded. "And so have you, finally. And there really wasn't any choice, was there? Powerful blocs of capital, labor, and governmental force are the circumstances of our environment, and those blocs aren't ruled by foggy ideals, Fellman, but by pragmatics."

Michael shrugged. "I still have the feeling that you expect some kind of protest from me."

Lynn curled his lip. "Don't you just make yourself the least little bit sick? Where are all those ideals you and your bunch held so dear?"

Michael motioned for another drink. "They went the way of the snail darter and the dodo, Mr. Lynn. As you put it, I have adapted." Lynn narrowed his eyes and stared at Michael for a moment, then he left his half-finished drink on the table, stood and walked quickly from the lounge. Michael took his fresh drink from the steward and gulped it down. As he held the glass in his hand, he glanced at the door through which Jacob Lynn had disappeared. He looked back at his glass and nodded. "Of course, some of us adapt better than others." He studied the glass until it shattered in his hand.

Armath squatted sullenly as his wives moved away from the eating fire. He watched Nanka, his head wife, as she went to the edge of the forest and brought back an armload of wood for the fire. He studied her short golden fur, her sleek flanks and gracefully arched back. He scratched at the long black fur on his shoulder. "Need not burn all wood in forest, wife. The eating is done."

Nanka tossed her head to one side, added another stick to the fire, then dropped the wood at the fire's edge. Armath frowned, then folded his arms. "You not speak."

Nanka squatted by the fire. "Husband. I speak for your wives. Our *Tueh* is almost ended—"

"Stop!" Armath reared back, then settled to the fire under Nanka's unblinking stare. "Hear no more of this, wife."

"Must talk, Armath. Your duty to your wives—"

"No!" Armath growled, then swiped at the snow with a clawed hand. "No talk! Enough!"

Nanka studied her husband for a moment, then looked down at the fire. "Last *Tueh* season, when you saw the male killed in the valley, then the teachers came. This started. Armath, you sired only six females last season. This season you have sired none. Is our *Dishah* to die, Armath?"

Armath scratched at his shoulder and frowned. He lowered his hand, then brought up both hands and folded his arms. "The school, Nanka. You have not seen it. You do not understand."

"The school." Nanka nodded, then drew her left arm down her flanks. "You get from this school what your wives exist to give you?"

Armath lowered his head and shook it "No You no understand the school . . . It . . ." He shook his head again. He looked up at Nanka. "Join the others. I talk no more." As she rose and loped off toward the edge of the forest, Armath looked back to the fire. The little gray human and his assistants had been teaching at the big houses for three winters. The Benda males would watch, listen and hear of the mighty human advance through space — a huge rock reeling down a steep hill, with other races nothing but feeble blades of grass. Armath looked up from the fire to see his wives talking together at the edge of the forest. He rose, shook his head and moved away from them to seek the solitude of the frozen river.

At his unit in the lavish instructors' complex, Michael Fellman put down his history of the Roman Empire, removed his glasses and rubbed his eyes. He looked at his watch, noted the time, then mentally calculated the remaining Bendadn minutes left before his self-appointed happy hour. He looked at the bottle on his clothes dresser, then stood. "To Hell with it." He went to the dresser, uncapped the bottle, and poured a glass full of straight gin. Returning to his chair, he sipped at the drink, closed his eyes, and let the familiar taste of juniper berries fill his mouth. He smiled, remembering that he had taken to drinking Martinis in an effort to curb his drinking. Michael had hated the taste of gin—once, long ago. Since then he had acquired a taste for the stuff. He raised his glass to take another sip, then the chimes sounded.

He stood, went to the door and opened it. Standing outside,

his overcoat collar hunched against the cold, stood a frowning Dale Stevenson. "Oh, it's you. Won't you come in? I was just about to have a drink."

Stevenson nodded, then walked through the door. "Doctor Fellman, I've come about something pretty important."

Michael closed the door, then moved back to his chair. "You can dispose of your own coat." He sipped at his drink as Stevenson removed his coat and tossed it on a chair. Stevenson pulled up his sweater as he turned and withdrew a large envelope that had been hidden there. "What have you got there, Dale?"

Stevenson held out the envelope, then walked to the dresser and poured himself a generous quantity of gin. "Something I want you to read."

Michael weighed the thing, then chuckled. "What is it? Your rough draft on the history of human conquest?"

Stevenson took a chair across from Michael, reached out a hand and tapped the envelope with his finger. "It's a confidential RMI report. It's a biological study that was done on Bendadn by the company five years ago."

Michael shrugged. "I have no interest in biology. And what are you doing with a confidential report? We're not exactly in the inner circle around here."

Stevenson took a gulp of his drink, twisted his face up until the fumes cleared his lungs, then lowered his glass. "I had it stolen from Lynn's office."

Michael raised his eyebrows. "How very imaginative of you, Dale. Would you mind informing me why you placed both of our positions in jeopardy in this manner?"

Stevenson lowered his glass after his second gulp, then nodded. "Doctor, do you know anything about the sexual habits of the Benda?"

"Not a thing."

"Didn't you wonder why males are the only students?"

Michael frowned. "The black-haired ones? I had no idea they were all male. I had supposed that the blonde ones were on a lower social scale—you know, something racial."

Stevenson shook his head, finished his drink, then stood and went again to the dresser. As he poured, he talked. "The Benda are all females at birth."

"Interesting, but how do they reproduce?"

Stevenson took his drink and resumed his seat. "It's all in the report. When they are young, all during their growing-up years, they have competitions, fights, and eventually combats to determine a pecking order of sorts. The ones who wind up on top become males. They then form a harem of females around each male. That's what they call a *Dishah*. That's the family unit on Bendadn." Stevenson paused as he took a long pull at his drink.

Michael looked at the envelope on his lap. "I suppose it's of some interest to someone, but why a confidential report on it—and, I might add, why did you steal it?"

"In college I had a minor in evolutionary biosystems. It's a hobby, I guess. That's why the Benda interested me in a biological sense. Because of their method of reproduction and the social organizations that were determined by it, it is almost impossible that the Benda evolved to become a sentient, time-binding race." Stevenson shook his head. "That's why my ears perked up when I overheard a couple of clerks talking at the executive complex about a proposed update on this report. To make a long story short, I heard enough to prompt me to spread around a few credits to get a copy."

Michael shrugged. "I only hope your dedication to history is as commendable as your interest in biology." He tossed the envelope onto his coffee table. "However, it's just not my subject."

Stevenson studied Michael for a moment. "Doctor, there's only two things you have to know about that report. The first is that males in this race are determined by conquest. Females are determined by being dominated."

"I know, the competition thing—"

"The other thing you should know is that the Benda look upon our little history course as a form of competition."

"What are you talking about?"

"Every reproducing male within RMI's claim area is in a position to compare his race's history with that of another race—that towering monument of lies called *Manifest Destiny*."

Michael sighed. "I still don't see what you're driving at, Dale. None of us are happy with the texts, but we knew what the job was when we took it."

Stevenson put his glass on the coffee table, stood and put on his coat. "I guess I misread you for all these years, Doctor. I'm sorry to have taken up your time."

Michael stood and faced Stevenson. "What do you mean?"

"You're rather a cynical character now, aren't you, Doctor?"

Michael sighed again and held out his hands. "Whatever does any of this have to do with me?"

Stevenson shook his head. "When a Benda male recognizes he is dominated, he reverts and becomes female again. What do you *think* will happen to the Benda after all the reproducing males have reverted?"

Michael's eyes widened. "Come now, Dale, I can't believe that."

Stevenson pointed at the coffee table. "Then, Doctor, I suggest you break your rule and read something in biology! I think you'll find it has a lot to do with the history you've been teaching."

"How?"

"In that report is an outline for *Manifest Destiny*." Stevenson opened the door. "RMI is having us—you, me and the others—the company is having us teach an entire race to death!" Stevenson walked through the open door, slamming it behind him. Michael picked up the envelope, pulled the report from it, then sat down and turned to the first page.

Jacob Lynn looked up in surprise as Michael Fellman burst into his office unannounced. Lynn's secretary followed in the historian's wake. "I'm sorry, Mr. Lynn, he just walked right past me, and—"

Lynn waved a hand. "It's all right." The secretary scowled at Michael, then turned and left, closing the door. "Now, Fellman, what's this all about?"

Michael took a bound sheaf of papers from under his arm and dropped it on Lynn's desk. "That."

Lynn raised his eyebrows as he read the title on the report, then he looked at Michael. "Where did you get this?"

"Transportation problems don't interest me, Lynn. What does interest me is are you aware of what's in that report?"

Lynn leaned back in his chair and half-closed his eyes. "Of course."

"Well?"

"Well what?"

Michael studied the project manager. With each sweep of his eyes, new information presented itself. "You knew all along about this."

"Of course."

"Why? This will mean the death of a race!"

Lynn smiled and shook his head. "You're overstating things, Fellman. We're not doing this outside the claim area." He shook his head again, then fixed Michael to the floor with his eyes. "Let me introduce you to a few realities, Fellman. Developed planets with advanced populations already are exploiting their mineral resources. Uninhabited planets are many, but expensive to investigate. Therefore, we, that is, RMI finds itself in a position where it always has to deal with semi-barbaric populations. To maximize our profits, it is necessary that the local population cooperate."

"And death is the ultimate cooperation."

"You said it, Fellman. I didn't."

"Which makes one Helluvalot of difference, Lynn."

Lynn smiled. "Is your conscience bothering you, Doctor? Is the size of the cynicism beginning to gnaw at you? You must know that any principle that you thought worth preserving was tossed down the toilet when you signed your contract with RMI." Lynn held out his hands. "What is this performance, Fellman? Are you trying to manufacture a rationalization for your own purity?"

"Lynn, you ought to be sporting a forked tail and red suit."

Lynn frowned, then laughed. "Are you complaining because I made a better deal when I sold out than you did? Or are old ideals beginning to shake their coffin lids?"

"You know, Lynn, you are the lowest form of life that ever crawled."

Lynn, still smiling, shook his head. "No, Fellman. There we disagree. I know what I'm doing, and I accept it. You are doing the same thing and crying about it. At least I'm honest. What does that make you, Fellman? You and the rest of your ivory-tower crew?"

"What does that make me?" Michael sat on the crude stone wall overlooking the encampments of five of the Benda families. Each family was removed from the others by distance and strict custom. The families had moved from their permanent sites in order that their males could attend his lecture at the local RMI auditorium. Michael pushed himself from the wall and began walking the rough path through the encampments back to his quarters. He thought of Stevenson's anger and Lynn's smugness, and the words Michael had uttered many years before when a young idealist at the university had sought his support in protesting some rights-diminishing law. "I am tired. Too tired to again break my back on the knee of another lost cause." A coldness had crept into his heart as he made his peace with uncontestable power; a coldness that allowed him to sweep together a few shards of career ruined by following impossible ideals.

As he approached the first encampment, he saw twelve young females competing to see which of them would have the strength, courage and stamina to become males. Michael remembered a line from the report. *The Benda cannot conceptualize of an organization beyond the family level. It appears, then, that the company must either treat with separate families—with the entailing impossible conflicts inherent in such arrangements—or devise a plan that will enable the Benda to be either treated as a unity, or eliminated.*

Michael shook his head at the frigid sense of purpose implied by the report. The cynicism of pragmatics brought to the ultimate cynicism: the elimination of a race to achieve the kind of political stability that would attract investment capital to the RMI coffers. He watched one of the Benda females deliver a savage blow to another, sending the stricken child writhing to the dust. The victorious female whirled around on her four walking hands, motioning to her sisters to come and try their luck. Most of them hung back, but one reared up and charged. The two met with a bone-crunching thud, then were lost to view in a cloud of dust.

Michael turned and saw the females of another family

similarly engaged. Then, he saw the family male squatting at the edge of the clearing, studying his children at their combat. The male's burly arms and strong back showed patches of fine blond hair amidst the black shag of his coat. The male turned his head, saw Michael, then jumped up, startled. Michael smiled and nodded his head at the Benda male. The creature only stared at the human, then hung his head and walked slowly away from the encampment.

Michael turned and hurried away.

Armath waited at the auditorium door for the opening to clear. At a break in the ingoing traffic, Armath spaced himself behind the most recent entrant the customary four paces, then moved into the huge, vaulted structure. Its size was necessary to seat the Benda students in such a manner that no two of them came any closer than four paces apart. Armath moved down the ranks, spotted an open place, then walked to it and squatted, facing the tiny stage at the front of the room. He noticed blond patches on many backs, and that the smell of *Tueh* was in the air. Armath bowed his head, sighed and waited. After a few moments, the auditorium grew silent. The frail gray human called Fellman entered at the front of the room and climbed up on the stage.

He placed his papers on the lectern, adjusted the microphone, then looked at the assembled males. "Humans will bury you." The words echoed throughout the auditorium. Armath frowned, for the human's style had changed. "If this were a classroom full of humans, there would be talking, laughing, playing about. But not with *you*." Armath could feel the scorn washing from the lectern across the students. "You *can't* talk with your neighbor, can you? Look at you. Look at yourselves squatting as though each one of you was an island unto himself." Armath looked and saw the other Benda males also looking around.

"Do any of you know why you sit apart like that? I'm asking a question? Do any of you know?"

Armath stood. "It is our custom."

Fellman nodded. "And how is it that it became a custom? Can you answer that?"

Armath held out his hands. "It has always been so."

The human motioned with his hand. "Sit back down." He looked over the audience for a long moment, then fixed one of the males in the front row with its eyes. "You!" The student stood. "Why are we speaking my language—the language of humans?"

The Benda frowned, then shrugged. "Our own language is not . . . it is not complex as is yours. Our only need of language is to care for our *Dishah*. We needed nothing more before the humans came."

Fellman nodded. "And we *are* here, aren't we? And you will all die because we came—because we are *better* than you!"

Armath swallowed as the last echoes of the human's challenge faded. Inside his chest he felt a tightening. The human walked from behind the lectern, then went from one end of the stage to the other, looking over the students. He returned to the lectern and leaned his arms on it. "The custom of separation dates back before the earliest memory of your oldest. Before the custom, a male chancing to meet another would enter combat to decide who was the stronger." Fellman nodded. "Of course you know what happened to the loser. You know because it's happening to all of *you*!"

The tightening in Armath's chest grew, and he recognized it to be anger. The human removed his arms from the lectern and held them behind his back. "Your ancestors were at least intelligent enough to see that this reduced an already small male population. Hence, it was agreed, long ago, that there was no challenge between males beyond four paces. This solved the problem, but it also eliminated the need for one male to talk to another. You cannot even talk to your own fathers if they can still reproduce, can you?" Fellman shook his head. "That's why you are nothing, and will remain nothing, until your race is extinct!"

Armath snarled and stood, along with several other Benda. His fingers ached to rip the little man apart, but other Benda had him boxed in on all four sides and corners. Fellman pointed his finger at Armath. "You!"

The growls among the Benda quieted. Armath held his head high, his eyes flashing. "Yes, human?"

"You want to come up here, do you not?"

Armath nodded and flexed his fingers. "Yes. Ah, *yes!*"

Fellman moved a little to his left and pointed at the four-pace-wide path between Armath and the stage. "There is a clear path. Walk through there."

Armath looked at the two Benda males flanking the entrance to the path. He saw the hair on one rise as the fellow stood. The male looked at Fellman, then back at Armath. He nodded. The male across from him nodded as well. The human screamed from the lectern. "Tell him it's all right! Tell him with *words*, damn it!"

The male to Armath's right looked at the human, then back at Armath. He held out a fist, then opened his hand, pointing it toward the human. "Pass."

The Benda male across from him nodded and held out his hand. "Pass."

Armath moved forward, his body tense, as he passed between the two males, then approached the next pair. They held out their hands toward the stage.

"Pass."

"Pass."

Armath walked between the two rows, stopping before each new pair, with each new pair holding out their hands toward the stage.

"Pass."

"Pass."

As he left the last pair behind and stood before the stage, he discovered to his amazement that he was no longer angry. Instead, his mind was filled with the wonder of what had just transpired. The auditorium was silent. Fellman walked to the edge of the stage. "Come up here."

Armath walked the five steps to the stage and moved to the lectern. He stopped four paces from the human. Fellman glared at him and pointed at a spot on the stage next to the lectern. Armath reared up a bit, blew in and out a few times, then stood next to the human. Fellman turned to the auditorium and folded his arms. To the Benda males seated in the ranks, he appeared foolish and small standing next to the tall, husky Armath. The odd couple stood together until the picture was firmly implanted in everyone's mind. Then the human spoke into the microphone.

"All over this Universe there is life that has a special quality. Humans have this quality; the Benda has this quality. You are not creatures of instinct, Benda. You are not slaves to the Universe's whim. You are creatures of choice. What you are is by choice; what you will become is by choice—*your* choice." Fellman looked at Armath, then returned his gaze to the assembled Benda males. "My job is to teach you about human history. That history has been one of expansionism, conquest and oppression." The little gray man rubbed his chin, then dropped his hand to his side. "But no race has a longer history of resisting human oppression, conquest, and expansion than do the humans themselves." Fellman tapped the papers on his lectern and spoke to Armath without looking at him. "Read this to the others." The man turned, left the stage, then left the auditorium.

Armath moved to the lectern, his heart stopping as he realized that he was about to talk—to talk to a room full of males. He swallowed, looked down at the papers, and studied them to keep from looking at the sea of faces before him. His eyes dashed over the hand-printed lines, then he frowned and looked back at the faces. "The human . . . the human has left us a story." He looked back at the paper, swallowed, then looked back at the males. "In a land far away, in a time long ago, there was a man. He was a hard man among hard men; he was a solitary man among solitary men. In the midst of a powerful empire, he was a slave, and his name was Spartacus . . ."

The winter closed, Bendadn saw its brief summer, then once again the winds brought the snow as two males met in the forest. Armath squatted in the field and turned to Januth. "Why do we meet here, Januth?"

Januth raised his brows and held out his hands. "Armath, can you imagine us meeting in my camp, or yours? Think of the females."

Armath nodded. "They would be disturbed." He rubbed his chin. "I wonder . . . about educating the females. What would Fellman think of that?"

"Armath, you are closer to the human than any of us. That is why I would ask you a question."

"What question?"

Januth frowned and scratched at the new black hair on his arm. "This human, Spartacus, and the few humans who fought the Persians at that pass..."

"Thermopylae."

Januth nodded. "And the human Hale who hung, and all those others. Humans who faced impossible odds, it is true. But they all failed."

"What is your question?"

"I feel that Fellman would have us... become something different, something better, stronger." Januth held out his hands, then dropped them. "But the examples he gives us all fail. What is the purpose of this?"

Armath studied the ground, then looked into Januth's eyes. "Can there be, Januth, something more important than the *Dishah*? We serve our own lives, and that of our *Dishah*. That is how it has always been, and it is good." Armath frowned, then held out a hand in Januth's direction. "But is there something more important? The humans Fellman talks of. They failed, but they... failed serving something more important than themselves. Perhaps that is the lesson Fellman would have us learn."

Januth shrugged. "He would have us serve something more important?"

Armath nodded. "It is what I think."

"Well, what would he have us serve?"

Armath shook his head. "I do not know. One thing I do know is that he teaches us that the contest with power is never won or lost until one side or the other breathes its last. Our contest is not over. Who is the stronger is still to be decided."

Januth smiled. "Do you... do you mean...?"

Armath grinned and held out his arms. "Yes. Soon my home will be crawling with screaming, squabbling brats!"

A month later, a strange human waited in the darkness at the back of the RMI auditorium furthest from the company administrative complex. He observed the Benda males, totally absorbed in talk, moving into the great room together and crowding toward the small raised stage where they squatted, shoulder to shoulder. When the auditorium was half-full, the Benda lowered their chatter, then became silent as a graying human entered and climbed up onto the stage. He moved to the lectern, placed some notes upon it, then adjusted the microphone. "Questions."

Several hairy black hands rose. The man pointed at one of them and a huge Benda male stood. "Fellman, if the Benda is to serve something larger, more important, than any one of us, or any one *Dishah*, what is it that we should serve?"

The human nodded. "I am a human. What makes me better than you is that I can devise and choose those things that I serve. You are Benda. It is not for me to devise and choose the things that you will serve. You are creatures of choice; then *choose*." The graying human looked to his notes. "Today I will talk of manifest destiny—"

A moan rose from the assembled males. One male close to the front stood. "Fellman, we *choose* not to hear any more of that trash. It is trash, and you have said so yourself." The male's comment was greeted with growls of approval.

The little gray man smiled. "You speak of a book; I speak of an ideal—the true destiny of humans, and of other intelligent races."

The male standing cocked his head to one side. "Is this the destiny of the Benda as well?"

Another male stood and spoke to the first. "Fellman said that such things are a matter of choice. We cannot choose until we listen and understand."

Both males squatted on the floor. The human turned to his notes. "Intelligent life rules other life. But it is not the destiny of intelligent life to rule intelligent life. The destiny of intelligent life is *not to be ruled*. As creatures of choice, it is our nature to be free to choose. Rule is existence by the choice of others as instinct is existence by the choice of nature. Today we will begin a study of the history of human progress and revolution..."

The Benda males, absorbed in thought, did not notice the other human at the back of the auditorium moving from the shadows, then walking rapidly out of the building.

Jacob Lynn leaned back in his chair and nodded at the biologist. "All right, Hyman. You've had a look around. Now tell me why things are not following the projections in your report."

Hyman pushed a thin wisp of brown hair from his watery blue eyes. "It's your boy Fellman."

"Fellman?"

Hyman nodded. "He's made the entire *Manifest Destiny* program into a laughingstock. In addition, he has the Benda males discussing matters that should be far beyond them. Dangerous matters."

Lynn frowned. "Such as?"

Hyman shrugged. "He's got them talking philosophy, politics, revolution—"

"What?"

Hyman nodded. "In addition, none of the males I've observed have reverted. By now they should have stopped reproducing altogether. Somehow, Fellman has convinced the Benda that they are, if not superior to humans, at least not to be dominated by humans. I'm afraid that simply removing Fellman and the other teachers who are helping him will not reverse the process. The damage is done."

"What do you suggest?"

Hyman sighed, then shrugged. "There appears to be little alternative. You must convince the Benda—once and for all—that they are inferior. And this must be done in a manner understandable to the Benda."

Lynn rubbed the back of his neck. "What are you suggesting?"

"A confrontation. A demonstration of force." Hyman smiled. "I'm certain that you can devise a pretext that will satisfy the Ninth Quadrant Supervisory Forces."

Lynn pulled at his lower lip, then nodded. "In fact, if it is worked properly, I might even be able to get the Quadrant Forces to do the dirty work." He leaned forward. "One thing more. Your report said that the Benda males cannot act in concert. How can we provoke something that will appear to be an uprising?"

Hyman rubbed his chin and studied the toes of his shoes, then he looked up. "Fellman has them sitting and talking together. Perhaps he has made our task very simple by making it possible for the Benda to act together in an attempt at force." He nodded and held up a finger. "One thing."

"What's that?"

"Fellman and his bunch must not leave the planet. Since they are aware of the report, it wouldn't do to have them wandering around Earth, talking." Hyman stood and walked toward the door. He paused and looked back at Lynn. "There is an alternative—but I suppose you know that."

"Know what, Hyman?"

"If Fellman's efforts result in a unified Benda race, RMI will have a political entity with which to deal for minerals. It will cut into the profits some, but no more than on any other planet RMI has invested in."

Lynn nodded. "I'll be getting in touch with you later, Hyman." The biologist nodded and left the office. Lynn swung his chair around and stared at the map behind his desk. On it were marked the many test-boring sites that had uncovered rich deposits of hematite, silver, tungsten, zinc, lead—a treasure house of metals. He tapped his fingertips upon the armrests of his chair, then he swung back and punched a code into his desk's tiny keyboard.

"Thorpe here."

"This is Lynn."

"Yes, Mr. Lynn."

"Thorpe, I want you to prepare to have a full crew move into the Javuud Valley tomorrow. I want full-scale production to be reached within the next two weeks."

"Yes, sir, but all the transfers of mineral rights haven't been completed."

"Let me worry about that. And Thorpe?"

"Yes, Mr. Lynn."

"I'll be having a full security company with your crew for protection."

"Is there a need? I mean, has there been some trouble that I should know about?"

"Just taking precautions." Lynn cut off the communication, then stared at the door through which the biologist had left. Lynn's eyes narrowed as he clenched his fists. "It's not profits, Hyman. It's *Fellman!*"

Dale Stevenson felt the bite of the morning chill as he walked from his quarters at the subschool to the local RMI auditorium.

There were many things that had to be prepared as Doctor Fellman made his circuit of RMI subschools. First, the auditorium had to be opened, which was the easy part. After the lecture, as the mass of Benda males divided into discussion groups, Stevenson and the other discussion-group leaders would again be embroiled in the telling questions and spirited arguments of the students for the next nine days. Then Fellman would appear for a lecture and begin the process all over again.

As he approached the door to the auditorium, he nodded at the students who had gathered there, then he motioned to the RMI security guard standing beside the door. "Let's open it up."

The guard shook his head. "My orders are to keep these doors closed."

Stevenson sighed. "Look . . . what's your name?"

"Bartlet, Mr. Stevenson."

"Then you know who I am."

"Yes, sir. But my orders come from Mr. Lynn. The auditorium is to remain closed for the day."

Stevenson held out his hands. "There is some mistake, Mr. Bartlet. This auditorium has to be open for Doctor Fellman to deliver his lecture."

The guard shook his head. "My orders stand until Mr. Lynn changes them. I'm sorry."

Stevenson fumed a bit, then moved to the door and tried the handle. The door rattled but would not open. He motioned to a couple of Benda males who were observing the conversation. "You two. Pull this door open."

The males grinned at each other, then moved toward the door. Bartlet pulled a solid projectile weapon from the holster at his side and aimed it at Stevenson. "If they go near that door, Stevenson, I have orders to shoot!"

Stevenson's eyes widened, then he laughed. "Nonsense!" He turned back to the two Benda and pointed at the door. "Go to it."

A sharp report deafened them all. The guard, his face red, looked around at the students, then back at Stevenson on the ground holding his thigh. "I told you! My orders are to shoot!"

Stevenson looked at the guard, his eyes wide and glassy with shock. "My god, man, have you lost your mind?"

"I got my orders!"

The guard turned and faced the circle of Benda males as a low growl began at one side. He pointed his gun at a particularly huge male who began advancing. "Stand back! Stand back or I'll shoot!" He squeezed the trigger again and again as hairy black hands reached for his throat.

Distath looked out of the door beyond his garden and examined with pleasure the rocks and fields of his *Dishah's* land. The human's lessons on property were complicated, but caused him many hours of profound thought. He rolled the words with his tongue. "Without a right to exist at some place, no other rights can exist." He nodded, then started as he saw a movement among the rocks. A Benda—a female, not of his *Dishah*. He ran from the house toward the movement, left the garden and vaulted the low fence. As he approached the rocks, a golden female stepped forth and bowed her head. "Forgive me . . . forgive me this intrusion. It is my husband, Virsth."

Distath glowered at the female, then held out a hand. "What of Virsth?"

"Distath, the humans have come with great machines to take my family's land." She hung her head, then looked into the male's eyes. "Virsth sent me to warn you."

Distath swung his head back, then looked down at the female. "You realize the impropriety of a female not of my *Dishah* being on my land?" He shook his shaggy head. "What care have I that the humans take *Virsth*'s property? He is to care for his *Dishah*, and I mine."

The female looked up into Distath's eyes. "The humans come for your land as well, Distath. This is the message I was given to deliver . . . as my husband died from a wound delivered at the hands of the humans. Do with it what you will!"

Lynn's office door opened and two guards pulled a struggling Michael Fellman into the room, then released him before Lynn's desk. "Lynn, what are you—"

"You're fired." Lynn returned to the papers on his desk. "If you are found anywhere on company property you will be arrested under Quadrant Savage Planet Regulations as a trespasser." He glanced up. "That's all."

* * *

Five days later, as his shuttle touched down at the RMI field on Bendadn, Damon Stirnak watched from his view port as Jacob Lynn crossed the tarmac toward the craft. He heard the shuttle door open, then he waited and watched. Lynn hesitated at the bottom step, then he moved into the shuttle. Stirnak did not rise as Lynn entered the passenger compartment, nor did he offer Lynn a seat. Lynn appeared to Stirnak to be having difficulties about what to do with his hands. They clasped in front, went into his coat pockets, jumped out and clasped behind Lynn's back, then went off to hide themselves in his trouser pockets. Stirnak leaned his head back against the seat and closed his ice-blue eyes. "Stop fidgeting, Lynn."

"Yes, Mr. Stirnak." Lynn took a deep breath and halted his nervous movements through sheer will.

"You know, of course, why I am here?"

"No, sir. I was only notified of your arrival a few minutes ago."

"Surely when your office applied for military assistance under the QSP Regulations it knew that the fact would come to the attention of RMI."

Lynn shrugged. "Of course, but everything is well in hand. I see no need for an Executive Office investigator."

Stirnak nodded, then opened his eyes and fixed Lynn to the deck. "Lynn, what is going on down here?"

Lynn wet his lips. "It's all in the application for assistance, Mr. Stirnak. There have been four attacks on RMI facilities by locals—"

"Why? Why have these attacks happened? According to the Hyman Report, submitted by your office five years ago, the locals should—right now—be a whipped and dying population."

"I can explain."

"Do."

Lynn wet his lips again. "It's Fellman and some of the other instructors RMI hired to staff the school system. They turned everything around, making the locals hostile."

"How did this happen?"

Lynn shrugged. "I'm not the one who screened the applicants for those positions. That's a Main Office headache."

Stirnak rubbed his chin, closed his eyes, then opened them again. "Lynn, I am going to give you a free hand with this problem."

"Thank you, Mr. Stirnak."

Stirnak held up a hand and shook his head. "Save your thanks, Lynn. I'm putting you on the spot."

Lynn frowned. "Sir?"

"The *Manifest Destiny* plan was cooked up and submitted by your office. RMI has made and will make no official notice of the plan. That includes, as well, your present attempts at resolving the situation. You are on your own."

"I see." Lynn nodded. "If everything works out, I'm a hero, but—"

"—But if this all falls apart, Lynn, you will find yourself in a high wind, and very much alone." Stirnak motioned to a seat opposite his. "First sit, then tell me what you plan to do about the Benda."

Several mornings later, Dale Stevenson, hobbling on an improvised crutch, spotted Michael Fellman at the edge of the clearing that the instructors had been camping in. He pursed his lips against the ache in his leg, and moved toward him. Fellman looked around and smiled. "It's good to see you up and around, Dale." Michael pointed at the leg. "And how is your badge of courage?"

Stevenson snorted as he came to a halt. "Michael, if you think for an instant that if I thought that guard was serious, I would have . . . well, you'd be as ready for a soft-walled room as the rest of us are." Stevenson cocked his head back toward the collection of rough lean-tos that housed the former RMI Department of History on Bendadn. "Look at us, Michael. Flabby, gray, weak, and without half an idea between us as to how to survive on our own, much less as savages."

Michael looked at the camp, saw several faces turned in his direction. As they noticed him looking back, the faces turned away. Michael looked at Stevenson. "Have you been put up as a spokesman of some kind?"

"I guess I have. Look, you know as well as any of us how impossible our situation is. You know what the winter is like on

Bendadn. I doubt if any of us can survive it like this."

Michael shrugged. "What would you have me do about it?"

Stevenson shook his head. "I don't know. Get in touch with Lynn. Ask for a deal."

"What kind of deal? We don't have anything he wants."

Stevenson looked into Michael's eyes for an instant, then averted his glance. "We have one thing."

Michael studied Stevenson, then as his mouth opened in surprise he pointed at the camp. "You . . . and the others. You want me to tell Lynn that we'll go back and implement his damnable *Manifest Destiny* plan?"

Stevenson kept his gaze down as he nodded. "What good are we doing like this? I ask you, what good? If Kurst over there hadn't had a smattering of medical training, I'd be dead right now. The same thing for those two Benda males who got wounded with me. Michael, in a couple of months we aren't going to have anything to *eat*!"

Michael sighed. "Is this the man who came to me with the Hyman Report? The same man who said that I *have* to do something?"

Stevenson shook his head. "I know. But, we aren't doing any good like this. What about the families that got tossed into the bush along with us? You and I are single, but what about the instructors with families? Could you sit and watch your son or daughter starve or freeze to death? What good are our ideals then?"

"Dale, that's when they're the most important. I'll tell you what good we've done. After you and the two Benda males were wounded, the rest of the students carried the three of you off and cared for you until we could get Kurst to you. Before we came, they wouldn't have done that—not for a human, not for a Benda."

Stevenson looked into Michael's eyes and shook his head. "But what good are we doing *now*?"

"We are abstaining from the commission of a crime."

"Aaah—"

"Listen, Dale. When you came to me with that report, what did you have as a limit on your so-called ideals? Do what you can, Fellman, just as long as I don't lose my job?" Michael turned away, then spoke with his back toward Stevenson. "First, Dale, I doubt if the *Manifest Destiny* program can be salvaged at this point. Our students, I am proud to say, have learned too well for that. But even if we could reverse what we've done, I doubt that Jacob Lynn would believe it, or, if he did, that he would take any of us back. In his mind, he is committed to the use of physical force." Michael turned back. "But if any of those in the camp want to try, I have no way of stopping them."

That evening, Armath and a scattering of Benda males looked with horror at the bodies littered across the Javuud Valley. Squads of scaled creatures moved out from the protection of the mineral extraction plant. Each one carried one of the weapons that had felled the Benda long before any of them had reached the RMI ramparts. A hairy hand shook Armath's shoulder. "The creatures seek the rest of us, Armath. We must run!"

The speaker ran off into the underbrush leaving Armath alone. The Benda male frowned as he felt the hair below his eyes and found them wet. He lowered his hand as a fist, watched the beings coming closer, then he turned and followed the other male into the forest.

Michael, Stevenson and several of the other instructors watched as the huge Benda male drew a seven-pointed star in the dirt. Armath looked up at the circle of human faces, then pointed at the star. "This is the sign they wore on their coverings, and on their flying boats."

"That's the Ninth Quadrant insignia." One of the humans stepped forward and turned toward Michael. "Those aren't RMI guards, Fellman. Those are Ninth Quadrant troops."

Michael nodded at the man. "I can see that, DuPree. What I want to know is how RMI got the Quadrant to use its troops." He looked up at DuPree. "You have experience in Quadrant law, don't you?"

DuPree nodded. "The only way I can figure it is that RMI asked for the protection of the Quadrant under the Savage Planet Regulations. What it amounts to, if a planet is savage, according to the law's definition of savage, then a private party on such a planet can request the Quadrant to come in as a police force if a threat has presented itself."

Michael nodded, then looked up at Armath. "Why did you do this? You cannot attack guns with bare hands."

"This is the only way we know, Fellman."

Michael nodded. "I know. I know. How many of you were lost?"

"A hundred of us charged the complex. Not more than ten escaped alive."

Michael nodded. "That a hundred of you would fight together for a common goal; this is good." He studied the star, then looked up at DuPree. "Savage?"

DuPree shrugged. "That's what they're called."

Michael turned toward Armath. "Do not be sad, Armath. Your companions joined in the right cause, but with the wrong weapons." Michael stood and turned toward the other humans. "School resumes tomorrow." He turned back to Armath. "I cannot travel the circuit as I did before. Can you spread word to the Benda?"

Armath frowned, then nodded. "I shall have them told."

As Bendadn's chilly winds gathered, sending the white flakes of winter through trees and across fields, little gray men and little gray women stood ankle deep in snow, surrounded by hulking black bodies. At night, the humans were quartered in Benda camps. They earned their keep during the days with their talk. The Benda males listened, questioned, argued, then listened some more. As spring darted warm fingers into frozen draws and hollows, the lessons ended.

Ninth Quadrant Force Captain Vaakne lifted his scaled head as the orderly entered. "Jazut, this is what?"

"Captain, the Benda at gate there are."

Vaakne stood. "Attack?"

The orderly gestured in the negative. "Talk it is they want."

Captain Vaakne buckled on his sidearms. "Guard to walls posted?"

The orderly gestured in the affirmative. "To walls posted, Captain."

*   *   *

Armath watched as the heavy Ninth Quadrant officer waddled from the mining complex gate. He looked up to see many of the scaled heads of the Quadrant soldiers looking back. The Quadrant officer waddled around the few remaining patches of ice and came to a halt in front of Armath. *"Negias si naad, Benda?"*

Armath shook his massive head. "Does the scaled creature understand English?"

Vaakne's slitted eyes narrowed. "The English I speak. What is that you and the others here want?"

Armath extended a roll of papers and handed it to the officer. "Take this, creature. The papers are our constitution, the record of our election, and our government's application for representation among the planets of the Ninth Quadrant Federation." Armath pointed at the roll of papers. "In there you will find my government's demand that Ninth Quadrant Forces be removed from Bendadn. Should you not leave, Bendadn shall request the United Quadrants to remove you."

Vaakne cocked his head to one side, looked at the roll of papers in his hands, then looked back at the naked, hairy creatures that had delivered it. "Government? This not understand."

Armath scratched at his shoulder with a clawed hand. "Study the regulations for savage planets, creature, and you will see. Bendadn no longer is a savage planet, and you must leave." The six Benda males turned and left Vaakne standing alone.

On the RMI ship back to Earth, Jacob Lynn frowned and turned to the two guards who had spent the first several days of the trip following him like a shadow. "Do you have to follow me around like that? It's not like I could escape."

One of the guards shrugged, then rubbed his chin. "Where'll you be, Mr. Lynn—just in case someone should ask?"

"I'm going to the ship's lounge to have a drink."

The two guards looked at each other, shrugged, then the first guard spoke to Lynn. "Okay, but don't get lost." They turned and went back to their quarters.

Lynn moved through the corridor until it widened into the ship's lounge. He walked directly to the bar, obtained a double whiskey, then turned to survey the open booth seats. He saw a graying man with glasses sipping at a Martini. He walked to the booth and looked down at him. "May I, Fellman?"

Michael looked up and smiled. "Be my guest, *sahib*."

Lynn made a wry smile, then sat down. He took a swallow from his drink, then lowered it to the table. "I suppose you know what's going to happen to me?"

Michael shook his head. "Only a little. Is it true that RMI is bringing charges against you?"

Lynn snorted. "Yeah. Like I did it all by myself. I'm their scapegoat so they can remain on Bendadn. It seems that they are willing to try and work within the framework of your government, Fellman."

Michael shook his head and smiled. "It's not my government, Mr. Lynn. It's theirs."

"I suppose in some philosophical sense you think you've created Utopia."

Michael sipped at his drink, then raised his eyebrows. "No, Mr. Lynn. The government of the Benda is far from perfect. Only the males can vote or serve in government. I advised them to extend those rights to the females to avoid a future headache, but as I said it's their government." Michael studied the former project manager. "Mr. Lynn, your problems stem from failing to take your own advice."

Lynn raised an eyebrow, then he turned back to his drink. "What advice?"

"Adapt to the circumstances of your environment, or go under. The environment changed, Mr. Lynn. RMI adapted; you did not."

Lynn took a swallow of his drink, then looked at Michael. "Why are you going back to Earth, Fellman? I would have thought that you would have carved a nice little place for yourself in the new society."

Michael leaned back and returned Lynn's glance. "I told you. My government isn't on Bendadn; mine is on Earth. Since leaving Earth, I've learned a little about environments, circumstances, and—if I may use the word—ideals. I'm going back to see if I can find ears willing to listen to what I have to teach."

Lynn laughed, then shook his head. "As a teacher, Fellman, you are poison on Earth. You'll die on the vine."

Michael finished off his Martini, then stood and faced Lynn. "Perhaps, Mr. Lynn, but at least I'll find the vine I die on quite comfortable."

Lynn frowned. "I don't understand you at all, Fellman."

Michael smiled. "I don't doubt it." Michael Fellman turned and left the lounge. Lynn stared at the door through which the history instructor had left, then he turned and finished his drink.

Legislative Assembly

of the

UNITED STATES OF EARTH

LEGISLATIVE RECORD

February 2, 2114

Speaker. Members of the Assembly, the President-General of the United States of Earth.

President-General Nataka. Madam Speaker, honorable members of the Assembly, distinguished visitors, people of the United States of Earth.

What I must say to you tonight is done with great pain. There is no easy way to say it, nor is there a way to soften the blow this knowledge brings. As a result of the Legislative Assembly's acceptance in principle of the entrance of USE planets into the Ninth Quadrant Federation of Habitable Planets, the eleven planets of the Rhanian Alliance have seceded from the union we call the United States of Earth.

The future of these many planets that the human race holds in its hands is part of the same future of every other race of this galaxy. The future is with the Ninth Quadrant and with the United Quadrants—a multitude of races living in accordance with law and justice. This is why the Assembly voted the way it did, and is why I endorsed the Assembly's resolution.

No human could tolerate the invasion of the Rhanian Alliance planets by aliens to achieve their unity with us in this great goal we seek. It is up to us—or, more accurately, our soldiers—to end the rebellion and let us enter the Ninth Quadrant as a whole people.

It will not be an easy war. Soldiers of the Rhanian Alliance have served the United States of Earth well and with great distinction many times. Many of you watching tonight, and several of those seated in this chamber, have friends and family on Rhanian planets. It will be little comfort to you that I talked with the senior representative of the Rhanian delegation prior to his leaving for Rhana, and that this burden weighs as heavily upon his heart as it does mine.

May God help us in our cause....

"Alpha team, prepare to advance into position." The amplified boom of the range officer's voice thundered across the range control frequency, shaking boot-squad leader David Merit out of his daydream about sleep. Automatically checking his sensor for overhead threats, Merit slowly stood in the trench where he had been crouching alone. Pressure sensors read the flexing of his muscles and instructed his armor to imitate his movements. Muscle control was important. An overflex, twitch or unthinking gesture could throw an ME II's occupant into a variety of silly, or deadly, situations. After three straight days and nights of range drills, Merit's muscles were sore and trembling. It took a conscious effort just to keep his iron pants from jumping off of him.

"Is the second battalion clear yet?"

"Zebra team of the last cycle has a wounded man, sir."

"An Overcontrol?"

"No, sir. Member of his own team flamed him."

"Vugg! Waller, get those clowns off the range and send their drill instructor to the range command center."

"Yes, sir."

Merit felt the perspiration gathering on his upper lip and reached for the chin control for the suit's air conditioner. It was on maximum. He didn't know anyone from the second battalion, but he knew what would happen to Zebra team after its D.I. got back from the range officer with a brand new excretory opening.

His armor in standing position, Merit checked his sensor again for deployment of the twenty-two other boots that made up his team, but the ground still obstructed his view.

"Is the second clear yet?"

"The medics are still working on the wounded man, sir."

"Keep me posted. I still don't see their drill instructor."

"He's on his way, sir."

Merit reminded himself that his team would make no mistakes, he hoped. The boots in his section had drilled until every one of them could do combat fire and formation drills in his or her sleep. He had called them out on free time to do even more drills, but mistakes could happen.

"Sir, the second battalion is all clear."

"What about the wounded man?"

"Didn't make it, sir."

Merit felt his stomach go sour as he listened to the crackle of his headset.

"Alpha team, third training battalion, advance into position."

Merit chinned his team's frequency. "Alpha team, this is Alpha leader..."—he liked the sound of that—"...net check." His headset popped and crackled as the team members called in.

"Two, Cooper."

"Three, Danzigger."

"Four, Watkins."

"Five..."

'Where in the Hell is that next cycle?"

"Sir, this is Private Merit, Alpha team leader..."

"What's the holdup? Where are your people?"

"Sir, we...Sir, net check, sir..."

"Get your animals up on the line, Merit. Do your goddamn net checks before you come on the range."

"Yes, sir."

"Move it, move it, move it!"

"Talpha deem..." began Merit, immediately damning his slip. "Alpha team, this is Alpha leader. Move into position." Through the open team net, Merit heard a few snickers. Talpha deem, thought Merit. Vugg, everything is falling apart.

His armor amplified his jump to the lip of the trench, and as he touched down he rapidly scanned the horizon through his sensor and saw his team stretched out along an irregular kilometer long line. Through his visor, he saw nothing but red sand, scrubby pines burnt brown-green by the Dathnia sun, and Training Force Sergeant Mordo.

The drill instructor stood facing him, squat and powerful, decked out in full combat armor. Mordo's visor was up and the face behind it was a study in unconcealed rage. Boots joked about Mordo looking the same whether he had his armor on or off; it was no joke. Shaved bald, his skin almost the color of blued gunmetal, the armor was Mordo's natural birthday suit.

Mordo chinned his net selector and cut in on the team's frequency. "So, this is the famous Talpha deem?"

"Sir," answered Merit, "Alpha team reporting in position."

"Demerit, izzat you behind all that Force-looking armor?"

Merit cursed his mother's fondness for the name David. David Merit. D. Merit. Demerit, get it? Mordo thought it was funny. "Sir, Alpha team leader Merit reporting Alpha team in position."

"Goddamn, it's the famous Demerit of Talpha deem and his internationally renowned meatbeaters." Mordo wiggled his armor forward until he stood less than two meters from Merit. Through the open visor, Mordo's ugly black-cratered face was twisted into a snarl.

"Zhatskull!"

"Sir?"

"You wanna tell me what a Talpha deem is, Zhatskull?"

"Sir, I...uh, got mixed up."

"Mixed up." As Mordo shook his head inside his helmet, his coal-black eyes fixed on Merit's, Merit concentrated on the top of Mordo's visor. "You know what a mixed-up forcer is, Demerit?"

"Sir, a mixed-up forcer is a dead forcer, sir."

"You betcher ass a mixed-up forcer is a dead forcer, zhatskull." Mordo raised his laser rifle and leveled at Merit's chest. "But you're not just betting your own ass, idiot child. You mix up and you put your team—your whole battalion's asses—on the crap table." Merit's air conditioner fought to keep up with the Dathnia sun in addition to the rivers of sweat running down his back as Merit stared at doom. Mordo's crazy enough, thought Merit, he's just crazy enough. Every boot in the platoon had heard of the time when Mordo had flamed a boot for being clumsy—and got away with it. Most of the boots, including Merit, believed the tale. "What's your team supposed to think, when you say 'Talpha deem,' Demerit?"

"Sir, I don't know, sir."

"Nobody else does either, zhatskull. You think the goddamn RATs are gonna stand by and play with themselves while your team tries to figure out what the hell you're mumbling about?"

"Sir, no, sir."

"Those Rhanians are soldiers, zhatskull, and you know what those Rhanian assault troops are going to do when they find your team milling around trying to figure out what you said?"

"Sir . . ."

"I'll tell you what those RATs'll do. They'll flame your ass, and your whole goddamn team. That's what." Mordo raised his rifle and took aim between Merit's eyes. "Demerit," he said calmly.

"S . . . sir?"

"You make one mistake out on the range today—just one—and make me look bad in front of the range officer . . . well, I'm gonna show you just how dead a mixed-up forcer can be. You copy, zhatskull?"

"Sir, yes, sir."

Mordo lowered the rifle and pushed it against Merit's chest, cutting the external control to his armor's air conditioner. "You're thinking too slow, Demerit. Probably too cold in there, and your brain went numb. You leave it like that. When it warms up in there, you'll be able to think straight."

As Mordo turned and leaped three times to a position centered and in back of the team, Merit breathed a sigh of relief and checked his temp indicator: 31°C and rising fast. As the drill instructor reported in to the range officer, Merit could smell his own body.

"Alpha team, this is a safe-fire range test. Targets representing Rhanian assault troops will appear downrange at irregular distances, groupings, positions and times. Kill them."

Merit raised his rifle, cut out the safety and crouched into position. Sweat dribbled into his eyes and he shook his head to remove it. God, I hate that son of a bitch. Merit's temp indicator stood at 34°C and still rising. He could feel the sweat gathering in his boots as he scanned the sensor display. The first group of green blips appeared.

"Alpha team," Merit shouted into the team net, "RAT squad at two o'clock, six thousand meters. Hold position, set weapons for full power and fire on my command." He quickly flicked his rifle's selector switch to maximum, and sighted it through his sensor. "Fire!" Merit hosed down an eight-degree arc back and forth three times and then released the trigger. The display had shown his team covering the same arc almost in unison. It was a righteous performance.

"Score: ninety-seven."

Despite the oppressive heat, Merit grinned at the score and tensed for the next shot. As he scanned the sensor, his eyes began to blur, his breath coming in short gasps. Shaking his head to clear it, he tongued some water, and brought his eyes back to the display—a mass of green blips, far to the left and close in.

"Alpha . . . Alpha team. RAT company at nine o'clock, five hundred meters. Half power, enfilade left and fire at will."

Merit sprang back into position and watched as the right wing of the team swung around and landed. An instant later, twenty-three lasers swept the target area.

"Score: ninety-four."

Merit barely heard the range officer as he fought to keep his chow down. His head split in flashes of light and pain, and he knew he was blacking out. His temp indicator read 41°C and rising, but all he could think about was Mordo. The son of a bitch would be all over him for passing out. Candyass. God, thought Merit, I hope I don't puke in here. Never get the smell out. Struggling his eyes open, he saw a lime-colored snowstorm all over the display. A RAT airborne assault—a full battalion. As he drifted off into a soft black nothingness, Merit remembered he hadn't issued the orders...

"Dad... Dad, I've joined the Force."

"You what?"

"The USE Force, Dad. I enlisted—"

"Don't be absurd. My son? A Quad?"

David shrugged and looked down. "I know... I know you don't think we should fight the Ronnies, Dad, but I really believe that the USE planets should join the Ninth Quadrant. Just about all the kids at—"

"Kids!" Mr. Merit threw his paper on the floor. "Kids! What do you know? David, the Rhanians are humans. Do you want to kill humans?" He shook his head. "Of all things; a Quad!"

David felt the back of his neck grow hot. "All of us should be in the Quadrant—"

"David, what you're seeing right now—between you and me—is just part of the ugliness of a civil war. Is this what you want? To war against your own father?"

"Dad, if we don't get Rhana to join, the Ninth Quadrant Forces will, and they aren't human. At least the Quadrant is giving us a chance to clean up our own mess."

"Some favor." Mr. Merit sighed, then looked up into his son's eyes. "Well... when do you have to report?"

"Tonight... I'll be gone before... before Mom gets back from Aunt Ruth's."

Mr. Merit raised an eyebrow. "That wasn't terribly courageous for a brand-new forcer, was it?"

"I guess not."

Mr. Merit shook his head. "What will your mother say?" He rubbed his eyes. "What am I going to tell her? You do know that her brother's family is on Rhana?"

"Yes. I know."

Mr. Merit shook his head again. "What will I tell your mother...."

... Ladies and gentlemen, please raise your right hands and repeat after me. I, then state your name....

...All right, you sorry bastards, you can put them down now....

The squat, horribly ugly DI padded softly down the rows of boots, standing at rigid attention. The naked light bars down the center of the squad bay cast ghostly shadows underneath his cruel eyes. "My name is Mordo," he came to a halt at the far end of the bay, turned and began walking back. "I am your drill instructor." He stopped in front of David, reached out a hand and slapped his face, sending David sprawling between the bunks where he came to rest with a bone-bruising thump against the cement floor. "You," Mordo continued, "are nothing..."

...Savvit looked around, pulled out the paper and began reading in a whisper, "Dear Mother, I am writing this letter to let you know I am fine, and to ask you to tell Carol that she should not wait for me. It's hard to explain, but, you see, Sergeant Mordo, our DI, shaves with a laser rifle, picks his teeth with a trench knife and wipes his bum with steel wool. These are all in the tradition of the Force, and, of course, the sergeant expects us to do the same. I knew the Force would make a man of me (it's done a fine job of making men out of several women in my platoon) and that this would entail certain changes. But Mother, I didn't realize how extensive these changes would be.

"It wasn't so bad when they tattooed the emblem on my forehead, and I didn't mind when they seared my pores shut with a blowtorch so I wouldn't sweat all over my armor. The fingers I lost on the grenade range simply balanced the toes I lost disarming mines. But yesterday, while shaving, a loose piece of steel wool jabbed me and I flinched, cutting off my nose with my laser. Even this wouldn't have been so bad, but in trying to catch my nose I dropped my rifle, which explains the stains on this letter. You see, Mother, dropping your rifle is the big sin here, and right now I am being flogged. Since this is the only free time I'm going to get for awhile, I'm taking this opportunity to write.

"I know Carol would understand about my fingers, toes, nose and other things, but there is one thing I haven't mentioned. You see, when I dropped my rifle it was still on automatic, and something else got cut off I know from experience Carol will miss. I'm married to the Force now, Mom, so please tell Carol, and take care of yourself. Your loving son, Zhatface."

As Savvit finished reading, the platoon squeaked, gasped and snorted as it fought to hold in its laughter. Merit felt tears coming to his eyes as he bit his knuckle to keep from guffawing out loud.

"TENHUT!" As the boots scrambled and froze at their bunks, Mordo strode down the center aisle and stopped in front of Savvit. Without looking at the boot, Mordo stuck out his hand and snapped his fingers.

"S . . . sir?"

"The letter, Zhatface." Savvit extended a trembling hand and put the offensive scrap of paper in the DI's hand. "Where's the envelope?"

"Sir? Mordo faced Savvit, their noses barely apart.

"The envelope, idiot! You know what an envelope is, don't you?"

"Sir, yes, sir."

"Answer me, Zhatface!"

"Sir, yes, sir, I know what an envelope is, sir."

"Where is it?"

"Sir, I, uh . . . haven't made one out, sir."

"Then make one out, Zhatface, and I'll mail it for you." Savvit looked around, confused. "Move it, Zhatface. Your mother wants to hear from you." Savvit half-turned to his footlocker, then turned back.

"Sir, it's . . . it's only a joke, sir."

Mordo looked truly stunned. "That can't be," he hissed. "Not a joke. Jokes make people laugh, and I gave orders that no one in this platoon will ever laugh again. You wouldn't think of countermanding my orders, would you?"

"Sir, no, sir."

"You better not, Zhatface, 'cause you laugh at a RAT, he's not gonna laugh back, is he?"

"Sir, no, sir."

"He's gonna take his beamer and fry a hole right between your horns, isn't he?"

"Sir, yes, sir."

"Then that can't be a joke. That must be a letter."

Savvit went pale. "Sir, it's a joke, sir."

Mordo shook his head. "More scared of your mother than you are of mè. She must be one jumbo woman, your mother." The DI read the letter through. "I guess it is a joke, Zhatface. But then why aren't you laughing?" Again Savvit looked confused. Merit clenched his teeth. You made your point, Mordo, slack off. Mordo jabbed Savvit in the chest with his finger. "You too good to talk to me?"

"Sir, no, sir."

"Then answer me!"

"Sir . . . I guess it's not very funny, sir."

"You're wrong. It's funny. I especially like the part where you cut your balls off. I guess everybody laughed when they heard it. Did they?"

"Sir, I couldn't say, sir . . . I didn't hear anybody, sir."

Mordo looked around the squad bay. "Zhatface says he didn't hear anyone laugh. Did anyone laugh?"

"SIR, NO, SIR!"

"Wrong again, people! I was down at the end of the bay listening to you silly people spending your guide-book time giggling like a bunch of school kids. Sergeant Allman?" The JDI came from the end of the bay and stopped next to Mordo. "Sergeant, this is too fine a joke to let go with a giggle." He folded the sheet in thirds. "So I want you to take this herd out for an hour of laughing drill. With buckets."

The JDI headed for the bay door. "All right, people. You heard it, so hit it, hit it, hit it!" As the boots scrambled out of the door, Mordo chuckled and put the letter in his billfold . . .

". . . That's his job, Merit. Don't take it so personal."

"But Sergeant Allman, you're not like that . . . crazy."

"I'm only a JDI, Merit. I don't have to be like that. He's got to be like that if he's going to turn you garbage heads into forcers."

". . . But . . ."

"Get your ass out of here . . ."

". . . Demerit!"

"Sir!"

"Puke out that first general order, Zhatskull!"

"Sir, my first general order is to circuit my post in a military manner, keeping always on the alert, and noticing everything within detector range, sir."

"Aren't you a sorry excuse for a human?"

"Sir, yes, sir."

"I hear you been crying on brother Allman's shoulder, Demerit. Well?"

". . . Sir, I . . ."

"Why, you candyass. You shouldn't even be here, crybaby. Why don't you put in for your walking papers?"

"Sir, I can make it, sir."

"Izzat a fact?"

"Sir, yes, sir!"

"Well, candyass, hook a sensor on this and copy quick. I'm making it my personal business to see that you don't. You think you got pressure on you now, Zhatskull?"

"Sir, no, sir."

"I'm real glad you feel that way, 'cause I'm putting down the heavy screws, Demerit; you copy?"

"Sir, yes, sir."

"From now on, you're first squad leader, and if you know me you know that's no reward. You're gonna have ten noses to wipe and ten little bums to keep clean. Anybody steps outta line, Zhatskull, and you go over the wall and join the freaks and Ronnies. You'll be a playboy again. Copy that?"

"Sir, yes, sir."

"Lay that second general order on me, pea-brain."

"Sir, my second general order is . . ."

Before Merit opened his eyes, he felt the symptoms similar to those induced through motion-sickness drills. Automatically he relaxed his arms and legs, and concentrated on his biofeedback responses. Opening his eyes, he saw the net of springs that supported the bunk above his. Turning his head to the right, he saw some of the boots from the platoon sitting on footlockers and cleaning their weapons and gear. Closing his eyes again, his gore rising, he wondered what the appropriate biofeed response to Mordo was. "Passing out in the middle of a range test," he whispered. "Mordo will be all over me like the Venusian crud."

Gingerly he sat up and swung his legs to the deck. Noticing he was still in skivvies and socks, armor dress, he stood and stumbled to his footlocker. Pressing his thumb against the sensor plate, the footlocker opened and Merit took out fresh skivvies and socks and changed. After pulling on his utilities, he sat down on his footlocker and began putting on his boondockers.

"Merit." He looked up and saw Watkins standing next to him.

"What?"

She sat down next to him and scratched her bald head. "You all right, Merit?" Her face was wrinkled in concern.

"Yeah. I'm okay."

"What's going on? I tell you, it's giving me the spooks."

Merit finished hooking his laces. "What are you talking about?"

Watkins pointed at three other bunks. Merit saw Drukakis, Bonini and Kuzik, the other three boot-squad leaders, flat and out cold. "What's going on?"

"I don't know. Mordo turned off my air conditioner. Cooper should have taken over . . ."

"Tenhut!"

Before the scream from the end of the bay died, the platoon stood motionless at attention, except for the three unconscious squad leaders. Mordo stood at the end of the bay, glowering.

"Pissant!"

"Sir!" answered a smallish boot named Alice Levy in the real world.

"Pissant, any of those candyasses up yet?"

Levy jerked her head left and right, then back to the front. "Merit, sir . . ."

"PISSANT!"

"Sir."

"What's the first word outta that filthy mouth?"

"Sir . . . 'Sir,' sir."

"So answer me, Pissant."

"Sir, Private Merit is awake, sir."

"Demerit?"

"Sir."

"Trot your candyass down to the hut at light speed and stand to."

Merit took one step forward, right-faced and ran down the bay past Mordo, clattered down the hall and came to a violent halt beside the door to the DI's hut, at attention. He could feel the muscles between his shoulder blades knotting in anxiety. As he heard Mordo's heavy tread advance slowly down the hall, he kept his eyes riveted on the green wall opposite the door. Mordo passed him and turned into the hut, leaving behind a scent of cigar smoke, cheap booze and the after-shave the platoon had dubbed Evening in Parris Island.

"Tickle that pine, candyass," growled Mordo from the depths of the hut. Merit about-faced and struck the door frame three times with the heel of his right hand and the fronts of his knuckles. "I couldn't hear that, candyass. How'm I supposed to know anybody's out there if they don't knock loud enough?"

Merit felt the ache in his knuckles and swore that every goddamn forcer in the goddamn Force must be as goddamn deaf as a goddamn post. He swung again at the frame with everything he could muster, causing tiny puffs of dust to erupt from between the frame and the wall. When he brought his hand down and resumed the position of attention, he could see small flecks of red among the cracked green paint.

"Trot your buns in here, Demerit." Merit right-faced, took one step, left-faced and took two steps into the hut.

"Sir, Private Merit reporting to the Drill Instructor as ordered, sir."

Mordo stood in front of him, the DI's hands on his hips and a thick black cigar jammed in his face. "Candyass."

"Sir."

"Candyass, you went asleep on the job out there today, didn't you?"

"Sir, yes, sir."

"I bet you're gonna blame me for turning off your air conditioner, aren't you?"

"Sir, no, sir."

"You're not worth much, are you, candyass?"

Tired and confused, Merit couldn't remember the right

answer to any of those are-you-worth-much, do-you-love-me kinds of questions—if there were any right answers.

"Aren't you talking to me, Demerit?"

Whatthehell, thought Merit. Whatever I say is going to be wrong. "Sir, yes, sir."

"Answer me!"

"Sir, yes, sir, I'm worth something, sir."

Mordo raised an eyebrow. "Izzat right, now? Just what are you worth?"

"Sir, broken down, the chemicals that make up my body are worth approximately twenty and a half credits on the open market, allowing for minor market fluctuations, inflation and..."

"Shut your goddamn face!" screamed Mordo, slapping Merit with his beefy hand. As he hit the floor, Merit's vision blurred and his head buzzed. He scrambled to his feet and returned to the position of attention, his cheek burning hotly.

"You got too smart a mouth on you, Demerit. I guess this came just in time." Mordo walked to his desk and picked up a sealed red envelope emblazoned with the USE Force insignia in gold. The DI held it in both hands, grinning. Merit recognized the kind of envelope wash-out discharges came in. Potter had gotten one, and Ramirez. He had seen theirs. The other wash-outs simply vanished in the middle of the night. Mordo held the envelope out. "Here. Take it, and get the hell out of my palace, candyass."

With a sick feeling in the pit of his stomach, Merit took the envelope, looked at it, and then looked questioningly into Mordo's cruel, mirthless face. "Don't look at me, candyass!" Merit returned his gaze to the front. "Did I tell you to get outta here?"

"Sir, yes, sir."

"What?"

"Sir, you told me to get out of here, sir."

"Then, do it, Demerit. Do it."

"Aye, aye, sir." Merit about-faced and ran from the DI's hut toward the squad bay. As he reached the bay, he began walking toward his bunk. He half-noticed the other three squad leaders were awake, their blanched expressions part of the preparation for their own ministrations at Mordo's gentle hands. Two boots came up to him, but seeing the envelope turned away, embarrassed. Reaching his bunk, he sat on his footlocker and stared at the envelope. As he stuck his finger behind the flap, Watkins came over and squatted beside him on the floor. Merit looked at her and she averted her eyes.

"Gee, Merit..."

"Forget it." He pulled the document from the envleope, unfolded it and began to read ... "This is to inform you that your team, Alpha of the Third Training Battalion, achieved an overall score of 91 points on the leadership takeover exercise conducted on the safe fire range, this date, July 17, 2117. 91 points breaks the previous range record of 89. You and your team are to be congratulated on a job well done..."

Merit reread the letter four times before he allowed himself to break into a smile.

"What is it?" asked Watkins.

"Here." Merit handed Watkins the letter. "Drag your orbs over that!"

Watkins quickly read the letter, stole a glance at Merit who was laughing and shaking his head, and then reread it. "Merit..."

"How about that, Watkins? Congratulations on a job well done."

"I don't understand. What about you passing out?"

Merit stabbed at the letter with his finger. "Look, dummy, a leadership takeover exercise. They wanted to see how you idiots would perform without me to wipe your bums. Our depth of training, remember?"

"Tenhut!" Merit and Watkins collided and just managed to get themselves untangled and at attention by their bunks as the clatter from the bay subsided. JDI Allman stood at the end of the bay, arms folded, campaign hat pulled down over his eyes.

"You silly people were slow getting up this morning." He paused, letting the accusation permeate the consciousness of the collective boot mind. "Sergeant Mordo is concerned because he thinks you people might not be getting enough sleep." Allman pushed himself away from the bulkhead and walked down the bay. "Sergeant Mordo thinks you will sleep better at night if you are more tired. Does that sound reasonable?"

"Sir, yes, sir!"

"I thought it would. Right after evening chow you animals will fall out for full pack and weapons drill . . . with buckets. We wouldn't want anyone to get a headcold, would we?"

"Sir, no, sir!"

Allman halted in front of Merit, who held his face in the traditional grim boot expression except for his eyes, which grinned from corner to corner. "Merit."

"Sir?"

"Sergeant Mordo said for you to leave your bucket behind and bring a GI can instead. Copy?"

"Sir, yes, sir."

"As Sergeant Mordo phrased it, 'That Demerit prob'ly ain't gonna be able to fit his head in a reg'lar bucket 'long about now." Allman turned and walked toward the hut. "That's all."

As everyone returned to doing whatever it was before the interruption, Merit sat on his footlocker and read the letter for the fifth time. Watkins walked over from her bunk and sat next to him.

"What'd he say?"

"What did who say?"

"Mordo. When you were in the hut. What'd he say about that?" Watkins pointed at the letter. Merit rubbed the welts on his cheek and thought a bit.

"He said congratulations—in his own way."

The gray, cramped hold of the *Sgt. Alfredo Gonzalez,* an outdated medium-attack transport, was dimly lit with faintly flickering light bars. The air recirculation system did little to relieve the smells of five hundred bodies strapped into racks stacked five high, with the rack above barely clearing the chest of the occupant beneath. Several of the forcers in the hold had gotten sick as the *Gonzalez* completed its first time-step phase, adding an acid-sweet odor to the already oppressive atmosphere. Some had no reaction to phasing, and others became dizzy or went into laughing fits. Still others became nauseous.

David Merit found himself in this last category as the *Gonzalez* began its first jump from the Schiller Force Base Sattelite toward the replacement depot three-quarters of the way to Rhana. Three years before, Schiller had been the replacement depot.

With phasing over for a time, David sleepily let his mind poke and prod his new surroundings and existence. In orbit around Earth, the Schiller Base contained the USE 7th Fleet School Headquarters. In addition, the base served as a transit station for USE Force personnel and as a rear-area assembly, outfitting and repair facility for the 7th Fleet. Space combat training took place there, while planetside combat training utilized Luna and Earth. The growing Luna colony, first begun to exploit certain minerals, was situated next to the huge Richter USE Base, which served as the principal supply point for all space fleets, as well as the 7th Fleet HQ. Stationed there, as well, were the 31st and 132nd Force Divisions. Far under the Lunar surface was Richter Force Hospital.

David and the other trainees were shocked at the treatment they received at Schille: Individual quarters, relaxed uniform and locker discipline and no harassment, as the school's staff concentrated on one thing—producing space-trained combat forcers. Complicated, thorough and demanding, David found the training both challenging and fascinating, even to the endless armor drills.

Navigation, survival, logistics, maintenance, space and planetside combat tactics and formations, shipboard protocol, tactical fire patterns and marksmanship, geography, planetary biosystems, first aid, Rhanian subversive efforts, sabotage and more were pounded and stomped into David's aching head. But although he griped along with the other trainees, he discovered he was having the time of his life.

Before he got to it, he felt apprehensive about the Rhanian Assault Tactics course. It couldn't help but remind him that the object of all the fun and frolic at Schiller was war. Once he got into it, however, his apprehension left him. The RAT's were human; they could be beaten. The battles of Dismas, AB-411.23, and Outpost Arthur showed that.

One hundred percent was passing at Schiller, since the slightest failure of knowledge or skill could be sufficient to jeopardize entire missions, not to mention getting oneself flamed in the process. It was in David's fourth month at Schiller, crouched over a desk piled with make-up exams, that he noticed Watkins among the four hundred similarly occupied trainees. He stared at her for a long time before he realized who she was and why it had been so hard to recognize her: she had hair; a soft cap of auburn, trimmed to frame her freckled face. Working hard on her make-ups, she felt David's stare and looked up, confused. Smiling in recognition, she pointed back to her papers. David nodded and she returned to work.

After turning in his make-ups, David waited outside the exam compartment hatch. As she stepped through, he called out, "Hey, Watkins!"

"Hey, yourself. I didn't recognize you with hair on your head." They both laughed.

"Same here. It looks good on you—you look good."

"So do you, Merit." She punched him playfully in the arm. He caught her fist and held it in his hands.

"No, Ann...I mean, you look good." David didn't know what was coming over him, and he didn't care. Taking both of his hands, she pulled them to her lips.

"That's what I meant, too."

With make-ups completed and graduation behind them, they went on liberty at Luna Colony while awaiting orders. They walked through the half-domed, half-underground city examining shops, the geological museum, markets stocked with Lunamade and Earth imported goods, and the first experimental mine converted into a tourist attraction. Arms around each other, they did the restaurants, bars and the colony's one lone ballroom, where they discovered that light-gravity combat training on Luna hadn't been sufficient preparation to attempt the Frenz in .2 gravity. Instead, they clung together and moved slowly, regardless of the music.

Later, in their room, they quietly nestled in bed, her head resting in the crook of his arm. The room lights were dimmed, and little of the clatter outside could be heard.

"David?"

"Mmm?"

"You're thinking that with me in the Thirty-first here on Luna..."

"And me with the Two Hundred and Third, wherever they are..."

"David, we'll probably never see each other again."

David raised himself on his left elbow and touched her lips with his fingers. "Hush." Moving his fingers to her eyes, he felt the tears beginning there and brushed them away. Lightly kissing her eyes, he dropped his hand to the clasp of her bed dress, opened it and placed a gentle hand on her breast.

"David..."

"Be quiet." Kissing her neck, he let his fingers glide from her breast down....

"*...Attention. Man your battle stations. Attention. Attention. Man your battle stations. This is not a drill. I repeat, this is not a drill. Attention...*"

Ripped from his dream by the hellish moan of the ship's Klaxon, David rolled from his rack and hit the deck running. An instant later, he realized he didn't know where to go, and neither did anyone else. All replacements enroute to the depot serving the 5th, 19th and 203rd Force Divisions had only been on the *Gonzalez* a few hours. Most of that time had been spent getting settled in, becoming familiar with the emergency facilities and accelerating from Schiller in preparation for the first-phase jump. From school, David knew where transport battle bays were on several kinds of ships, but the *Gonzalez* predated anything he had ever studied by fifteen years. From the confusion and milling around in the hold, everyone seemed to be realizing the same thing.

"You forcers in this hold!" shouted a voice from the hatch. "Follow me!"

Quickly peeling down to armor dress, socks and skivvies, David was among the first to run through the hatch. Several fully clothed replacements, seeing how David was dressed, began shucking their utilities and boondockers as they ran down the companionway. The high-speed parade whirled down the companionway to the battle bay. As David ran through the hatch and into the first dresser slot, a hand clamped on his shoulder.

"Number!"

"Seventeen oh sixty-four!" he shouted at the noncom, stating his suit nomenclature and size.

"Seventeen oh sixty-four!" the noncom repeated into a hand communicator. "Move out!"

David ran to the station displaying his number. As he turned into the stall, the dresser already had the armor cracked open and was checking the support system. David leaped on the step, grabbed the overhead bar and lowered himself into the iron pants. Leaning forward with his arms out in front and his head down, the dresser rapidly fitted him into the top half, sealed it, and pulled David up straight to seal the two halves of the armor. David chinned the environmental, transport and sealant test controls. As he finished checking the nutrition and medication systems, the dresser slapped David's helmet and handed him a laser rifle. David activated his armor, took the rifle, checked it and headed into the ejector. The ejector capsule closed and began moving into the ship's magazine along with other filled capsules. The number "13" appeared on the capsule's tiny briefing screen, making David the Number Thirteen member of the team, unless changes were made in organization prior to ejection.

"This is Number One," crackled his headset, "Lieutenant Pollack. You are A team." The first twenty-two forcers into the magazine plus a team leader became the A team, and an A forcer was considered the best. David knew he was A mainly because his rack was close to the hatch. "Anyone combat-qualified in this group?" asked the team leader.

"Number Five," answered a voice from the past David would never forget. Mordo; two-hundred ugly pounds of DI.

"Anybody else?" Silence. "Two and Five exchange. Stand by until we get the tactical readout."

Along with the rest of the team, David waited for the tactical information to appear on his capsule's screen. At the moment, all he could see was the number "13" glowing in soft red. Every aspect of his awareness had been occupied with following the drill; there had been no time for thoughts of fear. With the number thirteen hanging before his eyes and Mordo only a few capsules away, David's awareness began contemplating being sealed in armor, locked into a dark ejection capsule somewhere within the bowels of an ancient transport that someone out there was shooting at.

The red "13" was replaced with a moving red representation of the battle situation. Two USE cruisers, close together, were immobilized. Three Rhanian cruisers were standing by while a Rhanian attack transport moved in. The tactical computer showed David's team putting down the stick in split formation. Automatically David recalled that in split formation, Mordo would lead the first squad and 13 would lead the second.

"Thirteen, this is One. Can you handle that?"

"Yes, sir. I think I can, sir." You never know until you get there.

"If you have any doubts, we can exchange. Nothing's going to be said if you bug out. You're green and we're not supposed to put anyone who isn't combat-qualified into a leadership position, but you know the situation."

"Lieutenant, this is Two." Mordo's voice came across the team frequency without expression.

"Go ahead, Two."

"Permission to ask Thirteen a question."

"Granted."

"Demerit," Mordo called out, his words dripping with scorn, "Izzat you?"

David swore under his breath and cursed the day he ever laid eyes on a recruiting poster. "Yeah, Mordo! It's me!" The vehemence in David's voice produced a shocked silence on the net.

"He can handle it, Lieutenant," said Mordo, all expression removed from his voice.

"Right. Thirteen, you're it. Everyone stand by for the drop. Two, Thirteen, get your herds into position at light speed after they pull the pin. Copy?"

"Aye, aye, sir."

David was mixed up, and he quickly tried to get unmixed. Green, going into combat for the first time leading more greenies, and he was so happy he could sing. That "he can handle it" of Mordo's was all the diplomas and awards in the universe. I guess, thought David to himself, I never realized how much I wanted the respect of that sonofabitch.

"Ready A team," said Number One.

David stood straight in the center of the capsule with his arms folded over his rifle across his chest. With his chin control he locked his armor as the five-second warning beeped across the team net. The capsule moved, jarred to a halt, and its bottom opened to the vacuum of space. As the air in the capsule rushed out, it shot David down and away from the ship. He quickly established his relative position, checked to see that everyone in his squad had ejected successfully, and then hit his armor's jets and headed for the nearest USE cruiser. His sensor showed a team member out of position.

"Twenty-one, this is Thirteen. Hit that gas and get into position."

"Roger, Thirteen." David saw Twenty-one speeding up to make formation. The dull reflections from their armor showed the squad strung out in an irregular two-hundred-meter-long line, lasers at the ready. Off to David's right, the first squad sped toward its position.

"Thirteen, this is Alpha leader."

"Thirteen."

"You're going to have to kick some ass to get at that first cruiser. Tactical says the RATs have already ejected, and we got dropped too far from the target. The RATs'll be there when we show up. Copy?"

"Yes, sir." On his sensor, David saw the RATs pulling up on the other side of the cruiser while his squad had better then twelve kilometers to go.

"Holy Christ! We're the only ones out here!"

"This is Thirteen. Keep off the net." David's sensor should have been filled with the teams following Alpha into the fight, but all he saw behind him was the blip representing the *Gonzalez*. "Number One, this is Thirteen. The other teams . . ."

"I know, Thirteen. Something fuggered the ejections, but I'm not getting any change from tactical, so keep formation. We'll have to keep Ratso busy until the cavalry gets here. Open up as soon as your squad gets in range."

"Aye, aye, sir." David estimated the time to range. "Second squad, this is Thirteen. RAT platoon at twelve o'clock at the near cruiser, set full power for eight thousand meters, fire on my command." David sighted his own weapon and watched as his range indicator dropped to eight thousand. "Fire!"

As though they had trained together for months, the second squad hosed an arc back and forth across the front of the advancing RAT formation. A moment later, the first squad hosed a similar arc. David's sensor showed the remainder of the RAT formation dropping to place the near cruiser between themselves and Alpha team. Out of the blackness above them, a searing two-meter-thick beam of white light flashed square into the center of the second squad, exploding the armor it touched. David opened a channel to listen in on the story from tactical.

". . . This is Alpha leader. Ratso has a big light out there, and we can't touch it." Number One gave an approximate position as another beam flashed a few meters from David's head.

"We see him, Alpha leader."

David pulled a net check and reported three forcers out, then closed up the formation and continued the advance. Through his visor he saw the flash of a ship's engine firing full-attack power. Another flash sizzled close enough to warm his armor, and David saw the entire RAT formation had made it behind the cruiser and were beginning to return fire with smaller versions of the light beam that reduced his squad. David lost two more forcers.

"This is Alpha leader. Play your weapons along the edges of the ship. They have to expose themselves to shoot at us." The remaining forcers hosed the edges of the ship, and the RAT fire slacked off.

"Thirteen, this is Two."

"Go ahead."

"The lieutenant's had it. How many you got left?"

"Five."

"I got seven. I can't raise tactical, so here's what we'll do. I'm staying with the first squad and go around the bow of that first cruiser. Hold your herd in position and keep the RATs off us. Copy that?"

"Right." At two thousand meters relative, still firing, David

pulled his squad up while Mordo took his off, heading toward
the bow. Return fire was sporadic, but he saw one of Mordo's
squad get it as they streaked away. Before they made it to the
ship, Mordo lost two more. David could see vapor trails
marking the first squad's path, which meant that they had
dumped life-support air into their jets for extra speed. As they
disappeared behind the bow, pencil-thin red lines from the first
squad's lasers crossed with the thicker white beams of the
Rhanian Assault Troops.

"All right, Merit, we got their attention. Get around the stern
and hit 'em in the ass. It's only an advance unit; can't be more'n
fifty of 'em."

"Copy. Let's go, second squad." David hit his jets and air
dump at the same time. As they streaked for the cruiser's stern,
David's squad received no RAT fire. From the number of
beamers that could be seen flashing beyond the bow, Mordo
definitely had the RAT's attention.

As they reached the cruiser's tail assembly and swept around
to face the exhaust deck, David immediately opened fire on the
dozen RATs using the deck and exhaust nozzles for cover from
Mordo's assault. Following David's lead, the five remaining
squad members hosed down the exhaust deck. Most died, but
several RATs jetted away from the ship. Leaving two forcers to
guard their rear, David took the three others around the edge of
the exhaust deck, coming out in back of the main RAT position.

"Two, this is Thirteen."

"About time. Where are you?"

"Almost in your field of fire. I can see the RAT backs now."

"Okay, when you're set, open up."

Mordo and the first squad had driven the remaining RATs
toward the end of the ship. The ones the second squad hadn't
routed were bunched up close to the hull using the ship's frame, a
disabled torpedo launcher and an antenna blister for cover.
"Second squad. You see 'em. On my command . . . fire!"

The second squad's fire burned into the RAT position, while
Mordo's squad picked off RATs leaving the ship in an attempt
at escape. In seconds, the crossfire gave the ground to Alpha
team.

"Thirteen, this is Twenty-three."

"Go ahead."

"We're getting busy back here!"

David jetted away from the ship and saw that eight of the RATs the second squad had chased from the exhaust deck had reformed and were taking on his scanty rear guard.

David called the three forcers with him, and the four of them jetted toward the RATs.

"Thirteen," called Mordo, "keep an eye out for us. We'll be coming up the other side in about eight seconds."

"Right." As they saw David's group jetting around the stern of the ship, the RATs concentrated their beamer fire on the four forcers hosing them with lasers. The area around the stern was hazy with discharged gas, fragments of armor, weapons, bodies and a pink mist of frozen blood. As a beamer caught Number Nineteen square in the chest, his armor exploded, driving David toward the exhaust nozzles. He tried to counter the momentum with his armor jets, but they were empty. Just before he hit, David noticed that the two forcers he had left to guard their rear were smeared over the nozzles and plates of the exhaust deck. As he hit the edge of a huge nozzle, he could feel his chest armor caving in and his ribs cracking. The pressure made it difficult for him to breathe. Automatically David checked his suit pressure. It had dropped from .8 Earth normal to .65, but was rising as the armor's sealant system plugged the hole. Pulling himself around by hand, he sighted his rifle as beamers scorched the exhaust deck. Firing twice in quick succession, he exploded one RAT and nicked a second. Sighting again on the remaining RATs, they exploded before he could fire. David watched as the five remaining members of first squad jetted around the stern into view.

"Merit, any more of 'em?"

"No, Sarge. I guess that's it." David pushed away from the exhaust deck to meet Mordo. His remaining two squad members jetted in from the edge of the deck and joined them.

"That all you got left? Any wounded?"

"Just the three of us. No wounded."

Mordo's armor gave a spurt as he goosed his jets to position himself closer to David. Turning David's armor around by hand, Mordo inspected the damage. "You breathing okay?"

"I'll hold out."

"The rest of you?" Mordo pulled a net check. Two had wounds that had self-sealed and everyone was short of air. Dumping into the jets for speed had left them all in short supply. Feeling giddy from the pain in his chest, David tongued a mild peekay pill.

"What now, Sergeant?"

Mordo jetted away from the ship, looked around and jetted back. "RAT company's on its way over from the other cruiser. About all we can do is get on the exhaust deck of this crate, lash up and pick them off as they come around into view." Mordo waved toward the ship, and the remaining members of the squad jetted and hooked up at the edge of the deck, except Number Five. "What's the hangup, Five?" As Five's armor swung slowly around, the remaining members of the team could see that the right boot of Five's armor had been blown off. The armor had closed in the stump and filled in the cracks with fast-setting filler.

"'Sis...Five," the wounded forcer answered, his speech slurred by peekays. "Out of air...Used it up plugging the hole..."

"Two, this is Twenty-one. I still got a forty-percent charge."

"Go get him, and get back here fast." Mordo towed David to the edge of the deck and hooked a line from David's armor to an eyelet welded to the deck. As Twenty-one pulled in Five, Mordo lashed Five to the deck and then peeked over the edge. "Get ready. They're about on us."

David lifted his laser and sighted at where the advancing RATs would appear. He tongued another peekay, and as the pain subsided the first RATs came into view. Correcting his aim, he waited for Mordo's command.

"Fire!"

The eight forcers hosed down the advancing company and scored several hits before the RATs divided into two groups, sending the first toward the bow and the second toward the stern. Concentrated beamer fire began disintegrating the edge of the deck. David pulled on his line, backing himself up to the deck, and sighted his laser, waiting for the RATs to come around the edge of the deck. Checking his sensor, the area in view was clear except for battle debris. The ship blocked his view, and he waited for the tiny blips representing RATs to begin moving out from the big spot representing the cruiser the forcers used for cover.

The Rhanian beamer fire ceased, and David's trigger finger tensed. After two minutes passed, David relaxed. "Where'n the Hell are they?"

"Everybody stay put." Mordo pulled himself to the jagged edge of the deck, still glowing red from beamer fire, and stuck his helmet out. Pushing himself away from the stern, Mordo pulled himself around the edge and dropped from view. "Hey, anybody got a sensor that's still working?"

"Me," answered David, unhooking his line. David pulled himself over the edge and closed with Mordo. Through his visor he saw the RAT company jetting back to the far cruiser at top speed. His sensor was covered with overhead blips.

"What is it?"

"I don't understand...a battalion-strength assault." He motioned at the star-studded space forward and above their position.

"My, my. It's the cavalry. I guess somebody finally figured out how to open the door on the *Gonzalez*." In moments, the leading teams of the forcer assault came into eyesight, jetting at top speed toward the RATs. The Rhanians streaked for their pickup launches. "Tactical. This is Alpha leader."

"This is tactical, Alpha leader. Good work." A squad of RATs peeled off and streaked into the center of the forcer assault formation, beamers blazing.

"Tactical, Alpha leader. Send a pickup to the stern of the near cruiser. We can't make it back." In seconds the RAT suicide squad was evaporated, but the slight slowing of the forcer advance was all that was needed for the main body to make its pickups and blast away.

"Will do, Alpha leader."

David allowed himself to relax and take a heavy peekay while he waited for the pickup. Looking at the elapsed time indicator in his helmet, he figured it was broken. It showed a little over eleven minutes since the drop. As the pickup launch pulled into view, a bit of debris floated in front of David's visor. With a sluggish effort, he swatted it from in front of his face. It was a frozen finger.

Three weeks later on Earth, David looked at the blue and white Earth Medal Third hanging from his left breast pocket, then at the thin, gold lance corporal's slash across the left forearm of his dress blues. The increase in pay had been better than wiped out by the price of the blues David had to purchase for the lightly attended ceremony. Mordo had imparted a bit of Force lore regarding medals. "Never accept a Third unless you already got your blues. If you don't have blues, don't settle for anything less than a Second. They have to make you a full corporal and you can at least break even." Mordo's blues were shiny with age, but despite the six broad slashes of his rank and the kaleidoscope of medals blinking from his chest, he was still Mordo. The black, bullet-shaped head on top of that immaculate tower of Force blues was still the ugliest thing David had ever seen. Mordo's face would never appear on a recruiting poster.

David heard a laugh and looked up. His gaze traveled around the lobby of the Force's New York Office of Public Relations and stopped on Mordo shaking hands and back-slapping with another sergeant dressed in greens. The traditional Force greetings between lifers were exhanged: "You ain't dead yet?" Then the two continued by aiming harmless obscenities at each other. David watched for a moment, then turned to go back to his hotel, his mind half-made up to visit his parents for the remainder of his furlough. He had no desire to go home and pick up the Quads vs. Ronnies argument with his parents, but he hoped it would be better than wandering around alone in a strange city.

"Merit!" David froze at the sound of Mordo's voice, then he smiled, realizing that he was not all that far from boot camp. He turned to see the two sergeants looking in his direction. Mordo raised a hand. "C'mon over. There's someone you should meet." David walked across the lobby, stopping in front of the two Force sergeants. The one standing next to Mordo was tall, slender, and wore his greens as though they had been tailored, which they probably were. Mordo cocked his head toward David. "Jas, this is the kid I was telling you about. Merit, this is Jas Kolker. We did boots together."

David shook hands with Kolker, then frowned as he studied the sergeant's gleaming, even teeth and handsome face. "Sergeant, do I know you from somewhere?"

Mordo and Kolker laughed. Mordo jabbed Kolker in the ribs with an elbow. "Go ahead, Jas; show him."

Sergeant Kolker assumed a pose, his clear eyes staring at a nonexistent enemy, his hands holding a nonexistent rifle. David studied the figure for a second, then burst into laughter. "The poster! The recruiting poster!"

Kolker bowed. "The same."

"Sergeant, if you only knew how many curses have been laid on you by boots."

Kolker laughed again, then pointed at David's blues. "A brand-new set, I see." He turned to Mordo. "Why are you two in blues?"

Mordo clamped a hand on David's shoulder. "Merit picked himself up an Earth Third this morning, and I collected another pip for mine."

Kolker frowned. "That's what all that commotion was about in the press room. Why was the ceremony held in the PR building? Don't you two rate the Force HQ steps?"

Mordo shrugged. "The Ronnies. They were planning a riot or something, and the brass moved us here for the pin-sticking."

Kolker nodded. "It's getting bad. The Ronnies practically run parts of this town. The Legislative Assembly refuses to do anything about them, so it'll only get worse. If they like Rhana so much, they ought to move there."

Mordo snorted. "I don't think they want to be on Rhana, with the way the RATs are drafting anything that can still pull a trigger."

Kolker looked at Mordo, then turned his gaze toward David. "Say, what are you two doing tonight? Your Thirds get you a furlough for a couple of weeks. Any plans?"

Mordo shook his head. "Not me." He turned to David. "You heading home?"

David thought for a moment. "No."

"Well, where are you two dug in?"

Mordo rubbed his chin. "We're put up in a fleabag on Forty-fourth."

Kolker frowned, shook his head and waved his hand. "I won't hear of it. You two heroes come over to my place and set up your tents. I'll call my wife and let her know, then we'll see what we can do about drying up this town."

Mordo jabbed David in the arm. "Okay with you? I don't know how you feel about dragging the slopchutes with a couple of old duffers."

David grinned and shrugged. "Just as long as you two are buying, I can keep up."

Later that evening, all three dressed in Force green, David numbly tried to figure out the number of bars they had crawled before depositing themselves at a nameless place illuminated with blacklights and naked dancing girls. Kolker and Mordo were socking it away two to his one, but David could see no change in either of them. About the time he had heard the same war story for the third time, David's attention wandered to the dancers. As they bounced and shook, he lifted a hand and touched his face with his fingers. He drew his hand away, looked at it, then tried again. He couldn't feel his face. David raised an eyebrow and turned his face toward Mordo.

"Mordo?"

The ugly black face was hidden in the dark, but when the sergeant smiled, his teeth flouresced, giving the illusion of a disembodied smile. "What is it, Merit?"

David slumped back against the booth seat. "Mordo, did I ever tell you that you are the ugliest sonofabitch that ever put on greens?"

Mordo's suspended smile opened into a laugh. The smile shook. "I'm mean, too."

"Tha's right, Mordo. You are mean." David bobbed his head around until Sergeant Kolker came into view. "Kolker, Mordo is mean, mean, mean. He like that in boots?"

Kolker brought his glance back from the dancers and looked at David. "Sure. Mordo's like that in boots. He's always been like that."

"Always?"

Kolker nodded. "When Mordo's born, the doc took one look at him and said, 'Tha's the ugliest damn baby I ever saw.' Then Mordo, he looks at the doc and says, 'Yeah, 'n I'm mean, too'!"

David laughed, then faced Mordo. "You, you ugly sonofabitch."

"What?"

"You make sure I get home tonight. New hero in town, 'n' the Force can't get 'long without me."

"I'll get you home." Mordo finished off his drink, plugged another cigar into his mouth, then turned back to Kolker. The two picked up their war stories where David had interrupted them. David let his head loll to one side and saw a dark, standing figure looking back. The figure shook his head, then turned slightly to watch the dancers. As he turned, the medallion around his neck caught the light, and David saw the empty ring that marked a Ronnie. He jabbed Mordo in the arm and pointed at the figure. "What?"

"Tha's a Ronnie."

Mordo looked at the figure, then turned back to David. "He's not hurting anybody, Merit. Enjoy your drink 'n' keep your mouth shut." As Mordo put a light to his cigar, David saw that he had a fresh drink in front of him. He put his hand around it, lifted it to his lips and swallowed. As he lowered the glass he saw the forcers in his squad as they streaked toward the disabled cruiser. Men and women flashed into frozen shards of flesh and pink crystals of blood.

"Mordo."

"What's on your mind, Merit?"

"Mordo, those guys. Don't even know their names. Dead."

Mordo's smile vanished. "Don't want to know their names, Merit. Don't make any difference to them, but if you knew who they were it'd make a difference to you. Too much."

Merit felt tears striking the backs of his hands. "Don't even know their names. Give me a damn medal; what'd they get?"

Mordo turned to Kolker. "The kid's watering his booze. Think we better get'm home?"

Kolker nodded and slid out of the booth. He weaved for a

moment, then reached in and pulled Merit out and held him up as Mordo stood and joined them. Mordo threw some credits on the table, then the three started making their way through the crowd to the door. Merit saw the flash of another Ronnie medallion drapped on a heavy chain around the neck of a heavy-set man dressed in a white and gold smock. "God . . . goddamn Ronnies!"

"Shut up, Merit." Mordo faced the Ronnie. "Hero here is just feeling his anti-freeze." The Ronnie came over and stopped in front of the three forcers, blocking their way. Three other men sporting similar medallions moved and stood next to the first.

Kolker waved his hand. "Get out of the way. We don't want any trouble."

The first Ronnie laughed. "I bet you don't, Quad. You don't want to fight unless it's against cripples and babies."

"Step aside."

Merit studied the faces of the four Ronnies, then the tears blurred his vision. "Damn. Don't know their names! Can't even remember their faces!" He lurched toward the nearest Ronnie, grabbed the fellow's medallion and pulled him to the floor as he tried to break the heavy chain. He felt a fist strike just below his left eye, then hard toes kicking at his recently mended ribs. He struggled to his feet, placed a foot on the Ronnie's face, then pulled on the chain. It parted, sending David reeling back into an empty booth. White lights went on in the bar and David drifted off, watching the two sergeants grappling with at least six Ronnies. Images of exploded armor passed in his mind, the darkness of the ejection capsule, a ghostly number 13 floating in front of his face, his guts a hard knot. Rough hands shook him awake and David opened his eyes to see Mordo's face looking back. Mordo's right eye was closed, blood dribbled from his nose, an upper tooth was missing, and the left sleeve of his greens had been torn off. "Mordo, you are a beautiful human being."

Mordo pulled David to his feet. "C'mon, hero. It's time to go home."

David's head fell to one side and he saw Jas Kolker's handsome face, his strong Roman nose swollen and bent to one side. "You too, Kolker. You beautiful human." He looked down and saw the Ronnies among the debris on the floor. "Sure showed goddamn Ronnies." He looked at Kolker, the image stood on its head, then the room went dark.

The next morning, David opened his eyes for an instant, then closed them against the bright light. He lifted his hands and placed them gently on his head, surprised at not finding an anvil parked there. "Well, the hero lives." The voice was female. David shielded his eyes, then opened them. A trim, pleasant-looking woman in lounging trousers and housecoat stood next to his bed holding a glass filled with a dark red liquid.

"Who . . . who're you?" David sat up.

She held out the glass. "Drink this first."

David took the glass. "What is it?"

"Drink."

David tried to sniff at it, discovered that his nasal passages were swollen shut, then he shrugged and drank. The red liquid flamed a path down to his toes, then bounced and torched every extremity on the return trip. "Gah . . . god, what's that?"

The woman sat on the edge of the bed placed the glass on the bed table, then turned and began examining David's face. "Well, there doesn't seem to be any permanent damage." She lowered her hand to her lap and smiled at David. "I'm Della Kolker."

"Sergeant Kolker's wife?"

She nodded. "The way you three came reeling in here last night, you'd think the three of you whipped half the Ronnies on Earth."

David blushed, then smiled sheepishly. "I'm afraid that any whipping that was done wasn't done by me. I guess all I did was start it."

Della Kolker leaned toward the bed table and picked up an empty ring medallion, then placed it on David's lap. "Your trophy."

David looked at the medallion, then shook his head. "I'm sorry, Mrs. Kolker."

"Call me Della, and there's nothing to be sorry about. I've spent the better part of my life patching up Jas and Cos after their midnight wanderings."

"Cos?"

Della looked surprised. "Cos. Cosgrove. You mean you don't know Sergeant Mordo's first name?"

"Cosgrove?"

"That's right, but we've called him Cos since boots."

"Della, were you in boots with those two?"

She nodded. "But I'm not in the Force now. Not since Jas and I got married."

David looked over to the other bed in the guest room. It was empty and neatly made. "Where's Mordo... Cos?"

"He and Jas left for the PR building two hours ago. Something big is up, but I don't know what." Della saw David staring at her and she laughed. "Why are you looking at me like that?"

David blushed again. "Sorry. I didn't mean to stare. It's just hard to think of you being in boots with those two lifers. Isn't there some rule against forcers getting married to each other?"

Della nodded. "That's why I left the Force. Then, when Jas was assigned to PR, we decided to take a chance." She smiled. "You have a girl?"

"Sort of. From boots. Her name's Ann."

She frowned, then placed a gentle hand on David's shoulder. "With Jas out of combat now, I'm not too worried, but you be careful, David. Don't open yourself up for a big hurt."

"It's all right. She's with the Thirty-first Division on Luna."

"That seems safe enough." The apartment's doorbell rang, and Della rose and left the room, closing the door behind her. David took advantage of the opportunity to get up and get dressed. After returning from the bathroom, he found Mordo stuffing clothes into his bag. Mordo looked up.

"Get your kit together, hero. All furloughs've been cancelled."

David pulled on and sealed his green uniform blouse. "What's up?"

"The RATs have taken a planet called Dismas III. It's a nothing place but it puts them within easy striking distance of Earth, if they can ever get the place built up. You and me are detached right now, so we're being sent to the Twelfth Division. That's part of the lashup going to Dismas III."

David put his bag on his bed, opened a dresser and began

stuffing in his gear. "What happened to the forcers on Dismas III?"

Mordo shook his head. "They don't know for sure. They sound like they were wiped out to the last dogfoot. The RATs hit hard and fast." David turned to go to the door. Mordo stood and shook his head. "Don't go in right yet. Jas's been assigned to the Twelfth. They should be alone for a while."

David went back to his bed, buckled his bag shut, then sat down. Mordo finished with his bag, then pulled a long black cigar from his pocket and jammed it in his mouth. David heard soft crying coming from the other side of the door. Mordo pulled the cigar from his face and pointed it at David. "Well, hero, it looks like we'll be touring together. What do you think of that?"

David shrugged. "It's all right with me."

Mordo frowned, listened, then nodded toward the door. "Let's go."

David picked up his bag and followed Mordo through the door. Della was standing in the center of the small living room drying her eyes. Jas stood at the entrance to their bedroom and cocked his head toward Mordo. "Cos, you want to come in here and give me a hand?"

Mordo raised his brows, glanced at David, then back at Jas. "Sure." He patted Della on the shoulder then went into the room with Jas.

David lowered his bag to the floor and looked at Della. "Is there something I can do?"

Della walked over and placed her hands on David's shoulders. "I asked Jas to leave us alone for awhile, David. There's something I have to tell you."

"Tell me?" David frowned. "Tell me what?"

She lifted her right hand and stroked David's cheek. "It's the Thirty-first Division, David. It was on Dismas III when it fell."

David stared at her as he felt his skin prickle. "No. That can't be, Della. I told you the Thirty-first is on permanent station on Luna . . ." He shook his head. "The Thirty-first is on Luna. I got a letter from Ann . . ." He studied Della's eyes, then read the truth there. He half-closed his eyes, then removed her hand from his face. "I'm all right. I'm all right." His cheek twitched as he turned toward the apartment door and picked up his bag. "Mordo. You two going to take all day?"

... Her muscles, flat and hard from training, were softened by the filmy bedgown. She held out her arms and whirled in the tiny room, the hem of the gown spiraling out from her hips. "I am alive! So alive, David!"

He stretched in the bed, the lone sheet covering his body to his waist. His eyes drank in the whirling image. "You're not worried, then?"

She stopped, ran to the bed and threw herself on top of David. Her lips found his. When she raised her head, she looked into his eyes. "Nobody—the RATs, the Force—nobody can end what we have."

He reached up his right hand and pulled her head down to his lips while his left hand glided down her back...

"Corporal?"

"Oh, David, I love you..."

"Corporal?"

David opened his eyes as he felt a hand shaking his shoulder. He looked up and saw a dark figure standing over him, silhouetted against the dim light of the bunker. "What is it?"

"It's your cycle on watch, Corporal."

David sat up and rubbed the sleep from his eyes. "Has the CP moved?"

"No, but the watch lines have been moved around some."

"Is the rest of the watch up yet?"

The dark figure nodded. "They're assembling in front of the Captain's bunker. You get to wake up Mordo."

David nodded and the figure turned and slipped through the bunker's blackout sheet. He swung his legs to the dirt floor, hobbled over to the faintly glowing table light, then put his right foot on the crate that served as a chair. He pulled back the shreds of his trouser leg and examined the dressing around his thigh. It was dirty, but still intact. A figure wrapped in a heat sheet rolled over on the ledge next to the table. "Time?"

David nodded. "You're sergeant of the guard."

Mordo swung his legs to the floor as David removed his foot from the crate. "How's the leg?"

"I don't think it's infected." David reached out, picked up his gear and began strapping it on. "No damn medical supplies, no damn power packs for the armor, no damn food—just what'n the hell are we supposed to throw against the RATs, Mordo?"

Mordo pushed his heat sheet aside and strapped on his gear. "Just keep pluggin', hero."

David picked up his rifle and checked the charge. "Eight percent. Just great." He looked up at Mordo. "I don't know why I'm carrying this thing. What am I supposed to do; beat the RATs to death with it?"

Mordo smiled and shook his head. "Too light for that, Merit. Stick 'em in the eye maybe."

"Mordo, if the Thirty-first ran the defense of this damn hunk of rock the way Third Fleet ran the invasion, it's no wonder they were wiped out."

Mordo stood and headed toward the blackout sheet. "Come on, field marshal. Let's get our animals on line and see if we can get some advance warning for when we get run down."

David followed Mordo through the blackout sheet, then halted a moment for his eyes to adjust to the dark. In the four months since the invasion, the stars above Dismas III had become familiar enough to the 12th Force Division for them to be divided into constellations and given obscene names. David looked at The Impossible Act. Jas Kolker had named that one a month before getting killed as the RATs overran the 192nd Force Regiment of the 12th Division. David felt a jab in his arm and he turned and followed Mordo down the debris-littered trench to the captain's bunker.

As they approached the bunker, the familiar whine of a motion-detection probe caused both of them to freeze. In the dark, David could see the dozen forcers that made up the watch squatting around the bunker's entrance. The whine died out and David squatted next to a dark shape as Mordo went into the bunker, reappearing with the A company commander. The captain turned to Merit. "How's the leg?"

"Fine, Captain. How's yours?"

The captain turned to the watch. "You people gather around." The men and women huddled in the darkness moved closer. "All right. Be on your toes tonight. Just before Dismas peeks over the horizon, Division is going to put on a push and try and break this stranglehold the Sixty-third RAT Division has on us. Ronnie is getting in reinforcements and if we're caught here, we're last week's dogmeat."

"Captain," said a dark figure, "what about *our* reinforcements?"

The captain shook his head. "Orbital support is just barely holding its own and can't spare a bean. You know that Ronnie captured the time-step receiving station for this sector, which means we have to hang on for at least five more weeks. But Ronnie is in bad shape too, until those reinforcements arrive. So, if we're going to break out, it's now or never."

Mordo turned his head toward the captain. "Captain?"

"What?"

"The listening posts."

"Right." The captain faced the dark shapes squatting around him. "You people on listening posts, we need every squeak and groan you can pick up. Don't use your judgment; report everything. Copy?" The dark shapes mumbled their understanding of the orders. "All right, move out." He turned to David. "The CP is in the same place, but the lines have been moved. Mordo has the plan."

David nodded as the captain turned and went back into the bunker. He took the scrap of paper from Mordo's outstretched hand, then followed the string of dark shapes moving down the trench to post the night's guard.

The last post established, David climbed into a hole with one of the guards and looked over the edge at the rocky, twisted landscape below. He shook his head. With those rocks there, half the population of Earth could sneak up on them undetected. He turned to the guard. The forcer was examining the tiny screen of a nightscope. "Anything?"

"No." The voice sounded familiar.

"Antoine?"

"That's right." She turned from the scope and placed a hand on David's arm. He shrugged it off.

"Keep your mind on your scope, Antoine."

She turned back. "Why don't you call me Carla?"

"You know why."

"Because I'm from Rhana?"

David shook his head. "I didn't know you were from Rhana. I just don't need any complications—not with a forcer."

Antoine studied the field through her scope for a moment. "You're tied down too tight, Merit. One of these days you're going to come apart."

David bit his lip. "Not now; not here. Now stuff a sock in it." His gaze swept the landscape again, then he looked up and saw The Impossible Act, wondering where Della Kolker was, and if she even knew. He shook his head and turned to Antoine. "The other animals give you a rough time—being from Rhana?"

She shook her head. "There's a lot of us in the Force. We're just like anybody else."

"That's good." He heard her sniff. "What is it?"

"Good." She spoke the word through tears. "Out there is the Sixty-third RAT Division, Merit. I have two brothers—Dane and Stes—in it. At least I did. I don't know now."

David lifted a hand, hovered it over the forcer's shoulder for a split second, then lowered it to his side. "My father and mother are Ronnies. Back on Earth."

Antoine snorted. "Armchair revolutionaries. At least you don't have to worry about them." Her body stiffened. "Merit, I have something on the scope."

Merit pushed her aside and peered at the tiny red screen. Faint heat readings came from the rocks at the base of the hill. He tabbed his helmet communicator. "CP, this is post five."

"CP. What is it, Merit?"

"Mordo, the post-five scope is picking up heat about four hundred meters away." He checked the power indicator on the instrument. "The charge on this thing reads under zero percent, so I don't know if it's RATs or noise."

Mordo crackled through the headset. "Don't take a chance. I'll call it in, and you keep your ears open. As soon as you know for sure it's RATs, you and the guard bugg on back here after you call in."

"Right." David tabbed off, then studied the screen again. The image grew even fainter until he couldn't distinguish the heat images from the rocks. He turned, tapped Antoine on the shoulder, then pointed toward the rocks. "The set's dead. Keep a sharp eye out." He pointed at her rifle. "What kind of charge you have on that thing?"

"Eleven percent."

"Let me have it." David exchanged rifles with Antoine, then rested the weapon on the lip of the hole. He felt his eyes bug at trying to see the unseeable. Shadows appeared to blend and wave, then the rocks below erupted in a wave of beamer fire directed at the high ground. The dirt in front of Merit jumped as he hosed down two arcs, then threw the weapon aside, charge exhausted. He tapped his communicator. "Mordo, post five! This is it! Looks like the main body is heading toward post seven."

"What strength?"

"Battalion at least. Probably more!"

"Merit, you grab that guard and get your asses out of there!"

Merit tabbed off, then turned toward Antoine. "Let's go." She was crumpled against the wall of the hole. He squatted next to her and shook her shoulder. "Antoine, we have to move!"

She rolled over, gasping. David could see her utility blouse smoking below her left breast. He pulled open her utility blouse, found the sucking chest wound, and pulled the first-aid pack from his belt. Quickly placing a sheet of sterile plastic over the hole, he lifted her to a sitting position, pulled her blouse out of her trousers, then wrapped a bandage around her chest to hold the seal in place. After tying the ends, he pressed the tube of antibiotic/anesthetic against her arm, then placed an arm beneath her knees and his other behind her back. He stood, and found himself staring into the muzzle of a RAT beamer. He looked up at the dark face. "Very good, Quad. Bet you got straight A's in first aid." He waved the muzzle up and down. "Climb on out of there. The war's over for you."

As the sun called Dismas washed the cruel landscape with its hellish orange light, the Rhanian guards that had been nothing but shadows all night became dust-coated men and women, much like the haggard forcers they guarded. The thirty-odd Force prisoners sat huddled between two rocky outcroppings. David sat crosslegged, Carla Antoine's head nestled on his left leg, his heat sheet covering her to her neck. He shook his head to clear it, then checked his first-aid pouch. He had one junkshot left. Carla's pack was empty. "David?" she spoke softly.

He placed a hand against her cheek. "I'm here."

"David . . . wha's goin' happen to us?"

David smiled. "That junk making you happy?"

She giggled, then winced against the pain. "Not bad."

He touched his fingers to her lips. "Stuff a sock in it. You shouldn't be talking."

He looked up as Carla seemed to drift into spastic sleep. He recognized none of the other prisoners, although they all wore 12th Division insignia. A Rhanian officer came down from one of the rocky outcroppings and stood in the center of the group of prisoners. His uniform was filthy and torn. His eyes sported the classic thousand-yard stare. "Who's in charge here?"

David looked around, and the only prisoner ranking him was a sergeant who was staring blankly into depths only he could see. David looked up at the officer. "I guess I am."

"Name?"

"Merit." The officer looked around for a moment, then turned his gaze toward David.

"Merit, your bunch will join a larger group of prisoners when they get here. Keep everybody quiet until then."

David looked at Carla Antoine, then back at the officer. "What about the wounded?"

"We have our own wounded to worry about. You'll have to haul those that can't make it on their own." He turned and left. David watched several RATs making their way through the prisoners, examining their faces. One of the RATs stood and called another. "Sergeant! Sergeant Antoine, what about this one?"

The one called rushed over and looked down at the forcer indicated by the RAT private. He shook his head, then turned and began examining the other prisoners. David called out. "You! Your name Antoine?"

The sergeant stopped, looked at David, then slowly nodded his head. David looked at the sleeping head in his lap. "This is your sister, Carla."

The sergeant rushed over and squatted next to Carla. He

reached out his hands to grab her, but David grabbed his wrists. "Don't. She's got a sucking chest wound. She needs medical attention."

The sergeant stood, looked around, then shouted at a RAT medic. "You! Get over here!"

The medic rushed over. "Sergeant?"

"Get this forcer on one of the evac vans. Check this dressing while you're at it."

"Sergeant, we have our own wounded to look after."

The RAT sergeant stood, leveled his beamer at the medic, then fixed the fellow with a steady gaze. The medic dropped next to Carla and began checking the dressing. The sergeant looked from his sister to David. "Thank you, Corporal."

David cocked his head toward several other wounded prisoners. "What about them? They can't make it very far."

The sergeant looked over the group of prisoners, then turned back toward Merit. "I'll see what I can do." He noticed his sister's eyes were open and he squatted next to her. "Carla."

She coughed. "Hi, Stes." She turned her head slightly toward David. "He saved my life, Stes. Keep your goons off him."

The sergeant smiled, then nodded. He looked up at David. "I'll get your wounded on vans and back to the hospital. Anything else?"

David shook his head. The RAT sergeant stood and nudged the medic with the toe of his boot. "Well?"

The medic nodded. "She'll be all right, Sergeant, but we have our own wounded on the vans."

"Then kick off everyone who can still walk. Everyone of these Forcers who can't make it on their own is to be put on the vans. Understand?"

The medic glared at Merit, then nodded. "Yes, Sergeant."

The sergeant squatted next to his sister and placed his hand against her cheek. "Carla, I have to go. This clown will take care of you. Think you'll be all right?"

Carla nodded, then closed her eyes. David nodded at the sergeant. "Thanks."

The sergeant turned toward the RAT medic. "She dies, you die; understand?"

The medic glared at the sergeant, then returned to the

dressing. "You want to get out of my way, pig, and let me finish saving this girl?"

The sergeant stood, turned, then walked off.

The Ronnies had a name for Dismas III. As they stumbled under guard toward the Ronnie camp, the Force prisoners picked it up. Slag. Some of them repeated the name several times, Slag, wondering why they hadn't thought of it. As the sun sizzled off the rocks, nothing could be more obvious as a name for the planet. Slag. It fit the tongue.

In a daze, after five hours of marching through the rocky desert, David noted that the Ronnies guarding them were a ragged bunch. No armor, and as hungry as the forcers they guarded. At one point, the guards shoved and shouted the column off of the road to allow a column of spanking new vans to go in the opposite direction. David's heart sank as he saw that the vans were filled with fresh RATs in spotless armor. Ronnie's reinforcements had arrived.

"Corporal?"

David looked to his right and saw a dust-covered, blood-streaked Forcer stumbling under the weight of another, the wounded one's arm draped and clamped across the shoulders of the first. David moved to the other side of the wounded man, took his right arm, and took his weight upon himself. "Why didn't you get him into the medic vans?"

The Forcer staggered around, then turned to David. "The Ronnies with my bunch weren't so understanding. Chonnie's only got a burn in his gut, so they figure he's walking wounded."

David studied the forcer, realizing as something of a shock that she was a she. "What's this guy to you?"

"Husband."

David shook his head. "You know better than that. Both of you know better than that."

She laughed without making a sound, then turned her face toward David. Fresh tears cut tan paths through the dust on her cheeks. "We had our moment, Corporal. Whatever else happens, we had our...moment."

David looked over a couple of heads and saw one of the Ronnies, rifle slung, slogging it away along with the column. "Hey!"

The Ronnie lifted his head. "Quiet. No talking."

"What about a few minutes' rest? Some of these guys are near dead."

The guard nodded toward the front. "Almost there. Rest then."

David turned his head toward the front and looked over the heads of the Forcers in front of him. Ahead he could make out the wide spread of a military camp. The sky above it crackled with the pale yellow of overlapping repulsor fields. Again the column was ordered to the side of the road to let more armor-packed vans head in the opposite direction. David took a new purchase on the wounded Forcer's arm, then concentrated on putting one foot in front of the other. Endless footsteps later, the column was through the field, in the center of the camp, and behind wire. David sank to the ground and slept.

. . . leave after boots. David walked up the steps to his parents' house and rang the bell. The door opened and his mother's face filled his vision. "Go! Go away from my house, baby-killer! Go!" She raised her hands and tried to claw his face. David staggered back, shocked. "Baby-killer!" He stumbled backwards down the steps and stood open-mouthed on the sidewalk, half-noticing the heads of neighbors poking out of windows. He turned and walked away from the house, his mother's screams still in his ears.

"David! David!" He heard his father's voice, but David didn't look back.

David sat up, shook the dream from his mind, then noticed it was night and that someone had covered him with a heat sheet. Through the pale yellow of the repulsor field overhead, he could just make out The Impossible Act. He lowered his gaze to see a row of lighted posts following the wire around the Force prisoners. A figure squatted next to him and nodded toward the lighted posts. "If a man was to step between two of those posts, there wouldn't be enough left of him to make a sandwich." He faced David. "Ira Hayes. I'm a medic with the one-two-four Regiment, Twelfth Division."

David stared at the light posts. "Merit. First Battalion of the Ninety-second."

Hayes nodded. "What I hear, there aren't enough of you boys left to make up a half-strength fire team."

David snapped his head toward the medic. "What do you want, Hayes?"

"How's the leg?"

David reached under the heat blanket and felt for the wound. It was covered with a thin, flexible film. "You do that?"

"Uh huh. The Ronnie docs loaded me up with brand-new supplies and I've been like a kid under a Christmas tree. Fresh dressings, Plas-fil, knockout junk, the works."

David nodded. "Fine. It feels fine."

Hayes nodded. "The inflammation'll be down by morning. Must have smarted some to walk on that."

David pulled the sheet aside. "Ronnie hand out any chow?"

Hayes nodded and stood, pulling David to his feet. "C'mon. I know the headwaiter." The two walked between the still shapes of sleeping prisoners toward a dull red light. As they came upon it, the light became a small stove. Sitting cross-legged between the stove and a pile of boxes sat a bald Forcer. Hayes nodded. "Kazik, you want to see if you can ruin some chow for Merit here?"

Merit and Hayes sat down next to the tiny stove while Kazik opened a container, withdrew a can, then touched the can to the stove. Merit raised his eyebrows as Kazik held the can toward him. He took the container, pulled open the cap, then watched the steam escape from it. Kazik laughed. "These little RAT stoves cook it fast." He leaned forward and pointed at the still steaming contents of the can. "That's what you'll be if you step in between those light posts surrounding the camp." He pointed at the stove. "This is a low-power version, but the same thing."

Merit pulled his eating utensil from his belt, stuck it in the can, then put a spoonful of the steaming concoction into his mouth. His face wrinkled as he gnawed at the stew. "This stuff tastes like Hell."

Kazik shrugged. "Ronnie likes it."

Merit chewed on another mouthful, then put the can aside. He looked at Kazik, then turned to Hayes. "You see anyone in the compound from the Thirty-first Division?"

Hayes shook his head. "Nope. They'd be in the other compound."

"Other compound?"

"Yeah, the permanent camp. We'll be stuck there after processing." Hayes pointed toward a slight rise in the ground behind a long, low building. "It's over there." He lowered his hand. "What we got in here are a few Forcers from the Hundred and Twenty-fourth Regiment and what's left of the Ninety-second—all Twelfth Division. We'll know better tomorrow, but it looks like the other divisions managed to make it back into the hills."

Kazik snorted. "So what? I've seen enough new RAT armor heading toward the lines to chew up and spit out the rest of our so-called invasion force."

Merit looked at the stove and frowned. "If they can hold on for another five weeks, the relief force will be here. If they can keep the landing zone open—"

Kazik snorted again. "You can't fight beamers with rocks, Merit." He stood and half-waved his hand. "I'm calling it a night." The Forcer stumbled away a few paces, then pulled his heat sheet and curled up on the ground, covering himself.

Merit looked at Hayes. "Not exactly gung-ho, is he?"

Hayes nodded. "We got to face it, Merit. We've been whipped. There's not a Forcer in here that doesn't have a wound of some kind or other, and you haven't seen the stuff Ronnie has been putting down." Hayes shook his head. "It's not going to hurt Ronnie's position at the bargaining table to have just wiped out four Force divisions. Not to mention being within strike distance of Earth."

"Hayes, what's this about bargaining?"

"You haven't heard, I guess. Truce talks might start up. I guess the Force is getting too close to Rhana for Ronnie's comfort." Hayes pushed himself to his feet. "I guess I'll call it a night, too."

The medic walked off, and David fixed his gaze on the dull red of the stove light.

A week later, David was ushered into the building separating the two camps, along with a number of other prisoners. In line, he leaned against a wall, studying the RATs' entrance to the building. Beyond the entrance, under heavy guard, was a string of deenergized light posts. He felt a jab in his arm. "You are next,

Quad." He looked up and faced a Rhanian assault trooper aiming a beamer in his direction. He pushed away from the wall, turned left, then entered a small room. Seated next to the opposite door behind a desk was a RAT major. Next to the major was seated an operator before a computer terminal. The major looked up at David. "Name and serial number, Corporal."

David looked at the two armed guards leaning against the wall next to the table, then he turned back to the major. He noticed that the major's left sleeve was empty. "Merit, David E. Serial number USE117 3495 6692."

The major nodded at the operator who punched the information into the terminal. A moment passed, then the operator turned to the major and shook his head. The major looked at David. "Very well. You're clean. According to the agreement we have with the USE, the Force will be notified that you are alive and a prisoner of war. They will make the appropriate notifications to your relatives, if you have any." The major nodded at David's guard. "Next."

"Major, what did you mean, I'm clean?"

The major sighed, then leaned back in his chair. "No crimes have been registered against you or your unit by our forces or authorities. As long as you obey the rules here, you should remain clean. Colonel Wells will explain all of that." The major nodded again at the guard and David was pushed toward the closed door. It opened as he approached and two guards motioned him into the next compound. Directly in front of him was a small temporary shelter. David's guard nodded toward it. "Wells is in there. Move out."

David took several steps before he realized that none of the guards were following him. Before he entered the building, he noticed that the Force prisoners he passed wore Thirty-first Division insignia. He turned around, saw the three RAT guards watching him, then he entered the building. Immediately he came to a stiff attention as he noticed the shoulder stripes of a full Force colonel. Wells looked up. "At ease. Name?"

"Sir, Corporal Merit, David E."

"Relax, Corporal. The parade ground is a long way from

here." He cleared his throat. "I'm the ranking POW in this camp, and it's my responsibility to see to it that the POWs follow the rules."

David frowned. "Rules?"

"That's right. In essence there is only one rule: Don't make trouble. That means no escapes, no sabotage, no riots, no nothin'. Read me?"

David studied the colonel. The Force officer wore Thirty-first Division insignia. "I'm not certain I do, Colonel. Isn't it a POW's duty to try to escape?"

Wells studied David's face. "Son, I have over eight hundred men and women from my division under medical care at the RAT hospital facility. We made a deal—"

"A *deal*!"

"That's right, Corporal! A deal. We get food, medical attention for our wounded, and treaty communications to the USE. If we make trouble, we lose all that."

David closed his eyes for a moment, then looked at Wells. "Colonel, is this building under surveillance?"

Wells shook his head. "No. What I am giving you is the straight line. You follow it; understood?"

"Sir, isn't it part of the officer's oath to—"

Wells stood. "You forget your place, Forcer! Now, shag out of here and get settled in."

"Colonel, maybe you've forgotten *our* place. What about the pressure on the Third and Twenty-second Divisions? What about the rest of *my* outfit? If we raised some hell here—"

"Merit. You are a POW, and as such you are bound by oath to follow my orders. Those orders are for you to go out there and do nothing. Just survive. The war's over for us."

"Colonel—"

"That's all, Merit."

David turned and left the small building. He stopped a few paces from the door and studied the POWs standing around the compound. Several had set up light housekeeping, turning their heat sheets into puptents, lines of tattered wash hanging still in the hot air. Another Forcer, squatting in the shade of the building, looked up at Merit. "Go thou and do likewise."

Merit looked at the forcer and noticed that the fellow was with the Thirty-first. "You know a Forcer—a girl—Watkins. Ann Watkins?"

The fellow shook his head. "Out of the twelve thousand Forcers in the Thirty-first, we got maybe fifteen hundred here in the compound and about half that number in the RAT hospital." He pointed a thumb back toward the RAT processing building. "The only ones who know for sure are the Ronnies, and they won't tell."

Merit looked at the building, then back at the forcer. "What about you?"

"What about me?"

"You and the others—the war over for you?"

The Forcer stood, shook his head, then laughed. "Those are the orders. Sound good to me." He walked off.

As with all routines, after two weeks of life in the camp, it was as though life had always been that way. The rumblings and flashes far to the south became less the dying struggles of the Third Fleet Invasion Force and became, instead, something of the environment, like the stars or sun. The POWs did not notice it. Expedient friendships and circles developed, and in the absence of officers, makeshift authority rooted in who was strongest and who passed out the food. David remained clear of it all, spending nights watching the flashes in the south, and spending the days searching the Thirty-first Division survivors for some word about Ann Watkins. By the third week, the flashes in the south grew fainter, captured forcers from the 3rd and 22nd Divisions began processing in, and David had stopped searching for Watkins.

He would sit by the light posts, unblinking, flicking tiny stones into the heat field, watching the pebbles burst into tiny clouds of dust. The prisoners had found several uses for the fence. Trash thrown into it became little more than fine ash. For those who could not adapt, it offered a fast, painless route to oblivion. Two had chosen the fence's fire. For those who adapted too well, preying on their comrades stealing food, a rough shove at the proper moment served the camp's evolving brand of justice. But David noticed nothing, except that some of the pebbles that he flicked into the field did not burst. Instead, they sailed through and landed on the opposite side. He studied the pebbles before throwing them. Tan, black, gray-white and brown burst in the field; green and green-yellow did not. He picked up a number of the green and green-yellow pebbles and studied them.

"Merit?"

He looked up to see the Force medic Hayes looking down at him. "What is it, Hayes?" He returned his gaze to the pebbles in his hand.

"Major Tavis wants you to report to the rathouse." Tavis, the one-armed major, hadn't grown a nickname but his office had.

"What's he want?"

Hayes shrugged. "He doesn't confide in me."

David pushed himself to his feet, then held out his hand. "Hayes, look at these." He dropped the pebbles into the medic's hand. Hayes looked at them, then shrugged.

"So what? These things are all over the place."

"What are they; what kind of mineral?"

"I don't know. Why?"

David's face remained without expression. "Just curious. Know anybody who knows anything about rocks?"

Hayes scratched the back of his head. "I think Kazik does. I'll drop 'em on him and see what he says." The medic moved off and David got to his feet and headed toward the rathouse.

David stood in front of the RAT major's desk. "You wanted to see me?"

Tavis rubbed his eyes with his right hand, then looked up at David. "Who are you?"

"Merit, David E."

Tavis nodded, leaned forward and examined a slip of paper. He grimaced, then looked back at David. "Merit, we've just gotten word from the USE Force . . . It's your parents. They're dead. I'm sorry."

David looked blankly at the major. "Dead?"

Tavis nodded. "I'm sorry, Merit. Terribly sorry."

"How?"

Tavis pushed the slip of paper with his finger. "It's all in there."

David picked up the paper, turned it around and read of the madness that swept certain parts of Earth with the fall of Dismas III and the subsequent failure of the Third Fleet to take it back from the RATs. Window-breaking, paint slopped on house fronts, beatings, and in several cases Rhanian sympathizers were dragged from their homes, tortured and put to death. Several arrests had been made after the deaths of Mr. and Mrs. Arthur Merit of . . .

David looked at Tavis as he crumpled the paper. "Dead."

Tavis shook his head. "There's nothing to say, Merit. I wish there were." Tavis nodded at the guard who had escorted David. The guard took David's arm, but David turned to Tavis. "Major?"

"Yes?"

"Major, I know you don't have to, but would you do me a favor?"

Tavis looked into David's eyes, then averted his glance. "If I can."

David nodded at the computer terminal. "Can you find out what happened to a Forcer—Ann Watkins? She was with the Thirty-first Division."

The operator being absent, Tavis pushed his chair over and began pushing buttons. "I can't guarantee anything. The only ones we have on record are those who were captured or identified in the field . . . Ah, there . . ." Tavis turned and frowned at David. "What was she to you, Merit?"

"Was?"

Tavis nodded slowly. "Yes. She's dead. What was she to you?"

David hung his head. "A friend. Just a friend." He looked up. "Does it say how?"

Tavis nodded. "She and seven other POWs were tried and executed for war crimes."

David stared at the major. His skin prickled and red flashed before his eyes as he felt the blood thumping through his veins. "War crimes?" He laughed once, then narrowed his eyes. *"War crimes?"*

"She and seven others attempted an escape, killing two guards in the process. Under our military law, that is a crime." Tavis nodded at the guard. The guard pulled David from the room and deposited him in the compound. Without noticing anyone or anything, he returned and stood at his place before the fence. Through it he could see a RAT company in combat armor loading onto a column of vans.

"Pretty." David turned to see Hayes standing next to him. David looked back at the RATs.

"They can fight."

"So can we, when we have something to fight with."

Hayes raised an eyebrow. "Got some ideas, Corporal?" Hayes turned his gaze toward the RAT company. "For all practical purposes, there is no more Twelfth Division, and what's left of the Third and Twenty-second is in the hills with no food, damn little ammunition, and about as many Forcers left as we got behind the fence here. Between us and them is that brand-spankin'-new RAT division, not to mention the original three divisions."

David nodded. "That's it, then."

"That's what?"

"We've got 'em surrounded."

Hayes raised his eyebrows, then nodded. "Yes, Corporal, now that I think about it, I guess we do." He held out a handful of green pebbles. "How do these figure in?"

David picked one of the pebbles out of the medic's hand and flicked it through the fence. It landed on the other side of the field, unharmed. "That's how."

Kazik sat before his stove and turned the dark green pebble over in his hands. "Like I said to Hayes, you're always taking a chance trying to identify a mineral on another planet with Earth tests. But I'd say it's serpentine. It looks like it, feels like it, and it's the right hardness—can't remember any more of the tests. They're lab tests anyway."

David squatted across the stove from Kazik. "That's just a name to me. What is it?"

Kazik scratched the top of his head, then held up a finger. "You know what asbestos is?"

"Of course."

"Well, that's what this is, except it's not in fibers like asbestos. You know that ceramic glop that we smear in the armor?"

"Heat shielding."

Kazik nodded, then tossed the pebble up and caught it. "This is one of the ingredients..." He frowned, then dropped the pebble onto the contact plate of his stove. The pebble heated then cracked into several pieces.

David frowned. "You said the stove and the light posts work off the same stuff. These peb—"

Kazik rubbed his chin. "That's serpentine, all right. I just remembered the test." He looked at David. "Probably why the armor explodes when a beamer catches it for too long."

"But it does afford some protection for short periods?"

"It'll do that."

David looked down into his handful of pebbles. "Kazik, how can we make shields out of this stuff? I figure if we can get this stuff between the light posts and ourselves, we can break out of here."

Kazik picked up a few pebbles and studied them. "Maybe we could grind them up. They're soft enough. Then mix them with something—" He grinned, pushed himself to his feet, then looked around. "See any guards?"

David stood, examined the area surrounding them, then shook his head. "Not this far from the rathouse." He looked back at Kazik. "Why?"

Kazik pulled his heat sheet from his belt, then held out his hand. "Give me your heat sheet."

David handed his over, then Kazik wandered off among the POWs, returning in a few moments with three more heat sheets. He sat down next to the stove, folded one of the heat sheets into quarters, then wrapped it over his right foot, tying the loose ends around his knee.

"You figure on coating the heat sheets with the stuff? Won't it just crack and fall off?"

"Just watch." Kazik wrapped his left foot up to the knee, then spread out his three remaining heat sheets into a triple thickness. He stood, wrapped the triple thickness about his body, then walked toward the fence.

"Hey, Kazik!" David rushed to the fence, but before he could reach it Kazik had covered his head, then stepped through. On the other side of the fence, he opened the sheets far enough to grin at David, then he covered up and stepped back through.

As Kazik uncovered, David turned to the POWs in the immediate area. "All of you, keep quiet about this." He turned back to Kazik. "You zhatskull! You could have been killed!"

Kazik shucked the sheets and shook his head. "The heat sheets. They're lined with a flexible asbestos colloid. It gets warm going through, but that's all."

David pursed his lips, then shook his head. "Idiot, what if those sheets worked the same as the containers on the food? They don't even get warm, but everything inside gets roasted!"

Kazik looked at the ground and blanched. "I . . . I didn't even think—"

"I'll say you didn't." David picked up one of the heat sheets and examined it. "The covering along the edge is shot, but other than that it looks good for several more runs." He lifted up a corner and it crumbled away in his hand. "This corner must have flapped up when you went through. The fabric the lining was bonded to is gone." David wet his lips, then looked at Kazik. "See how many of these things you can scare up before nightfall, and be sure they are all folded with the linings out. Understand?"

Kazik nodded. "Where'll you be?"

David's eyes narrowed. "Putting together a small army."

Late that night, the last member of the recon party safely back across the line, David squatted, forming part of the ring of eleven Forcers who made up the party. David turned to Sergeant Chin. "What about the artillery?"

She smiled. "Easy. About half the heavy beamers are mounted on hover platforms and have self-contained power units. They have four separate power generators also mounted on hover platforms. Everything else is on wheels."

David nodded. "What about security?"

"Seven one-man stations pulling five-hour shifts. No remote equipment; nothing but eyeballs."

David turned to Kazik. "Food?"

Kazik shook his head. "There's no security on the commissary, but everything's on wheels. I'll need a hover platform and a couple of squads to load it. That'll take time, too."

"How long?"

Kazik shrugged. "With twenty Forcers, maybe two, two and a half hours."

David shook his head. "Too much time. Can we cut it down with more manpower?"

Kazik shook his head. "With more bodies, they'd just be getting in each other's way."

"Kazik, after the shooting starts you have to be out of there in no more than twenty minutes."

Kazik shrugged. "We could drive the vans up on hover platforms, but I don't know if the RAT platforms have enough lift for that. I'd need a platform for each van. Ten of them if we're talking about the entire compound breaking out."

David turned to another Forcer. "Otobe?"

"Right now there are thirty-two platforms sitting in the park. We'll need twenty to move bodies. I can let Kazik have ten."

David nodded. "Good. Now, about light weapons—"

Otobe held up his hand. "Corporal, what about the repulsor shields? We're not getting out from under this umbrella with those screens on unless we go on wheels."

David looked around the circle of faces. "I checked the shield projection battery. We can't touch it. A full platoon on watch, remote equipment, a reserve company standing by." He looked around the circle of faces. "But we aren't going to break out." Several of the dark figures muttered briefly. "Listen up. Once we break out, the RATs'll expect us to try and make it to our own lines. Even without the screens we couldn't make it through a couple of RAT divisions sitting and waiting for us." He looked around the circle of faces again. "We're going in the opposite direction." He pointed to his left. "Up there, into those low hills."

Otobe looked back, then faced David. "That is still under the shields."

David nodded. "First, we can get there fast and dig in before the RATs can react. Then, with the artillery covering the RAT landing site, nothing more comes in. Third, we won't leave enough under the shield to throw against us, and so Ronnie will have to pull troops off the line to throw against us, taking the pressure off of the Third and Twenty-second Divisions."

Otobe nodded. "That will keep our own landing area open for when the reinforcements arrive..."—he nodded again—"...and they can't bring anything heavy against us without turning off the shields unless they bring it in on wheels."

David leaned his elbows on his knees and clasped his hands. "And if they turn off the shields, our orbital support will fry them." He studied the faces in the circle. "I didn't want to lay out this much of the plan so soon, but you have to know sometime. Still, we can't afford word of this getting to Wells or to the RATs,"

Another Forcer held up her hand. "Merit, in this bunch we have two sergeants, three corporals, a lance corporal and the rest privates."

"So?"

The forcer shrugged. "I don't know. I think I'd feel a little better about this if we had a few officers in on it."

"The only officer we ever see is Colonel Wells. The rest are in another area. We'll try and bust them out when we go, but we can't get to them before then." David turned to another Forcer. "Now, about the light weapons..."

The next morning David was startled awake by the sounds of angry shouting. He sprang to his feet and saw a double line of RATs working their way through the POWs—collecting heat sheets. Colonel Wells and the RAT Major Tavis walked behind them.

Later that morning, after being dragged there by two RAT guards, David stood in front of Colonel Wells' desk. "Merit, there is something you don't seem to understand. You are a corporal—a stinking dogfoot who takes orders and keeps his mouth shut. I am the ranking Force officer in this camp—not you. Is that clear now?"

David, standing at attention, looked down at Wells, then returned his gaze to the wall above the Colonel's head. "It's clear."

"It's clear, *what*?"

David looked down and into the officer's eyes. "It's clear, *sir*. What is not clear is how you ever became an officer."

Wells averted his glance, drummed his fingers on the desk, then looked back at David. "Merit, I'm going to let that pass. In boots you were trained to think like that—to not know when you've been whipped." Wells leaned forward and pointed at David. "But this isn't boots, Merit. That gung-ho, over-the-top stuff is out of place here. There are seventeen hundred Forcers in the RAT hospital who will suffer if you do manage to succeed at whatever crazy scheme you're thinking of. We've been licked, Merit. Get that through your thick skull, go out into the compound, find a piece of sand, stick your ass on it and keep it there! Do you understand that?"

David nodded. "But I don't think you want to know what it is that I understand, Colonel."

Wells pointed toward the door. "Dismissed!"

David about-faced and stepped into the compound. A group of Forcers stood about the entrance watching him. He paused, studied their faces, then noticed Hayes and Kazik among the group. He motioned them to follow, then he began walking. Hayes came up on David's left side and Kazik on the right. David turned to Kazik. "Those Forcers near the fence when you went through, do you remember who they are?"

Kazik scratched the top of his head. "Some of them. Why?"

"We'll get together and compare notes. I remember most of them." David turned to Hayes. "Wells didn't seem to know anything about the plan—just the heat sheets. One of the Forcers who saw Kazik must have talked."

Hayes frowned. "What'll you do if we figure out who it was?"

David turned his eyes to the front. "I'll make the sonofabitch wish he still had a heat sheet." He turned back to Hayes. "How many bodies do we have?"

"About eighty. We can trust them all."

David shook his head. "That won't be enough. All we can do is hope that more join us when we bust out."

Hayes raised his eyebrows. "Bust out?"

"We go tonight." He turned to Kazik. "You know how that pebble cracked in the stove? If you had a big enough chunk of that and rolled it in next to one of the light posts, with the increased heat, would it shatter with enough force to blow out the post?"

Kazik shook his head. "No. At least I don't think so. Anyway, we have a lot better things to use. Just about all the rocks that won't go through the field." He frowned. "A big enough chunk, and at that heat . . ." He nodded. "Quartz'll work. But it's going to make one helluva racket. The RATs'll be all over us."

David nodded. "That's why eighty won't be enough." He looked at Hayes. "What do you think?"

Hayes rubbed his chin. "The light-weapons station is close, and if we can grab a couple of guard beamers along the way . . ." He shook his head. "It's going to be expensive, but I think we can do it if another two, three hundred join in."

David nodded, then stopped, pulling Hayes to a stop beside him. "Hayes, the RATs let you into the hospital, don't they?"

"Yeah. For supplies, and sometimes I help out the docs there. Why?"

"Something Wells said. What will happen to the Forcers in there if we break out?"

Hayes looked at the ground and rubbed his chin, then shook his head. He looked at David. "I don't know. The Ronnie docs seem pretty square, but you never know." He looked into David's eyes. "But they knew what the deal was when they enlisted, right?"

David looked up at the hills behind the compound, then back at Hayes. "Get all our people out and see how many more bodies you can scrape up before tonight."

That night on the side of the compound closest to the RATs' light-weapons dump, Sergeant Chin moved through the Forcers feigning sleep to find David sitting up and staring at the fence. She squatted next to him. "Merit, I have enough bodies to man nine heavy beamers and all four power platforms."

David nodded without looking from the fence. "The first group through the fence will head for the light-weapons stores, then it will divide into three groups. The biggest group will head for the artillery park to help your people." David turned his head and looked at Sergeant Chin. "Until they get there, you're going to have to use meatpower to get through those guards. Understand?"

Chin nodded, then turned toward the fence. "The second group hits the commissary, but what about the third? Will it try to pin down the RAT security?"

David nodded. "That and one other thing. We're going to try to bust out the officers."

"What makes you think they'll come along? Wells must have given them their sit-down orders."

"They're not all like Wells."

Chin shook her head. "Maybe not, but any brassie is going to think real hard before disobeying a direct order." She looked at the fence, then noticed several dark shapes, one moving up on each light post. "Kazik and company?"

David nodded. "We'll have to get down and cover our faces when he gives the signal. Kazik figures there'll be rock slivers flying all over the place."

"Merit . . . what if we're wrong?"

David turned and looked at Chin. "What do you mean?"

"What if we shouldn't do this? A lot of Forcers are going to die. Then there's the Forcers in the hospital. What if the relief force can take this hunk of rock without us doing anything?"

"You're dreaming, Chin." David looked down at his feet, then back up to the fence. "Kazik's giving the signal. Let's cover up."

"Merit, I'm the senior noncom in this lashup. The only reason I've let you bull this thing along is that artillery is the only thing I know—that, and you seem to know what you're doing . . ."

David rolled over onto his stomach and covered his face with his arms. "Those are questions that should have been asked when we first started this thing. Now cover up." David listened as Chin stretched out beside him, then waited for sounds of the explosions. He bit his lip. The same questions the artillery sergeant had asked, David had asked himself countless times. He still hadn't thought up enough answers to satisfy himself.

"Now!" Kazik's voice broke the silence, followed by a succession of sharp explosions. David felt something strike his left leg. He sat up and looked at the fence. Six of the light posts were out. David jumped to his feet and ran toward the opening. "Let's go!"

A roar of voices erupted from the compound as the prisoners stood and moved toward the gap in the fence. Just before he reached the fence, David saw the one called Kazik lying flat on his back, his face a pulp. David blinked, then ran through the gap into the darkness of the Ronnie camp.

David moved through the following hours as though he were in a nightmare of confusion built on blood. The wide eyes of frightened RAT guards, the screams from behind as their beamers tore into the prisoners, the limp bodies of the guards as their weapons were taken from them. The light-weapons dump fell, then frantic, eager hands took beamers and extra power packs as fast as they could be distributed. The group divided and David took his against the RAT security company. As they reached the area, the RATs were just beginning to pile out and get organized, only half of them carrying weapons. Against six hundred angry Forcers, the Ronnies fell. By the time David's group made it to the officers' compound, two full RAT companies in armor stood between them and the compound. After a brief exchange of fire, David pulled his group back toward the artillery park where they mounted hover platforms, rose toward the pale yellow repulsor shield, then headed toward the hills behind the POW compound. Two hours after arriving, the seven remaining heavy beamers were dug in, defense lines established, and a RAT infantry assault launched against them. As Dismas lit the sky with its orange light, David watched as the survivors of the two RAT companies that had been sent against them stumbled off into the camp. Another Forcer standing next to David pointed at David's left leg. "Corporal, think you ought to look at that?"

David looked at the Forcer, then looked down at his leg. Below the knee, his utilities were brown with dried blood. He stooped over, felt at his calf, then stuck his finger in a hole in the cloth and ripped the fabric. He stood holding a ten-centimeter-long sliver of quartz. Fresh blood dribbled down his leg. He turned to Sergeant Chin who was standing above and behind him at the number-one beamer emplacement. "Burn them."

As Chin shouted her orders, David turned back to watch the artillery park, landing area, weapons stores, ammunition dump, and several bivouac areas go up in flame and smoke.

He felt something handling his leg and he looked down to see Hayes wrapping his calf with a bandage. "What are you doing?"

Hayes looked up and smiled. "I know you world conquerors hate to be bothered with little things, but you need this red stuff."

David turned his attention back to the camp below. Several areas couldn't be hit because of intervening terrain. In days—perhaps hours—units from the front lines would be ordered against them. They had to hold out for—David did some mental calculations; funny how you lose track of time—nine days. They had to hold out for nine days, then the relief force would arrive.

"Post number seven! Here they come!" David opened his eyes in the half-dug hole that was his bunker. He stood and saw a Forcer running at a crouch to his left. In the early evening David could make out the dim lights and dust of a large column approaching the camp on the other side of the screen.

"Chin!"

"I see them."

David looked back and up to see the artillery sergeant squatting on the edge of a rocky outcropping. "Can you hit them as they come through the screen?"

Chin shook her head, then pointed. "Look. The column is heading toward that range of hills and gullies to the left of the landing area."

David wet his lips. "Chin, by now they have a good fix on where we are—especially the heavy beamers. With all the stuff they're moving in, they'll be able to just burn us out of the ground."

Chin looked at the nearest heavy beamer, then back to David. "Pack it up and move it out?"

David nodded, then looked at the advancing column. "We'll wait until full dark, and everything has to stay out of the line of sight from the camp. I don't want them to know we're moving."

*   *   *

As they were digging into their new positions, the artillery batteries of a full division opened up on the original site. The Forcers watched, open-mouthed, as the area became red, then white from the heat, with the dust from decrepitating rocks climbing the hot air looking like a column of steam. David turned and moved through the dark, around rocks and crouching Forcers, until he came to one of the heavy beamers. "Where's Chin?"

A dark shape moved toward him. "Right here."

"Chin, if the RAT artillery finds us, we're cooked. Can we hit it from here?"

Chin shook her head. "These beamers are strictly line-of-sight. The only way we could hit them would be to go airborne, but I wouldn't advise that. They have enough stuff to burn us away before we could do much damage."

David turned and watched the RAT beamer fire cut across the foothills below. "Ronnie'll be sending foot troops come morning." He turned to Chin. "Get two of your beamers set up to cover the approach to our old position, and get the other five ready to move out. We're going to establish our fallback position now."

Chin turned and began shouting orders, while David turned and began searching the landscape for a defensible position that would cover the place where he was standing. As he looked at the hills, black against the yellow of the screen, he saw them blur. David rubbed his eyes, but couldn't clear them.

The next morning, the Rhanians mounted a full-battalion ground assault against the position they had beamed the night before. As they came abreast of Chin's two heavy beamers, the field was crisscrossed with death. In moments, the RATs withdrew while another RAT battalion grouped to assault the new position. The Rhanian artillery couldn't reach the position due to the intervening terrain, and the RATs went in cold, while Sergeant Chin withdrew her two heavy beamers. From the fallback position established the night before, David waited with two more heavy beamers for the assault to begin on the second position. This was to be the pattern for the next five days: lay down fire on an old position's assault, withdraw while the newer position's assault drew fire from a still newer position.

Early evening and David rested with his back against a rock. The RATs had launched no assaults for hours, and the Forcers were taking advantage of the breathing space. He gently rested his head against the rock, his eyes closed, his mind a collage of flame, shrapnel, and dying RATs and Forcers. Images passed before his eyes, Ann Watkins, Sergeant Kolker, Della . . . Mordo, his parents. His body began shaking, while his head rocked back and forth on the rock. That private—Carla something . . . You're tied down too tight, Merit. One of these days you're going to come apart.

"*Sergeant of the Guard! Post three!*"

Not now; not here. Now, stuff a sock in it . . .

"*What is it?*"

"*It looks like three men—Forcers. Making their way up here.*"

David rocked his head against the nightmare of the RAT assault, the air sucking through the hole in Carla's chest, the pitiful smallness of her blood-streaked breast . . .

"*You down there; hands on your heads and come up here in single file.*"

Voices, small, far away.

"*Sarge! They're officers! Three of them busted out!*"

David opened his eyes, the dark shapes of rocks and running Forcers swimming before his eyes. He used the rock he was leaning against to push himself to a standing position. The medic, Hayes, swam into his vision.

"Merit! Three officers—a captain and two lieutenants—busted out! Did you hear me?"

David nodded as the scene before his eyes grew darker. "Thank god." He sank back against the rock, slid down and closed his eyes.

The next morning, David opened his eyes and found himself covered with a coat. The odor of coffee tickled his nose, and he sat up and looked around. Eight other Forcers still lay sleeping on the sand of the small, rock-walled area. A ninth Forcer squatted next to a small stove brewing some coffee. David stood, tossed the coat aside, swayed for a moment, then walked over to the stove. The Forcer squatting there looked up. "Want some coffee?" He lifted a cup.

David nodded and took the container from the Forcer's outstretched hand. "Seen Hayes or Chin?"

The Forcer shook his head. "No. I was told to tell you to see the captain when you wake up. Sergeant Chin'll probably be there. I don't know about Hayes."

David sipped at the coffee and closed his eyes as the scalding bitterness cut the dust in his throat. He turned, walked between two rocks, then surveyed the scene before his eyes. From where he stood, he could see five of the heavy beamers—not dug in, crews nowhere to be seen. David frowned and rushed to the edge of a rocky outcropping. No pickets, no defensive positions, a few Forcers stumbling around getting food, the rest sacking out. "What in the hell is going on?" A Forcer passed by David. "You. Where's the captain holed up?"

The Forcer pointed back in the direction from which he had come. "Straight that way, Corporal."

David nodded, threw his cup aside, then he hurried down the path. After making a turn, he stopped as he came face to face with an armed Forcer. Behind the Forcer were two other armed guards, and behind them, sitting on the sand, were Hayes, Chin and the other Forcers who had served as David's section leaders. He looked at the prisoners, then back to the armed Forcer. "I'm supposed to report to the captain."

The Forcer waved the muzzle of his beamer up and down. "Turn around."

David did as he was told, then felt a hand slapping down his sides and between his legs. "What is this?"

"Captain'll explain everything, Corporal. Okay, you can pass."

David turned and looked at Hayes and Chin. Both of the Forcers kept their eyes down. David moved off between two rocks, the armed guard following him, and saw a Force captain standing and talking to two other officers. The captain looked up and turned toward David. "Yes?"

The guard spoke from behind David. "The corporal said he was told to report to you, sir."

The captain frowned. "Are you Merit?"

"Yes, sir."

"I'm Captain Divak." David looked and noticed the Thirty-first Division insignia. "Merit, I've taken command of this . . . mutiny of yours—"

"Mutiny?"

"Shut up, Corporal!" The captain shook his head. "You must be *insane*. By what authority did you and these others break out—"

"Captain, it was our duty to escape—"

"It was and *is* your duty, Merit, to follow orders!"

The images of the three officers swam before David's eyes. "Wells. You didn't bust out of the officers' compound. Wells sent you. You're working for the RATs—"

"Merit—"

David held his hands to the sides of his head. With his eyes shut, he saw explosions of light. "Yyyyaaaahhhhhhh!!!!" He turned on the guard behind him, wrested the beamer from his hands, then swung on the three officers. When his vision cleared, the three officers were crumpled on the sand, dead. David swung around and faced the guard. The Forcer put his hands up in the air. "You! Get out! Get out!" The guard nodded, turned and fled. David turned back and examined the three officers, then backed away from them.

The guards and prisoners were standing and facing David as he emerged from between the two rocks. He looked at the two guards. "What about you two?"

They exchanged glances, then the one closest to David shrugged. "I was just following orders, Corporal. Might as well be yours as anyone else's."

David looked at the second guard. The guard shrugged, turned his back and walked off. David turned to Chin. "Chin, get those heavy beamers out of here and to the next position. This spot'll be hit anytime now." He turned from the artillery sergeant. "The rest of you, get your people off their asses, out of here and dug into the next position." They looked at him then turned and moved off. Hayes remained behind.

"Merit. Are you all right?"

David studied the medic's face, then he pointed back toward the officers with his rifle. "They're dead. All three of them. I killed them."

Hayes returned David's stare. "So what do you want me to say, Corporal?"

"I don't give a damn what you say."

Hayes shrugged. "Then I won't say anything."

"Fine!"

Hayes nodded, turned and moved off. "Have to look after the med gear."

Alone, David moved to where he could see the approach to the position. Far below he could see telltale wisps of dust marking the movement of troops and heavy equipment. He hung his head for a moment, then grabbed his beamer by its barrel and smashed it to pieces on the rocks.

The next day, moments after an intense RAT assault, pickets saw a flag of truce being waved from the RAT position. Two men advanced into the open and were ushered through the Forcer lines. David was sitting on a rock, hardly noticing Hayes rebandaging his leg, when the two RATs were brought before him. The shorter one had only one arm. David frowned. "Tavis. Major Tavis."

Tavis nodded, noting David's half-closed, dark-circled eyes and expressionless face. "Corporal."

"What do you want, Major?"

"It's simple, Corporal. Your position is hopeless. We want you to surrender and end this senseless bloodshed."

David nodded. "I see." He looked up at the Forcers who had brought the two RATs. "Throw them back. They're too small."

Tavis shrugged off the hand placed on his arm. "Listen, you maniac! We've been counting your dead. You can't have more than two hundred Forcers left. That's less than a quarter of the number you started with." He pointed a finger toward the battle lines. "We have almost two divisions down there ready to run you into the dirt."

David cracked a weary smile. "Pulled another division off the line, did you?" He nodded. "Good."

Tavis flushed. "Look, why haven't I been brought before Captain Davik?"

"He's dead."

Tavis frowned. "The other two officers?"

"Dead."

The RAT major studied David's face. "Corporal, further resistance is pointless. You are no longer harming us. We've established another landing area and our reinforcement continues."

David nodded. "Then, Major, why don't you turn off the repulsor screens and come after us with your flying stuff?"

"I tell you, this is a pointless gesture. Surrender before you all get killed."

David pushed Hayes' hands aside and stood, then pointed a finger at the RAT major. "If we surrender, we'd be criminals, wouldn't we? We'd be put up for war crimes by one of your quickie courts and then have holes fried between our horns. Thank you for the offer, Major, but no deal."

"Corporal, you—"

"Get him out of here." As the guards escorted the two RATs away, David resumed his seat on the rock. Hayes stooped down and finished putting the dressing on David's leg. David stared blankly at where the RAT major had stood. "Hayes?"

"What?"

"How long has it been?"

"How long has what been?"

David shook his head. "I've lost track. Since we busted out. How long?"

Hayes thought for a moment, then shrugged. "Eight, nine days. Can't remember."

David looked up at the orange sky. "The relief force must be close. That's the only way I can read that number."

Hayes stood, picked up his med kit and slung it over his shoulder. "There's another way to read it."

David looked at the medic. "What?"

"Maybe they're tired of killing and being killed. You ever stop to think that the relief might not show on schedule? Maybe they show up a week or a month from now, or maybe they don't show up at all. You ever stop and think about that?"

David looked up at the medic. Then he hung his head and nodded. "I think about it maybe a thousand times a day." He pushed himself to his feet. "Tavis isn't bringing back happy news. We better get the hell out of here. The artillery from two divisions'll be enough to burn the top off this hill."

Late that night in their new positions, the Forcers crouched behind or in any cover they could find as heavy beamers heated and exploded the rocks around them. David crouched between two boulders, wincing as near misses rained rock splinters down on him. He felt a shape slam into him from behind. He turned to see Sergeant Chin ducking against the blast of an explosion.

"Chin, can't you knock out some of that heat?"

Chin shook her head, then both of them ducked as a shower of hot splinters fell on them. "They're washing the entire ridge for a kilometer on either side of us. Even so, they've knocked out three of the heavy beamers. We open up on them and they'll zero in on us. We won't have anything left to break up their assault."

"What about the next fallback position?"

"That's getting it worse than we are here. All we can do is sit it out and hope enough of us are left to fight back when it's over."

David nodded and Chin turned and ran at a crouch through the dust and smoke. David got off his knees and stayed low as he ran to a defense trench, then rolled in. He sat up and looked into a face as expressionless as his own. "Got an extra beamer?"

The face nodded, then looked down the trench. "Take your pick."

David followed the man's gaze and saw seven Forcers broken and twisted in death. He moved down the trench, found a beamer in operating condition, and pulled two power packs from bodies no longer needing them. He looked up and down the trench, counted fourteen forcers still alive, then he took up a position against the wall of the trench and waited for the barrage to lift. Silence came at last, and David placed his back against the rocky dirt and looked up toward where two of the heavy beamers were dug in. "Up there! Do you see them yet?"

He saw Chin's face peer over the lip of an overhanging rock, then her arm shot out and pointed. "Merit, look! They're falling back—it's the relief force! The relief force, Merit!"

Shouts rose from the holes and trenches as David stood and looked over the edge. In the distance, beyond the screen's edge, he could see the flashes of intense fighting, while at the landing area RAT troop carriers were putting down. "Chin!"

"I see them!"

David watched as the troop carriers began exploding. He felt a punch in his arm and he turned to see a Forcer's smiling face. "C'mon, Corporal! Say it. You'll never get another chance."

David looked down at the retreating RATs. "Which do you prefer: Gung-ho, or over-the-top?"

The forcer rubbed his chin, then held up the bloody stump of a finger. "I always preferred over-the-top."

David looked down and giggled. "I don't believe this." He looked up, climbed to the lip of the trench, then shouted as he waved his hand. "All right, boys . . ." He laughed. "Over-the-top!"

Forcers looked at each other, then up at the madman on the edge of the trench, and back at each other. A deep roar came from the trenches and holes, then torn and weary men and women, some without beamers, some without a hand or an arm, rose to the edge of the defensive line and followed the corporal down the slope into the night.

Five weeks later on Earth, garbed in dress blues, David entered a hospital room. The sole patient in the room lowered his newspaper and peered at David's uniform. "Well, hero, I see from your duds that the court-martial went all right." He looked at the three gold stripes on David's sleeve, then at the Earth Medal First hanging from around his neck. "Well, I see you finally got your blues paid for."

David smiled. "How are you doing, Mordo?"

The sergeant shrugged. "Good enough."

"How's the leg?"

"Gone."

"I know, but how are you? You know—"

Mordo snarled. "Look, hero, in two months I'll have a tin prostho strapped on this stump and I'll be back pushing boots. That way I won't hurt my foot every time I have to kick a little sense into those garbage heads." Mordo turned back to his paper. "What do you want, hero?"

David slumped down into a chair. "I need a little advice."

"I look like a chaplain?"

David leaned forward and placed his elbows on his knees. "Mordo, you know that the Ronnies get to pick five of the negotiators on the USE team for the truce talks."

"So?"

"So I'm one of the five they picked."

Mordo lowered his paper, raised his hairless brows, then went back to his reading. "So?"

"So I'd have to resign from the Force if I accept."

Mordo turned a page. "Why wouldn't you accept?"

David stood and began pacing. "Damn it, I don't want to leave the Force. Besides, why'd the Ronnies pick me?"

"Because you're a soldier, hero. The same as the other four Ronnie picked."

David stopped. "You knew?"

Mordo shook his paper. "What do you think I use these things for, Merit? To keep the sun out of my eyes?" He laid the paper on his lap. "Look, Merit, the Ronnies picked Forcers for the same reason that the five we get to pick turned out to be RATs. You people are going to be the only ones on those teams that know anything about being in a war." Mordo pushed himself into more of a sitting position. His ugly face winced with the effort. He lifted a heavy hand and pointed a finger at David. "Look, hero, even with that shiny new medal around your neck, you got no future in the Force."

"What're you—"

"Just shut up. Merit, you disobeyed orders, caused a mutiny and popped off three officers. The right or wrong in the thing doesn't matter. No officer you get in the future'll ever forget it."

"If I hadn't done what I did, Rhana wouldn't be at the truce table right now!"

Mordo shrugged. "True, but it doesn't matter. Any officer you get is going to be wondering when you'll try and second-guess him. Besides, a lot of people aren't too thrilled at Ronnie being beaten to the truce table."

"Like who?"

"Like me, for one."

David raised his eyebrows. "What?"

Mordo nodded. "I never wanted the USE planets to join the Ninth Quadrant. Never could see humans being run around by a bunch of toads and lizards."

"But ... but you fought for the USE. Why ...?"

"I'm a Forcer, Merit. Been one since I was sixteen. I follow orders. That's the beginning and the end of it. The orders said to fight Ronnie, so I fight Ronnie."

"But if you didn't believe you were right—"

"Orders, Merit. That's what I believe in. If that jerk Colonel Wells had ordered me to flame you for disobeying orders, that's exactly what I would have done." Mordo lifted a hand and scratched his head. "That's why you should accept the position on the negotiating team."

David frowned. "But, if you think I'm wrong—"

Mordo shook his head. "You're right." He swatted his newspaper with the back of his hand. "Everybody says so. See, Merit, you know when to disobey orders. I couldn't do that. That's why the Ronnies picked you. My guess is they figure you to work for what you think is right." He lifted his paper and held it in front of his face. "People like you are supposed to protect everybody from people like me. Now beat it. I'm tired."

David moved to the door, pulled it open, then turned toward the bed. "So long, Mordo."

The sergeant lowered the paper a bit. "Say, kid, did you really yell 'over-the-top' like it says here?"

David grinned. "I'm afraid so." He left the room, closing the door behind him. Mordo held the newspaper up and shook his head, then laughed.

"I'll be diddled."

THE RESOLVE, AMENDED

WHEREAS the United States of Earth, with the advice and consent of the Legislative Assembly, has become a signatory to the Charter of the Ninth Quadrant Federation Of Habitable Planets, and has, therefore, become in turn a signatory to the Charter of the United Quadrants of the Milky Way Galaxy, and

WHEREAS Legislative Assembly Resolution 991 (2032) conflicts with both of the aforementioned charters,

NOW, THEREFORE, BE IT RESOLVED:

That Resolution 991 (2032) is amended to read as follows: That the Legislative Assembly of the Government of the United States of Earth, in all related matters that shall come before it, will decide all such matters in accordance with the Manifest Destiny of Intelligent Life, that it shall be self-determined and free from either the coercion of its own kind, or from any other kind of life, in this and in all other galaxies of the Universe.

Legislative Assembly Resolution 252
11 December 2120 A.D.
Adopted without dissent

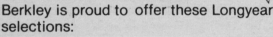

86